Raised by the River

Raised by the River

Jake MacDonald

Turnstone Press

Turnstone Press
607-100 Arthur Street
Winnipeg, Manitoba
Canada R3B 1H3

Turnstone Press gratefully acknowledges the assistance
of the Canada Council and the Manitoba Arts Council.

Cover design and illustration: Doowah Design

Text design: Manuela Dias

This book was printed and bound in Canada by
Hignell Printing Limited for Turnstone Press.

Second printing: January 1994

Canadian Cataloguing in Publication Data

MacDonald, Jake, 1949-

Raised by the river

ISBN 0-88801-166-0

I. Title.

PS8575.D631R3 1992   C813'.54   C92-098046-5
PR9199.3.M36R3 1992

for Selma

It was settled from the start that I would build near the water. After my wife's death in 1955, I felt an inner obligaton to become what I myself am. To put it in the language of the Bollingen house, I suddenly realized that the small central section which crouched so low, so hidden, was myself.

—Carl Jung
Memories, Dreams, Reflections

1

ONE HOT JUNE AFTERNOON IN NORTHWESTERN Ontario, a small and insignificant forest fire named Kenora 27 licked a thick stand of mature white spruce and turned into a monster. Flames shot a hundred feet in the air and the towering wall of smoke, white and ominous, rolled up into the blue summer sky.

Miles away from the fire, a big red car sped along Highway 17 at eighty miles an hour. The car, a twenty-year-old Buick Wildcat convertible, was driven by Michael Saunders. His face was that of a man in his late thirties, still boyish and handsome. Only a few crinkles around his eyes suggested the pressures of work and the passing years. He kept looking at the distant forest fire, not because he was concerned, but because June was forest fire season in northwestern Ontario, and the great, hydrogen bomb-shaped cloud above the trees meant he was coming home.

Mike Saunders' companion was his old friend and business partner, Skip Carter. Skip's open-necked Hawaiian shirt, gold necklace and bug-eye sun-glasses seemed to mock Saunders' conservative, lightweight summer suit. Skip seemed to be having a whale of a time. He drummed his hand on the door frame and bobbed his head in sync with the song on the radio. He owned the car, but he liked to let Saunders drive it.

"Last time I was here," Saunders said, "there was a fire going right across the road. I stopped to watch. There were these great birds made out of fire jumping across the highway."

"You don't say." Skip Carter glanced toward the monstrous cloud. He took a long pull from the can of beer on his lap, then shot a finger accusingly at Mike Saunders. " 'Spotlight on Lou Rawls now, he's the king of them all, y'all.' "

A big green sign flashed by on the side of the road and Saunders turned his head to look back. "Whoa." He hauled the car down to a stop, shifted into reverse and backed up at about forty miles an hour past the sign. He wasn't mad, he just drove that way.

MINAKI TOURIST AREA.

"This is it," Saunders said. He spun the steering wheel and stepped on the gas.

"Where's Kenora? Don't we go to Kenora?"

"Not until we finish our job."

"I thought we were going to get an ice-cream in Kenora."

"First our mission," said Saunders. "Then ice-cream."

A few minutes later they were speeding down the humped asphalt secondary road, the music from the radio loud enough to reverberate over the rush of the wind. Saunders hadn't been here for a few years and things looked different. Road construction. But the land never changed: endless bony white ridges and green forest and lakes. They were driving straight towards the forest fire now, a white rage of clouds in the west. Skip lobbed his beer can with a hard overhand and reached into the back seat for another. The little radar detector on the visor beeped and Saunders slowed down. A minute later a police car went by. Skip threw it a friendly wave.

Finally, Saunders turned onto a gravel road. The Wildcat had worn brakes and he came into the corner too fast. The big car swayed and slammed its undercarriage on the stones. "Whoa big fella," Skip barked. They drove through the forest with the sun pinwheeling down through the pines. On the left side of the road flashed wooded driveways, glimpses of cottages and blue water. Eventually they reached the end of the road and a wooden placard bolted to a metal barricade.

Saunders shut the car off, got out and walked up to the sign. STONEHOUSE INN — CLOSED — NO ADMITTANCE. He nodded and muttered to himself, and then walked around to the back of the car.

"Whatsa matter?" Skip asked. Saunders didn't answer. Skip unwrapped a stick of gum and popped it in his mouth. He chewed thoughtfully, then got out of the car.

Saunders cleared his throat. "You know how you always forget one little thing and you can't even remember what it is until you arrive?"

"Uh huh."

"Well . . . I forgot the gaw-damned key to the gate."

Skip turned and looked at the gate. "Break it."

Saunders came around from the rear of the car. "Can't. My old man built it."

Skip shook the gate. "To hell with it. Let's go back to Winnipeg."

"Don't you understand? I *have* to do this."

Skip shrugged. "Well, in the meantime let's go get an ice-cream."

"MAN, I CAN'T BELIEVE the chicks," Skip said. "Did you see that little thing getting out of the van back there? A real pistol-packin' mama. And look at these two here. Look at these two pistol-packers."

Two pudgy blonde girls, perhaps eighteen years old, minced barefoot across the parking lot, tiptoeing on the hot asphalt, and stood in line at the chip wagon. The chip wagon was a panel truck; the guy inside made French fries in a deep fryer and sold them out the window.

Saunders stepped up to the window. "Two fries and two Cokes."

"Cokes in the machine," the guy said, gesturing towards the supermarket bordering the lot.

Skip turned to the two girls. "So listen . . . could you lovely young ladies tell us where a man can buy a hack-saw in this town?"

The girls exchanged nervous looks and giggles.

Skip was poker-faced. "I'm serious, ladies. But to change the subject, how 'bout this lovely summer weather we're having?"

They half-turned away from him, clamping their hands over their mouths and shuddering with mirth.

Saunders handed Skip his hot French fries. "Fix your own salt."

They walked across the parking lot and got their drinks from the vending machine. Skip kept looking at the chip truck. "Did you see the billies on the tall one? Man . . ."

"They're too young," Saunders said. "Besides, we have a mission."

"Right. We have a mission."

They descended the hill to the waterfront. At the wharf, boats bobbed in the blue waves. Chrome hardware flashed in the sunlight. On the other side of the mile-wide bay were the green forest, a spindly bridge, the puffy white clouds of a stable summer sky.

A bush plane growled overhead, then banked and slid down towards the water. Saunders sat on a timber guard-rail at the foot of the dock and popped open his Coke. He laid his attaché case on his knees to use as a table. Skip did the same. They ate their French fries in silence, then Skip belched emphatically and tossed his empty can towards a distant trash container. A woman with a baby carriage detoured warily past him.

"Maybe we should take a boat over," Saunders suggested.

"Can we get to the place by boat?"

Saunders nodded. He pointed to the bridge across the bay. "It's seven or eight miles past the bridge."

"Sounds feasible," Skip said. "So where can we rent a boat?"

Saunders folded up his paper tray and lobbed it into the trash can. "I'm not sure, but why don't we try this place?" He pointed to a marina at the end of the dock.

A few minutes later they were climbing into a small, dirty aluminum boat, assisted by an apathetic teenager. "Can we pay you when we get back?" Saunders enquired.

"Sure, no problem."

Saunders scrutinized the outboard motor. "And this is just the standard equipment? Any funny little things I should know about?"

The kid shrugged. "Not really."

Skip untied the front rope and sat down, propping his feet up to avoid the heel of dirty water that slopped back and forth on the floor. "Nice boat . . . I guess we really hit the big time."

Saunders scrubbed his hands together, studying the international symbols on the outboard engine's switches and controls.

Skip watched him uneasily. "Are you sure you want to do this?"

"Look. I came fifteen hundred miles. I'm not enjoying it any more than you."

"And what about keys? We still don't have keys."

"We'll break in."

"And you're sure you know the way to the property? You don't need to buy a map or anything?"

Saunders just looked at him.

"Sorry," Skip said. "I forgot who I was talking to." He watched Saunders pump the bulb on the gas line, humming to himself, then muttered, "Mike of the Wilderness."

An hour later they were cruising through a labyrinth of islands, none of which looked familiar to Saunders.

Raising his voice over the bawl of the motor, Skip shouted, "I thought you knew the way."

Saunders nodded.

"Well, it's almost two hours now."

Saunders slowed the boat down. "I'm not sure where we are, if you want to know the truth."

"That's great, Mike." Skip was still trying to keep his feet out of the swill in the bottom of the boat.

Saunders glanced at the gas tank. International symbols or not, he couldn't read the guage, but when he hefted the tank, it seemed alarmingly light. He shut the motor off and they drifted. A sea-gull circled overhead, chuckling. The tall white plume of the forest fire still dominated the horizon.

"Well, that's just great," Skip said, propping his feet up on the seat. "We go for a little Saturday morning drive and we end up lost in the barrens."

"We're not lost. We're just turned around."

Skip nodded. "Whatever you say, Captain Ahab."

Saunders reached into his suit pocket, withdrew a toothpick and stood it up on the crystal face of his wristwatch. He stared at the wristwatch, then fiddled with the arrangement so that the sun threw a shadow on the watch face. "This makes a compass, if you do it the right way."

"I'm going to flag down this boat," Skip said, nodding toward a big outboard coming toward them. He waved and the boat pulled over. The two fishermen offered Saunders the use of their map.

Holding the boats together, Saunders examined it. "Here's the Stonehouse Inn," he said. "See that, Skip? We just go around this long island, go through a channel, turn left, turn right, and we're home free."

When the boat pulled away, Skip said, "I thought we were going to die out here."

Saunders yanked the starter rope. "Don't be a crybaby."

They cruised past a big island and entered a long, narrow channel. Funny, Saunders thought, how it always looks different from the map. Further on they passed another maze of islands, then a familiar-looking marker buoy. He nodded to Skip. "Not much further."

They entered another long channel, then came out into a big bay. Cottages. A railway bridge across the water.

The town of Minaki, right back where they started from.

"THIS IS RIDICULOUS," Saunders muttered, slamming down the phone. He scrawled some instructions on a cigarette package and walked out of the phone booth. "Have you got a quarter?"

Skip said, "I gave you my last one." He sat behind the wheel of the Buick, the motor running.

"Okay, there's one last chance. His cleaning lady has a key."

"The cleaning lady?"

"Yep."

"Why didn't we go there in the first place?"

"My father owes her money."

"You mean *you* owe her money."

"Right."

"So where do we find her?"

Saunders squinted in the afternoon heat, searching through the beer cans and cassette cases in the back seat. He found his overnight bag. Just when he was starting to get the upper hand on a vicious hangover, that hot boat ride had made him feel woozy again. He unzipped the bag and pulled out a white tennis pullover, then peeled off his dress shirt and threw it in the car. The air was nice and cool on his armpits.

"Strip show," Skip said. "You gonna drop your skivvies too?"

Saunders sniffed the tennis shirt, then pulled it over his aching head. He and Skip had been out on the town last night, a night of fluorescent lights and weird women. At one point Skip made some calculations on a napkin and announced they were under the influence of five different drugs. If you counted alcohol.

Saunders and Skip were a troublesome combination. They were business partners, had been for years. Their company, New Age Associates, provided consulting services to small business: tourist resorts, native groups, roadside innkeepers, and so on. The government had grants available to small business, but before giving the cash away the bureaucrats liked to protect themselves by having independent consultants examine the project. If the feasibility study was positive, the money was granted. Saunders and Skip ran a consulting company that could see merit in almost anything.

There were six full-time staff members. A feasibility study that came in at around $18,500 might involve four or five days' work for each of them. Skip, who saw his role as chiefly that of liaison man, sales director and in-house philosopher king, often spent less than an hour actually working on projects of that size. The federal government sent down a whirlwind of obscure and ephemeral funding programs, and New Age Associates was borne aloft on the updraft. The company had grown to the point where it now maintained two offices, one in Winnipeg and one in Toronto, and after celebratory nights like the one they'd just had, Saunders was glad he and Skip lived a thousand miles apart.

Skip shifted impatiently. "Okay, cleaning lady," he said. "Talk cleaning lady to me."

"She lives in a houseboat. We just go straight over, get the keys and we're done."

"Where to?"

Saunders looked at the scrawled instructions. "Move over. I'll drive."

They drove out of town and down a wooded road to a parking lot alongside the river. A houseboat was tied to a tree with yellow rope. It wasn't an aluminum houseboat, but a home-made floating cabin, finished with rough cedar shingles, flower boxes and round windows. Saunders parked the car and got out to look around. "No car," he said. "No boat."

"There's a note on the door," Skip said.

Saunders followed Skip across the gangplank, which rocked unsteadily above the swampy water. " 'Raymond,' " Saunders announced, peering at the note, " 'I'm working at Minaki Lodge. I'll call you later.' "

Skip popped another stick of gum in his mouth. "Well, that does it. Let's get out of here."

"Where are we going?"

"Back to Winnipeg," Skip replied. "Come on, let's go. This is bullshit. We gave it our best shot."

"I can't go home until I get this done."

IT WAS DARK, and a storm was coming. Saunders lounged on a rattan stool at an outdoor bar on the lawn behind Minaki Lodge. The vinyl awning overhead luffed and fluttered in the wind. Faint rumbles accompanied a distant stuttering of blue light. He could smell the faint scent of fire-smoke on the air. It was going to rain tonight. Thunderstorms started the fire. Thunderstorms would put it out. Nature took care of everything. Saunders drained his drink and clicked the glass down on the bar top. "Another, please."

The bartender refilled his glass.

Across the patio Skip entertained some wedding guests with a long, complicated joke. "So the boss looks at the kid and says, 'Ex-*cuse* me, but my wife happens to come from Minaki.' And the kid says, 'Oh yeah? What position does she play?' "

The group erupted into laughter.

A woman in a white smock walked by and Skip deftly lifted a glass of champagne off her tray. "And then there's the one about the guy who wanted to be Billy the Kid."

The wedding party was winding down, and Saunders and Skip had managed to slip in unnoticed. The Stonehouse Inn's cleaning lady was helping with the food preparation here tonight, and she'd promised to get them the keys when she finished. Her name was Maggie Chavez. She'd turned out to be a handsome young woman, nice figure, chestnut hair knotted back in a pony-tail, and sharp, intelligent eyes. She didn't seem overly pleased to meet Saunders, however. Which was understandable, given that he'd owed her money for almost a year. Glancing at his watch, Saunders was surprised to see that it was almost ten-thirty. He wondered if she had forgotten them.

He stood up and studied the crowd of wedding celebrants. No sign of Ms Chavez. He drained the glass, lit a cigarette and glanced up at the rain-scented black sky. Time to get this show on the road. Or we're going to get soaked. He walked across the grass. Someone else was telling a joke and for once Skip was listening. "Skip," Saunders announced. "I'm going to look for her."

"I just saw her a minute ago."

"Where?"

Skip pointed. "Thataway."

Saunders walked down through the trees to the dock. Waves sloshed among the boats. Far away, obscured by the tall trees and fallen darkness, the storm boomed like the guns of a battleship. It's been years since I visited this place, he thought. A sad mission, but an essential one. And not without a certain element of adventure. They had to negotiate several miles of dark, weed-grown road and search through a dark, spooky building. Fortunately, they'd had a few drinks. A pair of heels clickety-clicked onto the boards of the dock behind him.

It was Maggie Chavez, with Skip bringing up the rear. She reached into the pocket of her white windbreaker and produced a flashlight. "Are you ready to go?" Her voice was business-like.

"You bet," he replied. "Should we take the car?"

"It's easier to go by boat," she said, "and I don't have a lot of time."

Maggie Chavez led them to a wooden boat tied up beside the dock. It was an antique cruiser with a canvas top, chrome running lights and a little Union Jack on the stern. Maggie untied the ropes and started the engine. They accelerated into the darkness. Black wind scooped in through the side window. It was impossible to see anything but Maggie obviously knew where she was going. After a long ride the boat slowed down and Maggie shone a spotlight towards shore. Through the windshield was a glimpse of staircase, a For Rent sign.

Saunders climbed up onto the bow of the boat, searching for the rope. Maggie handed him a flashlight. "Be careful." She slowed the boat. The wind was wild and it was hard to see. "Watch your footing," she said, gunning the engine in reverse.

"Stand by to board," Saunders exclaimed.

"There are planks missing in the dock," Maggie warned.

The boat lurched against the dock and Saunders almost lost his balance. He sprang forward and landed on his hands and knees on the rough wooden planks, clutching the bow rope. Lightning cracked overhead and the spotlight threw crazy shadows on the dock.

"I got it!"

"Good work, Mike," Skip shouted.

Maggie shifted the boat into forward. "I just want to move up a bit."

Saunders stood up. "I'll give you a hand." He turned around and stepped into a hole. The ground dropped out from under him and the dock slammed his face.

He clambered painfully to his feet. The entire right side of his body felt like pins and needles. He could taste blood in his mouth.

Maggie and Skip jumped out of the boat. Maggie shone the light in his face. "Are you hurt?"

"I'm fine."

She shook her head. Annoyed. "Just stay behind me."

They followed her carefully across the broken planks towards the shore. The flashlight played across the For Rent sign, then probed through the trees as they moved uphill. Soon, Saunders could make out the black outline of the old building. He kept tripping over roots. Pausing, he looked up at the high stone walls. Dead ivy rattled around the windows on the third floor. He felt as if he should be depressed, returning like this to the family home. But it was really quite a lark.

Maggie stopped at the back door to fiddle with the big padlock. "Your father has so many keys," she muttered, sorting through a jingling key-ring. "I have no idea what most of them are for."

"That padlock is about a hundred years old," Skip said. "You got a crowbar?"

"Just wait," Maggie said. "It's rusted. But there's some penetrating oil in the tool shed." She moved off into the darkness.

Saunders waited a minute. "Well, listen," he said. "Let's not be silly." He shrugged out of his jacket, balled the fabric around his fist and administered a light punch to one of the small mullioned windows. The glass exploded. He reached in and loosened the wing-nuts on the window, and lifted it out of the door. "Who needs keys?" he said.

Maggie appeared. "What's that? What in *hell* are you doing?"

Saunders leaned the window against the stone wall. "Don't worry, I'll get it fixed. Can we use your flashlight?"

"No," she replied. "I don't want to let either of you out of my sight."

Skip climbed through the open window first, then Saunders, then Maggie. Saunders tested the light switch but the power was turned off.

"What is it you need?" Maggie asked.

"A few things. I'll have a look around."

He shuffled carefully across the kitchen floor, feeling broken plaster underfoot. In the living room he stood in front of the fireplace and used his Bic lighter to study some old photographs on the wall. He moved into the velvet darkness of the lounge, feeling his way by memory. At the bookcase he stopped to examine the row of books. Lightning illuminated the diamond patterns in the old leaded windows. Walking on, he passed cobweb-draped furniture and stuffed animals with glass eyes. Everything looked weird and dream-like in the flickering half light of the storm. The small office was still under the stairs, still had its desk and file drawers, an old wooden swivel chair. Saunders lit a candle.

He peered at the walls of the little room as if they were painted with prehistoric symbols. Photographs. One showed the entire family standing by the water, many years ago. His mother looked like Lauren Bacall—padded shoulders, sun-blonde hair. About the same age as he was now.

He opened a file drawer and searched for his father's records of receivables and payables. Whatever seemed vaguely relevant, he stuffed in a padded envelope. As always, his father's bookkeeping system was mysterious. Telephone expenses were filed under a tab entitled "Christmas mailing list." After about ten minutes he had assembled a bundle thick enough to keep his father busy for a couple of weeks. His father hated inactivity. Stubborn old war veteran with half-amputated feet, wild grey hair. Tough as an old railway tie. Saunders had been trying to persuade him to rent his place, or sell it, or do anything to get away. Move to Florida. Forget this fallen-down tourist lodge.

He tucked the bundle under his arm and carried it out into the dining room. Not every son would go to these lengths, he told himself, to humour an ailing father. Skip and Maggie Chavez were sitting at the big oak table. Saunders thumped the bundle down. "Enough financial stuff to help Gordie do one of his creative tax returns. Two months late. But that's normal."

"What now?" Skip said.

Saunders glanced around. "That's about all, I guess."

Maggie Chavez looked straight at him. "I think you should just get in your car and go back to Toronto."

Saunders blew out the candle. "I can hardly wait."

2

IN THE WAITING ROOM OF THE TORONTO GENERAL
Hospital, Saunders sat reading the *Star*. It was hot but
he hadn't taken off his raincoat. His hair was tousled
and his face unshaven. Occasionally he glanced up from
the newspaper and down the hall towards his father's
room. The nurses were in there and every once in a while
he could hear the arguing.

He put the newspaper on the floor and took out a
pack of cigarettes. After patting down his pockets he
noticed the No Smoking sign on the wall, so he put the
cigarettes away, leaned back in his chair and crossed his
legs. Hurry up and wait. The distant chop-chop of an
accelerating motorcycle drifted up from the street.
Saunders stared out the window. A river of red
tail-lights flowed along Wellesley Avenue. It was hard
to believe that this time last night he'd been in Minaki.
After visiting the Stonehouse Inn he and Skip had

returned to Winnipeg. Saunders intended to stay for a few days and do some business, but a phone call had come in the middle of the night. It was the family doctor, telling him his father had an emergency decision to discuss with him. For two or three months now his father's condition had been up and down. It was constant pressure. Saunders had caught a morning plane. Now here he was in Toronto, waiting.

Saunders' father had spent part of World War II in a German POW camp in Belgium. He wasn't a model prisoner, according to the stories that Saunders had heard. Once, for example, he refused to work. An officer came out and pointed a pistol at his head. Saunders' father told the young officer to shove the pistol up his ass. Of course, who knows, stories grow over time. But he could easily see his old man saying that, with that stubborn set to his jaw. And he could see the young SS officer shaking his head angrily, holstering the pistol and walking away. His father spent a lot of time in the cooler, which was a corrugated iron shed, hot and filthy. And when he came home from the war he brought diabetes with him. But the old man still insisted on having a few belts of Scotch every night. One by one, his toes had been amputated. He'd get drunk, stub his toe stumbling around the Stonehouse Inn, and get a minor infection that wouldn't heal. So the doctors would take the toe off. Then the strokes began. Through it all, his father maintained a stubborn belief in the Stonehouse Inn. He kept swearing that in one more year he'd have it squared away. Just one more season. For years, Saunders had watched the old hotel, rotten in its joints and leaky-roofed, sink slowly with every dime his father owned.

"We're finished, Mr. Saunders."

A nurse appeared in front of him. Saunders stood up, bundled the financial records under his arm and followed her into his father's room. A curtain divided it, and diagnostic equipment cluttered the space between the beds. Even after psyching himself, each time he visited the hospital it was a shock to see his father looking so feeble, flat on his back, an intravenous tube taped to his hand, his arms as pale and emaciated as the wings of a thawed chicken. He was muttering some complaint to a large black nurse as Saunders walked in. From the other side of the curtain came the sound of someone whimpering in his sleep. It was a smelly and claustrophobic room, but the sight of his father's grizzled hair, his reading glasses propped on the end of his nose, gave Saunders a bit of a lift. He still liked to pretend that this time next week his dad would be up and walking, trying to find someone to play cards with.

"Hi Pop."

"Well, look who's here."

"How are you feeling?"

"Lousy. Did you bring my month-ends?"

"Yes sir."

The man behind the curtain gave a sudden cry for mercy from Jesus.

"And?"

"I haven't had time to look at them. I got your message and caught an airplane right away."

"Well, I want you to call that little Jewish kid over at H & R Block. He does a real good job and he knows the company."

"Sure. But the doctor said something was up. Are you okay?"

His father stared at him. "First things first, all right?"

Saunders nodded.

"Have Shel do my taxes. Tomorrow."

"Let me do your taxes, all right? You're late anyway, at this point, so it doesn't make any difference."

His father chuckled. "What do you know about taxation?"

"I'll FAX it to Skip in the morning. He'll have the whole thing done, perfectly, in a day or two. Why pay someone?"

After the usual back-and-forth argument, with Saunders insisting on doing the Stonehouse Inn's taxes and his father arguing that he wasn't qualified, Saunders relented, as usual, and said he'd deliver the materials to his father's accountant in the morning.

The old man in the next bed was now weeping softly and pleading for God's help. "Oh Jesus help me. Oh God help me. . . ."

Saunders' father glanced at the curtain in irritation. "I have to listen to this all day. Where the hell's the nurse?"

Saunders activated the call light. He half-stood. "I'll go get her."

"Never mind. They'll come in a minute." His voice had a weary tone, as if he'd gone through this before. "So anyway, did you meet my gal?"

Saunders nodded. "She let us in. We had to jimmy a window. The lock was wrecked."

"Great lady. Helluva woman. Cooks. Bangs nails. Knows accounting. Got those pretty dark eyes, long legs. If I was a young man I'd never give her a minute's peace. Did you see the houseboat?"

"Yep."

"She built the whole thing out of recycled lumber. You oughta see it."

"I saw it."

"Anyway, I think she's going to manage the inn for me. I want to catch the last half of this tourist season. Did you go over it with her?"

"No," Saunders replied. They hadn't discussed anything. This Maggie Chavez individual obviously was mad at him for cutting off the cheques. Every first of the month Saunders was supposed to use his power of attorney and send her five hundred dollars, "maintenance." Sure thing. No receipts in return. No record of her hours and activities. No wonder Gordo was going broke.

"So I want you to work it out with her. Can you do that?"

"This is the emergency you wanted to discuss?"

"Yes, dammit."

Saunders exhaled. There was no end to it. The inn, the inn. Skip was right. They should have torched it. "What do you want me to do?"

"She'll need start-up inventory. Food and supplies. Money for advertising and part-time staff. Six or seven thousand dollars to start off. Can you send it to her?"

"Where am I supposed to get seven thousand dollars?"

His father stared at him belligerently. "From my corporate account."

"Your account has fourteen hundred in it."

"What about my line of credit at the CIBC?"

"It's overdrawn to the limit. You know that. I get calls from the manager every three days. He's concerned about your health."

"I'm sure he is, the little prick."

Saunders crossed his legs. He felt hot and irritable. He'd hurried back from Winnipeg for this. There were noises from next door.

His father scowled at the curtain and then at Saunders. "Okay. I guess I have to dip into my pension. I've got sixteen thousand left. I want you to . . . "

"You're not doing that."

His father paused. "What did you say, Mikey? You're telling me how to spend my pension?"

"You're not spending it. You're wasting it. Listen, that place is—"

"No, *you* listen," his father exclaimed. "You don't know shit. Do you think you know everything? I worked my ass off for that hotel and—"

"Did you ring, Mr. Saunders?" The nurse peered around the corner of the curtain.

"Oh God help me," muttered the voice from next door.

"Yeah, I need some paper, sweetheart. Can you get me something to write on? I need to tally some numbers here. And will you do one other thing?"

She smiled.

Saunders' father gestured with his thumb. "Will you go next door and tell that guy that God doesn't exist?"

AFTER LEAVING THE HOSPITAL, Saunders cruised down Queen Street in his BMW. His girlfriend Deborah was still at work. Maybe he could drop in for a visit.

He parked and walked up the street, holding his raincoat shut with pocketed hands. A chilly night for early summer. The rain drizzled on the cobblestone street. Deborah's fitness club was an old brick building that had once been a police garage. Up on the second floor they'd knocked out a row of walls and installed big picture windows, presumably so that passers-by could admire the physiques of the scissor-jumping young people inside. Saunders wasn't big on the health and happiness movement. Life is a bitch and then you die. He jogged up the steps past the neon Hollywood's sign.

The receptionist greeted him with a smile. "Good evening."

"Hi there. Is Deborah here?"

"I'll check." She stood up, a lush blonde in a half-unbuttoned blouse and a leather mini-skirt, and left the room.

After a few minutes, Deborah materialized. Her face was flushed and she had tucked her flax-coloured hair out of sight under a headband. A thin film of moisture shone on her face. "Hi," she said. "I thought you were out of town."

"I just got back. Do you want to go have a coffee?"

"I'm in the middle of a class. And I have a meeting afterwards."

"I'll wait."

Deborah studied him. "What's going on?"

Saunders shrugged. "Nothing." After a moment he said, "It's Dad."

"Drinking again?"

"He wants to spend his pension money reopening the inn."

Deborah rolled her eyes. "Why do you put up with this?"

"It's his money, remember?"

"I can't really talk now."

"I'll wait."

Deborah thought for a moment before she said, "I'll see you at my place."

"Sure."

"Just let yourself in." She reached into the bodice of her electric blue gym suit and handed him the house key. It was still warm from her breast.

"Got anything else in there?" he said.

"I beg your pardon?"

"Never mind."

She looked at him. "Are you all right?"

"No."

DEBORAH LIVED IN THE BEACHES, a wooded enclave along the Toronto lakeshore. Her house was a cute, granny-style brick one-and-a-half, a couple of blocks up from the lake, with a landscaped yard and oak trees. Across the street was a deeply wooded park.

Saunders walked up the driveway and checked Deborah's mailbox. Mr. Nosy Parker. He went into the house and flipped on the light. The kitchen was as neat as a pin. Pegged oak floors and all the latest equipment. In the evenings he liked to come in here, put on the FM radio and flip through *Fortune* magazine while the coffee grinder hummed. Coffee was about as wild as it got at Deborah's house. The fridge was full of green vegetables and mineral water and weird, muddy-looking concoctions in plastic containers that were supposed to make you healthy. Saunders would have been happy if, just once, he opened her fridge and found a big, slobby, cold pizza and a family-size Coke. The thing that bothered him most was that you couldn't argue with her. She was thirty-four years old and had the body of a teenager. Saunders was pushing forty. No doubt, in a couple of decades he'd be slapping the dirt with his face, courtesy of a left aorta packed with animal fats.

He went into the living room. They'd had some good dinner parties in here, six or eight people, drinks, good food, Stan Getz or Van Morrison providing the music. What a classy life this had turned out to be. No war. No starvation. All that's asked of you, really, is to behave. Do a few honest hours of work every day. Pay your taxes. Keep your lawn clean. Don't shoot the prime minister. If this business with his father was shaping up to be a trial, he was probably due for it.

He wandered into the sunroom in his wet raincoat and sat in the swivel chair at the writing desk. He gazed out through the ivy-hung windows at the yard, the oak trees and the rain scribbling down through the streetlights. What am I going to do? he asked himself. If I step in and try to take control of financial affairs, he'll have another stroke.

The telephone rang. Saunders picked it up, wondering whether it would be a man.

Deborah. "Michael. I'm terribly sorry but I simply can't make it tonight."

Saunders was silent for a moment. "Problems?"

"Not really. Can we meet tomorrow?"

"I don't know. I have to make a decision. I can't let

him spend every last penny on that place. He's killing himself."

"Michael . . . excuse me. Have we discussed this before?"

"Yes. But—"

"But nothing. *Go* to the lawyers and get some help. It is your *responsibility*." When Saunders said nothing, she went on. "They have this legal manoeuvre called 'an order of committeeship.' They don't declare him insane," she said. "They just examine the evidence and decide if he's capable of making decisions in his own best interest. I've explained all this. I don't know why you won't listen."

With the phone against his ear he sat quietly, thinking. Deborah had scored this house as a result of her mother's going to the funny farm. At the time, Saunders had thought it was disgusting. Now here he was, in the middle of it. He listened to Deborah's breathing. In the background he could hear the robotic knock of work-out music. "Okay," he said. "I'll talk to you tomorrow."

He drove back to his apartment and went to bed. He fell asleep right away but woke later in the night. His chest ached. A nightmare. He looked around the room, at the vague shadows on the ceiling. Usually, when he woke up he had to lie there the first few minutes, thinking, where am I? Often, he was in some little hotel in Cornwall, Thunder Bay, Gravenhurst, Sudbury. The travelling consultant. He got out of bed and went to the bathroom for a leak. Starting to worry again, now that he was awake. What the hell am I going to do? Should I have him committed? Where's a guy to go to get advice on stuff like this?

He walked into the living room and lit up a smoke. Through the caulked aquarium-like window the lights of the city glittered in the distance. Far-off neon throbbed in front of the girlie clubs. Miss Penthouse

All-Nude Review. Girls. Girls. Girls. They're Alive and They're Naked. Off to the south, on the concrete loops of the freeway, a thin stream of tail-lights twinkled. A siren looped through the air. Someone dying. He glanced at his watch. Past two a.m. Later, he would wonder if that was the precise moment it happened.

He went to bed. He hadn't even fallen asleep yet when, in the living room, the phone began ringing.

3

~~~~~
~~~~~

SAUNDERS SKETCHED THE OUTLINE OF A BUILDING SITE
on the back of the place-mat. "This is where they want
to put the trailer pads."

Skip nodded. He crunched an ice-cube between his
teeth. They were sitting in sunshine at a sidewalk cafe
in Toronto. "So what's the problem?"

"Health Department wants a separate sewage line or
they won't approve it. I can't get them to see our logic."

Skip bit into another ice-cube. "I'll call Ernie. He
owes me one."

Saunders laid the pencil down. "I'm sick of this
project."

Skip fired up a menthol cigarette with his gold
butane lighter. The jewellery around his wrist twinkled.
"Don't worry. I'll take care of it." He went into the
restaurant to call the Health Department.

Skip was here to help out while Saunders managed

the after-effects of his father's death. The end had come suddenly from a blood clot that travelled to his brain. Killed him cleanly. A bolt of lightning. You stop breathing. The doctor told him afterwards that he'd half expected it. Saunders hadn't been very close to his father for the last few years and there'd been plenty of warning. But he felt stunned, nevertheless.

The funeral was all prearranged by his father's will. He wanted to be buried beside Saunders' mother in Mississauga, a place Gordo hated, but spending eternity there would be a last gesture, like buying a round for the house. The service was a dismal affair in one of those nouveau-style churches that looks like a cedar ice-cream cone. Saunders stood off to one side with Deborah and didn't talk to anyone. He wondered why the end of every life must be celebrated with this awful farce.

The mourners trooped to the cemetery with headlamps burning. Saunders and Deborah trailed in his little BMW. It was a dull, cold, rainy day, as befitted the occasion. Green Valley Memorial Gardens looked like an industrial park with its clumps of shrubbery and long vistas of humped lawn. The Queen Elizabeth Way poured a torrent of trucks and cars past the fence.

The coffin was set down on canvas straps and the preacher launched into another brain-numbing oration. What would these jokers do if they had to work for a living? A hundred yards away, behind a curtain of hedges and slanting rain, a yellow backhoe coughed blue smoke. Then a set of electric motors whirred and the canvas straps automatically lowered Gordo down into the hole beside Alice. Green Valley Gardens didn't allow big tombstones. All his parents got for their final monument was a small bronze plaque that looked as if it had come from K-Mart. That, and a run-down old lodge somewhere up in north Ontario.

So here he was, a couple of days later, explaining the Toronto case-load to Skip, who'd volunteered his assistance for a few weeks. They were scheduled for a trip to Kingston in the morning with their business associate, an Indian chief.

After lunch, driving back to the office, Saunders was quiet. His mind whirled with details. Things that needed to be done. Brief flare-ups of anger. Depression. Skip tried to be depressed too, but he wasn't very good at it. Every once in a while he'd break into a snippet of song, then catch himself.

New Age Associates was situated in a renovated warehouse building. In his trench coat and silk tie, Saunders led the way up the back stairs. He pushed open the door to their office.

"Maybe I'll work in Shelley's office," said Skip. "She still on the road?"

"Yep."

Saunders went down the hall, followed by Skip. Shelley was one of their college researchers and was away on assignment. "There's no files in here," Saunders said, turning into an office, "but you can help yourself to mine."

Skip threw his raincoat on the chair. "Hey, no problem."

Saunders went into his old office, hung up his trench coat and umbrella, then sat down in his swivel chair. Out the window he could see nothing but brick warehouses and grimy fire escapes.

He took a manila envelope out of his attaché case and emptied it on the desk. Old brochures, price sheets, magazine articles. Some old photographs. That was it, everything he had on the Stonehouse Inn.

He looked at an old photo of his mother and father standing in front of the Stonehouse. His dad was in his Princess Pats uniform, just back from the war. Or maybe just leaving. His mother wore a flowered dress, her blonde hair long, her head held high and stern.

Must be thirty years ago.

Around that time, he remembered, he went with his dad and Eddy Crogan on a fall moose-hunting trip, up to the English River. Late one night, lying in the tent, he'd heard his father tell Eddy, who was another war vet, the story about the time he was walking point on a sweep through an olive grove. And six young German soldiers came out waving a white flag. Their heads were bandaged and they were afraid. The oldest one in the group was maybe eighteen. His father put baling wire on their wrists and took them prisoner, marched them back to his sergeant. Who told him to take them up to the CP and hand them over. The officers were in a tent looking at maps. His lieutenant, a man named Markham, came out and said, "What have you got?"

Private Gordon Saunders of Minaki, Ontario, nodded towards the prisoners. "Sir, these men have surrendered."

The CO gave the prisoners a mildly reproving look. "Private Saunders . . . we're stretched to the limit today. We've got wounded, we've got supplies coming up. We can't babysit these people. Just uh . . . just take them down to the olive grove. Just take them down there and shoot them."

"I beg your pardon, sir?"

The CO gave his father a curious look. "You didn't hear me?"

"No sir. I mean yes sir."

The CO threw him a stiff salute. "Then take care of it. Dismissed."

An order is an order. His father pointed his Thompson at the six teenagers and marched them down to the end of the olive grove. The prisoners whispered to each other. One of the youngest was crying. Another comforted him and held him by the elbow, awkward with his wrists wired. Private Saunders took out his pack of Navy Cuts and offered each of the boys a cigarette. They all took one. The young one was crying so hard his cigarette fell apart. The boy with the gun gave the other boys, who didn't have guns, more cigarettes. They finished their cigarettes and he passed the pack around again. Eventually, they worked their way through an entire pack of Players. Saunders' father was cracking open a fresh pack when an American soldier walked up. "What's going on?"

"I captured these men," said Saunders.

"Well, you better take them back to the CP."

"I did."

"And?"

"Lieutenant Markham said to shoot them."

The American shrugged. "Then shoot them."

Private Saunders studied his cigarette, then dropped it to the ground and crushed it under his boot. The American was a Special Forces commando on loan to their unit. He was supposed to teach them things like how to set booby-traps and cook lizards. Saunders could not look at the German boys. "I'm not going to shoot them," Saunders said. "They're wounded. They're prisoners of war."

The Special Forces guy drew his Colt. "*Mach schnell,*" he ordered, motioning the prisoners to kneel down.

"You better not do it, either," Saunders said.

The specialist just stepped past him.

The prisoners knelt down quickly and held their hands in front of them. They bowed their heads. Receiving a sacrament. The commando cocked the hammer on the big .45 and walked up to the boy who was sobbing. He put the gun against the boy's head and shot his brains out. Private Saunders jacked the bolt on the Thompson and aimed it at the American. "Christ," he said. He turned on his heel and walked away, followed by intermittent bangs from the pistol.

A few days later they were sweeping a wheat field. It was a sunny, cold day. Streaks of white strata marbled the autumn sky. They hadn't heard a shot all day. The American guy was out in front, walking point, when a loud, shrill whistle suddenly fell from the sky. It was a stray shell, the biggest shell Private Saunders had ever heard. "Incoming!" someone screamed. They hit the dirt. The shell landed with a ground-shaking BOOM. Clods of earth clattered down. The air was thick with the luscious stink of cordite. Private Saunders cautiously looked up. Thirty yards ahead, where the American had been walking point, was an excavation the size of a church basement.

An army boot lay at the rim of the hole.

Saunders put the photograph on the desk and tilted back in his chair. His father's youth had been pretty rough, compared to his own. Here he was, sitting in his spiffy little office, and the biggest decision he'd faced all day had been whether to have poached salmon or pasta verde for lunch. His father lived through a time when you had to make up your own rules, and people lived or died according to the results.

And there was more to the story. His dad came home from the war and built the Stonehouse Inn, the finest small resort in the Kenora District. Alice Saunders was the dame of the mansion. She was a pretty lady with the sort of wavy hair you saw on Hollywood's movie heroines. Son Mikey, an energetic kid, was being groomed to take over the resort business.

Years after the war, Gordon and Alice went to a Princess Patricia's Light Infantry reunion in Kenora. They walked into the Legion Hall and Gordon saw the guy who'd ordered the shootings, Markham, a Major

General now. Everybody in the receiving line was laughing and embracing, shaking hands. Gordon was shaking too when he told Alice they had to get out. Alice didn't know what the hell was wrong with him. Curly and Ray and their wives stopped them to see why they were leaving.

Gordon didn't answer.

Later, their friends came over to the Stonehouse Inn. They didn't come alone. Major General Markham came. He had a big job at the DND in Ottawa now. Quite an honour that he would have a nightcap with enlisted men. It was around midnight when they arrived. Headlights swept into the yard. Horns honking, shave and a haircut. Mikey Saunders was sleeping in his Pumpkinhead bunk on the third floor of the inn. A sound like animals growling woke him up. Mikey jumped out of bed and pressed his nose against the screen. Down in the swaying shadows of the big pine trees on the lawn, a man was sprawled on his behind, shaking his head. Above him, restrained by two other men, was Mikey's father. The Major General rolled forward onto one knee and balanced there for a moment, unsteady. "What's his problem?"

"Get up," his father ordered.

"Is this guy crazy?"

"Get up," his father said again. "Get up you sonofabitch."

Saunders put the photograph of the boy soldier into a white envelope, arranged the brochures and newspaper clippings and photographs, and slipped them into their large manila envelope. He opened the attaché case and tucked the envelope into the file labelled Stonehouse Inn.

The rain drummed the thermopane window. Outside, pigeons wheeled past the ugly rooftops of downtown Toronto.

Skip walked in, punching out a number on his

hand-held portable phone. "Mikey . . . what's in your horoscope? . . . Hello? Hello? Oh shit, sorry . . . wrong number . . . hello? Forget it." Skip palmed the aerial and sat on Saunders' desk. "What work is there to do?"

Saunders sipped his coffee. "Why don't you call Chief Leo, make sure he's going to be there tomorrow?"

"Right." Skip tapped out several numbers on the cellular phone, listened, then rapped it on the edge of the desk. "American-made junk."

"And when you're done that, put together a proposal for the Health Department. We need to bomb them with paper."

"How far is Chief Leo's place?"

"I don't know, maybe three hours. It's right there on the map."

Skip looked up at the big map on the wall. Chief Leo's reserve was marked with a red thumbtack. There were several dozen thumbtacks spread across the map. Some of them marked New Age Associates projects, some of them held the map on the wall.

Saunders said, "We should be able to make the round trip in one day. Can you finish the proposal today so we can give him a copy?"

"As long as I'm just writing for weight. Have you got resource stuff I can use?"

"Sure." Saunders went to the file drawers. "We're looking for any feasibility studies we've done on rehab centres, right? So we just thumb through, go past Production Line (Time & Motion), past Retailing to . . . Rehabilitation." Saunders pulled that file and tucked it under his arm. "Knowing Chief Leo, I assume you'll want a Native Awareness section," Saunders pulled another heap of floppy material out of the cabinet, "and because you want a section on how we've walked all over the Indians in the last hundred years, you look up a few of your old eloquent passages from the Liberal

Guilt file." Saunders dumped the pile of documents on the table. "And after you're done . . . patch it all together and you've got your PPCS."

"Thanks," Skip said.

Saunders threw Skip a gallant wave. "You're welcome, grant-breath."

Skip paused to look at the old brochures on Saunders' desk. "Hey neat . . . Stonehouse Inn?"

Saunders nodded. "Back in the 1950s."

The coloured brochures showed a bulbous Buick roadster parked in front of the inn. Green trees, stylish ladies. Skip leafed through the brochures. "So what are you going to do about the place?" He sounded tentative. He knew Saunders was touchy about the inn.

"I'm going to sell it."

"What do you think you'll get for it?"

"Frankly, I don't care. It's not worth much. I'm going to ask what's her name, Maggie Chavez, if she wants to act as the agent."

"Why her? She doesn't seem to be one of your bigger fans, old buddy."

Saunders drank his coffee. "Well, I owe her a yard and a half anyway. So this way at least I'll get something in return."

Skip bundled up the research materials and headed for the door. "Well, that's too bad, Mike. End of an era."

And then Saunders got down to work, reading mail and reciting responses into his dictaphone. Every once in a while, his gut twisted. Jesus, I'll be glad, he thought, when I get this settled.

The phone rang. It was Maggie Chavez.

LATER THAT EVENING, Saunders leaned back in the swivel chair with the phone cradled against his ear. "I'll pay you to do it," he said.

Neil Olson was their engineer based in their

Winnipeg office. Skip referred to him as "Chief Engineer Olson." Neil was a burly farmer in a checkered shirt and bushy sideburns. A round toothpick usually drooped from the corner of his jaw. He was a construction guy, not a real engineer, but he could, as Skip often said, "sure as hell put up a building." Saunders wanted him to get a crew together, drive out to the Stonehouse Inn and clean it up for sale.

"Why don't you do it yourself?"

Saunders tapped his cigarette on the ashtray. "Because I'm fifteen hundred miles away."

"When does this need to be done?" Neil's voice was flat.

"Tomorrow, if you can. I talked to the caretaker. She thinks there's a fair amount of work there. I figure if you take three or four of the boys, it's a day's work. It's worth a thousand to me."

Long pause. Neil hated old buildings. Anything that didn't have aluminum siding, he'd rather demolish. "What's this broad's name?"

"Chavez," said Saunders. "Maggie. She lives in a houseboat."

"How do I find her?"

Saunders fed Neil the information and then, with a feeling of relief, hung up the phone. Everything was working out. Neil would go out and clean the place up, saving him the grief of doing it in person, consigning old teddy bears to the dumpster and so forth. Maggie Chavez would sell it for a reasonable commission, some of which he owed her anyway. Two or three weeks from now the inn would be gone. He'd frame one of those old brochures and hang it on the wall.

He went into the other room to work on the presentation for Chief Leo. He like working at night, in the silence and austerity of a deserted office. Normally, writing proposals was dull work, cutting and pasting, slamming PPCS materials through the copying machine. A PPCS was a Proposal to Provide Consulting Services. The members of New Age Associates were always sending proposals to each other. What Skip had done this afternoon was propose to provide consulting services to the Powatami Indian band, where, coincidentally, one of their business partners, Leo Redsky, was chief. The way it often worked out, Chief Leo would hire his own partners, Skip and Saunders, to study the matter carefully. After a preliminary study they would come up with an initial recommendation, which was usually for further study. At that point they would approve the project and move on to the implementation phase. Chief Leo would then hire them to search for a good contractor. After an exhaustive tendering process, New Age would select the highest bid, submitted by their own contractor, Neil Olson. The invoices would all be sent to the government. Skip worked the lunch meetings. It was a living.

Saunders shut off the coffee machine. Slipping on his trench coat, he left the office. It was still raining. Now what?

Skip had borrowed his car so he was on foot. He walked the long stretch down the back alley. Life in the big city. You have to watch out for poor people with knives. On Queen Street, restaurant lights gleamed on oily pavement. Cars whisked by, towing tatters of rain. At a hip bagel shop Saunders peered in the window, checking for lonely witches. He felt tense. Maybe a shallow and cheap sexual encounter would cheer him up.

At a corner store, he bought a pack of cigarillos, which he had heard were healthier to smoke than cigarettes. A lonely rapist browsed through the dirty magazines. Outside, Saunders lit a cigarillo. Dark and rainy. Castanets rattled in the trees overhead. He was smoking.

He was going to die. Just like his father. He felt his stomach twisting. Who had made up this lousy game?

He walked across to the Don, cupping the cigarillo. At his apartment complex he cut across a wooded lot, a shortcut to the front door. He swung the attaché case aggressively and fired the glowing red eye of the cigarillo end-over-end as he strode through the wet woods. Rotten world, the city. The only cheerful prospect in sight was the possibility of devising a Final Solution to the goddamned Stonehouse Inn problem.

He rode the elevator up to his shag-carpeted apartment, hung up his wet trench coat and slipped off his shoes. "Hello Skipper!" he called. No answer, but then he heard Skip singing in the shower. He went into the living room and switched on the big TV before he mixed a drink. In the window the misty night skyline was constellated with the lights of a thousand high-rise apartments. He sat in the leather recliner by the limestone fireplace.

I'm beat, he thought.

Skip came out, wearing a Club Med bathrobe. He towelled his hair. "Hi there pretty boy."

"Hi there Skip."

"What's new?"

Saunders thought for a while. "Absolutely nothing."

NEXT MORNING THEY DROVE out to the Indian reserve. They arrived after noon and took a side road to a rain-streaked clump of buildings with a few battered pick-up trucks in the gravel lot. A Bingo sign was painted on the side of a large metal barn nearby. Saunders parked in front of the cedar and concrete wigwam that was the band office. After a long wait in the reception area, a willowy girl in a fringed vest came out and ushered them into the band council chamber, where Chief Leo sat with other men. He wore a longhorn string tie and a ten-gallon hat with an orange feather stuck in the band, and he was smoking a White Owl. "Howdy boys," he said.

"Hi Leo," Saunders said. "Artie, Frank . . . Albert, Elijah."

The councillors and the consultants shook hands.

"So what have you got?" Chief Leo asked.

Saunders explained what he had in mind for the alcohol rehab centre, then the sources of funding. "You sent us a letter of transmittal," he said, "which we wrote for you. Then we reply with a PPCS, which we have right here." He brandished a sheaf of paper. "Then we apply to NEBLA through Plan 21. The PPCS will then get processed through the selection panel, then the department committee, then the ministerial sub-committee, then to NEBLA head office in Ottawa, back to the province, back to Ottawa, back to the province and so on."

Chief Leo nodded, making notes. "Sounds pretty straightforward."

Saunders handed him the envelope with the Stonehouse Inn materials. Chief Leo emptied the contents on his desk. "What's this?"

"It's a country inn," Saunders said. "I recently inherited it from my father."

Chief Leo sifted through the photographs and brochures.

Saunders waited. Finally he said, "What do you think?"

Chief Leo puffed a great plume of cigar smoke. "What am I supposed to think?"

"What I mean is . . . maybe you'd be interested in buying it."

"What for?"

"The alcohol rehabilitation centre. It's a long way from the community, right? So there are no distractions. No temptations to take off and go home. You could get NEBLA funding to renovate it to your exact requirements."

Chief Leo nodded.

Saunders said, "I've got an agent named Maggie Chavez who'd be glad to show it to you. Do you want her number?"

Chief Leo stared at the documents. "You can talk to my cousin Norris," he said. "He's on the selection committee. But I doubt he'll go for it. He's already got a site picked out."

"Where does Norris live?"

"The blue house," Chief Leo replied.

"Blue house," Saunders said. "They're all blue. Come for the ride and show us. And you can introduce us to Norris."

"No way I'm going down there. That's where the Clearsky boys live. They shot my truck last time. Just leave it and I'll put it on his desk."

IT WAS EVENING when Saunders and Skip got back into Toronto, pouring rain again. Skip had a date, so Saunders went home alone. He turned on the answering machine, sat on the couch and threw a quilt over his legs. The machine bleeped and whirred, delivering several spectacularly uninteresting messages, one from the dentist reminding him of an appointment and another from the Rug Doctor. The last message was from Neil. "Call me at the office in Winnipeg, Mike. I'll be working until about ten."

Saunders called Winnipeg. He could hear country music in the background when Neil answered.

"Olie. It's Mike."

"Mikey."

"What's the deal?"

Neil's voice was gruff. "I drove all the way out to Minaki and looked at the place."

"And?"

"Well, for starters, I'd get another real-estate agent."

"Why?"

Neil grunted. "She'll never sell it. She's too fussy. She says she wants to make sure that whoever buys it 'preserves the character' of the place, all that. Do you think buyers want a lecture from this individual?"

"So did you clean it up?"

Neil laughed. "Are you kidding? The wiring's shot. The plumbing is a mess. The chimney is going to tip over. The window casements are rotten. And there's carpenter ants eating the foundation. All that place really needs is a good snowy winter day and about five gallons of kerosene. Then you got a pretty nice fire and no more headaches. No . . . I didn't clean it up."

"So you're saying it needs work."

"Well, I would say yes, it needs work. That's one way of putting it."

"What does it need?"

"I just *told* you, didn't I? Why don't you go and see for yourself? Compile a list of things you want done, and I'll cost it out for you."

"All right."

"And get rid of that woman. She thinks she knows something about the building trades."

"All right."

Saunders hung up the phone. Well, that's that. It was dead silent in the apartment except for the sound of rainwater running down a drain.

4

Saunders OFTEN WONDERED HOW THE HELL HE'D
ended up being a consultant. He was in college in
Vancouver when he met Skip. Every Friday Saunders
and his Fine Arts pals used to go to the Cecil Hotel on
Granville Street to drink beer and play pool. The place
was full of hair, the air thick with smoke. The jukebox
thundered out "Sky Pilot," the version with the machine
guns chattering over the bagpipes and the falling plane.

Saunders had no idea why he did this every Friday.
Inevitably, by suppertime he'd be walking out into the
grey Pacific dusk with a headache. One afternoon he
met Skip Carter, an odd-looking Commerce student
with pastel leather shoes and the personality of a
game-show host. Skip kept following him around,
laughing, buying drinks and generally behaving as
though Mike Saunders were the most fascinating fellow
he'd ever met. Saunders' woolly-headed pals kept

looking at Skip as if to say, Who is that capitalist swine and why is he in our bar?

One night Skip persuaded Saunders to join him on a double date. Skip had a Studebaker Avanti with an elaborate bar in the glove compartment and a trap door in the floor. If the police pulled him over, he explained, he just poured his martini onto the road. They took their dates to a movie. Skip talked all through it. When the on-screen lovers had a tender tryst in the meadow, Skip made sucking noises. At the White Spot coffee shop afterwards he enraged an immense, leather-garbed lesbian by repeatedly asking her if she'd "grown a bit." In the parking lot Skip's date slapped him in the face and ran crying to the bus. Saunders' date complained of a headache so they took her home. She dutifully invited them in for coffee. Her black cat met them at the door. "Do you like cats?" she asked Skip.

"Sure," Skip replied. "I like to tie a big rock to their tails and throw them off the Second Narrows Bridge."

End of conversation. Skip drove Saunders home. He kept rolling down his window and shouting at pedestrians. "Big improvement, guy! One hunnert percent." They parked in front of Saunders' house and had one last cigarette. Skip couldn't understand why no one seemed to like him.

Saunders lost touch with Skip for a while when Skip moved east, but a friend of theirs was killed on a motorcycle, and they met at the funeral in Winnipeg. It was one of those hot days in early May. No leaves on the trees. Dusty dog shit on the boulevards and gravel on the streets. Skip and Saunders had a smoke out on the church steps, waiting for the car to the cemetery. Skip was telling Saunders about this new thing, consulting. You had all these ex-flower-power types in government. The prevailing attitude was, there's no social problem you can't fix if you throw money at it.

Skip said the government regarded native groups, women, the unemployed, the handicapped, as programming targets. That's what they called them, "targets." All these liberal young bureaucrats in Ralph Lauren neckties were lobbing cash at them. "The trouble is," Skip explained, "a lot of them haven't noticed they're targets yet. And some of the ones who've noticed can't catch. And the ones who can catch can't manage their cash. So that's where I come in. I'm a consultant. I catch their cash for them."

Skip had worked in the Toronto area for several years and then moved to Winnipeg. Apparently his move was triggered by some kind of scandalous event in Toronto. Saunders didn't have the complete story. One source said Skip had gotten into apartment blocks and was torn asunder by the infamous OPEC collapse/interest rate spiral of '81. Another said he'd gotten into trouble with the law. Whatever happened, Skip didn't want to talk about it. He claimed that Manitoba, with its dying towns and desperate economy, was a consultant's paradise.

Skip had incorporated his own consulting company, a one-man show called New Age Associates. Saunders' girlfriend was pressuring him to make a little money, so he joined up with Skip to handle the design and copywriting work, and they split everything down the middle. Neil Olson came on board to handle the sod-kicking and the general contracting, and they went to thirds. Then Chief Leo showed up with a whole bag full of Indian Affairs construction and renovation contracts, and then the Brain, who defected from Consumer & Corporate to run their accounting. Everyone split the loot.

It was nice having cash and all the toys that came with success but sometimes there were dues to pay. Family debts. After talking to Neil, Saunders realized that dumping the inn was not going to be as easy as he thought. He really had no choice but to return to Minaki. Pay off Maggie and get her out of the situation. Assess the cost of renovating and then compare those costs to the potential increase in market value. If it's worth fixing, fix it. If it's not, then bulldoze the buildings, sell the property and be done with it.

He discussed his options with Skip and Chief Leo during a meeting at the Toronto office. Chief Leo had mentioned Saunders' offer to Norris Redsky and several of the councillors, and they weren't interested. He said he recognized that the Stonehouse Inn had been in Saunders' family for years but, you know, so what?

"Don't you want to think it over?"

"Don't beg," Chief Leo said. "It doesn't look good on your resumé."

"But will you think it over?"

"Yeah, yeah."

They swapped car keys. The last Saunders saw of Skip and Chief Leo, they were peeling away from the office in his car, bound for Ottawa and further skulduggery.

A couple of hours later Saunders climbed into a jet with sixty other strangers and bid adieu to the Toronto vortex. The plane sat back on its tail and punched up through the rolling overcast. Saunders unclicked his belt and relaxed with a cup of vile airline coffee. He scanned the weathered brochures and odds and ends in his Stonehouse file. He'd save some of them for his scrapbook. The rest he'd put in the garbage. When he arrived, he'd retrieve letters, photos and whatever was left. Through the plastic porthole he stared at the slow-passing clouds and the turquoise expanse of Lake Huron. It occurred to him that he just might spend the rest of his life like this, sitting silently among strangers, a courier of documents.

After a seemingly endless flight he landed at

nightfall in Winnipeg, the centre of the continent. Drizzling rain. He threw his bags in a cab and headed for Skip's apartment. The fridge contained sour milk.

Too late to work but too early to go to bed. He cruised downtown in Skip's vintage Buick. He was allowed to drive it around but not to wreck it. What a laugh. Skip had systematically destroyed every car he ever owned. And was probably doing the same at this very moment to Saunders' BMW.

He found a parking spot and continued on foot, searching for a bar, his heels clicking on the wet concrete. The cops were grilling a drunk driver across the street. Red lights splashed on the brick building as Saunders walked by. He felt like ducking into a phone booth and calling Maggie Chavez to ask if she had slept with his father. If so, well, good for both of them. She was young and lithe. But more than that, she evidently had no liking for consultants. Which made Saunders regard her with a grudging respect.

Next day by train to northwestern Ontario. A rainy day. The late summer woods were mottled by changing leaves. His hotel, the Bayview, was a two-storey brick structure with purple carpets, red wallpaper and a picture of a matador above the bed. The room was almost directly over the pub, which was bad, but there was a TV chained to the wall and a telephone. He called a realtor and made an appointment. He wanted an official appraisal, and to find out whether the property was worth more with the building or without. He managed to set up a meeting with a Ben McNabb for the following day.

Rain and thunder. Another lonely night. He walked down to the BoBo Cafe and ordered some dinner. The cafe was empty with the exception of one large, dull-looking guy in the corner who snuffled at a bowl of rice like a feral hog. Saunders took a booth. The glass window beside it had been patched with a sheet of plywood. He could make a pretty good guess at what had happened. The BoBo was located next door to one of Kenora's roughest beer parlours and sometimes loggers came hurtling through the windows, landing on the table in a spray of broken glass and Chinese food.

Back at the hotel, the TV had only one channel. Pretty bad, he thought, when you're so lonely you have to call your business partner. He picked up the phone and tapped out the area code and number for the Château Laurier.

The desk rang Skip's room. "Yo."

"Skip?"

There was a pause. "Mikey!" Saunders held the phone away from his ear. Even at eighteen hundred miles Skip was a loudmouth. "Mikey, are you there?"

"I'm here."

"Where are you? Are you still in Toronto?"

"I'm in Kenora."

"How are you doing? How did you find me?"

"The same way I always find you. Call the most expensive hotel in town."

"How are you doing? Where are you?"

"I'm in Kenora."

"Jus a sec. Jus a sec . . . Mike, will you?"

The phone clattered in Saunders' ear. He could hear music and a woman's voice in the background. Skip's voice came back on the line. "Mike."

"Yeah."

"Giselle doesn't want to say hello. She's too shy."

"Who's Giselle?"

Skip was whispering now. Saunders could visualize him standing there with his hand cupped over the phone. "Mike . . . something unbelievable has happened."

"Where's Chief Leo?"

"Mike . . . something unbelievable has happened.

You know what happened? We were at this reception, this cocktail party, and . . ."

Skip's whisper was so low that Saunders could barely hear him. "Skip, tell me later, all right? I just want to talk to Chief Leo I want to find out if he made a final decision on my idea."

"Oh yeah, right."

"I'm meeting with the realtor tomorrow. Ben McNabb. I'm going to arrange to have it appraised."

"What do you think you'll get for it?"

"How do I know?"

"What about the houseboat lady?"

"Like I said, I'm going to pay her off. And get a realtor. Is Chief Leo there?"

Saunders could hear whispering, then the phone clattered again. Skip came back on the line. "Mike? Sorry . . . I just had to get something."

"Skip," Saunders said, "will you listen to me? I want to talk business for a minute."

"Okay good," Skip said.

"I'm meeting with McNabb tomorrow. I'm going to—"

"Can you call me back?" Skip whispered.

"When?"

"First thing in the morning."

Saunders ran his hand through his hair. What did he ever do to deserve this? "Is Chief Leo there?"

"No, he went home. Listen, Mikey?"

"What?"

"I have to tell you about the unbelievable thing that happened. We went to a reception last night, Chief Leo and I? And we're standing there, talking to all these Quebec assistant deputy ministers, and—" There was the woman's voice again, an embarrassed protest. "Mikey, wait a sec . . . just wait a sec, will you?"

"I'll talk to you in the morning," Saunders said, hanging up.

AT NOON THE NEXT DAY, Saunders went to the hotel restaurant for his meeting with the realtor. He bought a *Globe and Mail* from the newsbox in the foyer and stood by the Please Wait to Be Seated sign. The restaurant was dark inside and, except for a few people having coffee, deserted. He thumped the newspaper against his leg. Joni Mitchell belly-ached softly in the ceiling. A Chinese girl in a black dress came out of the kitchen and spotted him. "Hello."

"I'm meeting another fellow, Ben McNabb?"

"Oh yes, he's here," she said. She led Saunders outside onto a sundeck above the harbour.

A portly grey-haired man in a madras jacket jumped to his feet and extended a hand. "Mr. Saunders," he smiled joyously. "I've heard so much about you."

"Oh really?"

"Isn't this a great sunny day?"

"Yes it is."

Saunders sat down, sliding his briefcase under the table. The waitress stood by. "I'll have ice water and the house salad," he ordered.

"Just coffee for me," McNabb added.

Saunders leaned forward. "Well, how's the market?"

"Good," McNabb said. "Very active."

"You're familiar, I suppose, with the Stonehouse Inn?"

"Of course I am. Knew your father very well. And was very saddened, by the way, to hear of his passing."

Saunders nodded, then explained he was trying to determine if the inn was worth repairing. If not, he would clean off the property and sell it as lake frontage.

McNabb squirmed, clearly excited at the prospect of listing the property. "I have some ideas," he said. "Tenants-in-common cottage lots. And I'll get in touch with various people I know who are involved in trailer parks, motels, that sort of thing."

Saunders laid his arm across the Stonehouse file, protecting it from the wind. He said, "My first preference is to sell it with the buildings intact. I'd rather not demolish the inn if I don't have to."

McNabb scribbled notes on a sheet of yellow paper. He looked up suddenly and smiled. "You know, I feel better, talking to you. I spoke to Margaret Chavez last night, from Minaki? She said you'd hired *her* to act as your agent."

Saunders nodded. It's hard to do business in a small town, he thought. There's no such thing as confidential information. "I've decided not to . . . use her. I think you'd do a better job."

McNabb tapped his pen on the table. He was a nervous little dynamo of a man, with the plush face of a sixty-year-old working on his second cardiac. "Good, good. So are you going to talk to her?"

"I fully intend to. Later today, most likely. Can we drive up to Minaki this afternoon and take a look at the property?"

McNabb flipped open his day book. "Golly Mike. I can't manage it until tomorrow. I've got meetings all afternoon. I can run you up to Minaki, but I can't do much more than that. But why don't I come by tomorrow and do an appraisal?" McNabb said. "Both with the buildings and without them."

Saunders sat for a minute, quiet. "What's your hunch? Do you think the place is worth fixing up?"

McNabb looked apologetic. "From a realistic point of view, I think your best bet is to sell it as a serviced lot. With hydro, road, septic field, lawn and what have you, a big waterfront parcel like that is going to list at a handsome price. I'm almost certain that the buildings are a liability. Go in there with a crew and tear them down. Takes a couple of days. Then you're done with it."

5

$\approx$

MAGGIE WALKED SLOWLY UP AND DOWN THE TRAIN station platform. Her heels knocked on the wooden planks, and bugs cracked and whirred in the weeds beside the railway track. The smell of creosote drifted on the hot air. She sat on the bench under the big Minaki sign and crossed her legs, waiting for a brown Econoline.

They were late. Michael Saunders had called to say he wanted to stay overnight at the inn and he needed to get the keys from her. There were some other changes. He was coming in person to explain. She couldn't help smiling. For some people, money was a subject that could only be mentioned in a whisper. The almighty dollar. She didn't give a damn about her commission. She only cared about the disposition of the inn. She'd done a lot of work on it and she didn't want to see it torn down if she could do anything about it.

She stood up, restless, and paced another circle

around the platform. A police car honked and she waved. She could sit here all day, walking in circles and waving to people. She'd lived here three years now and knew most of the people. The first winter was the worst. Everybody ignored her —she was just another fly-in schoolteacher from Ottawa who would disappear after her contract expired. But she stayed, bought an old houseboat to live in. Who can afford property around here? She renovated the houseboat, put some R20 in the roof, a wood heater, triple-pane windows, and for fifteen thousand dollars had a comfortable house. Ottawa be damned. By the second winter the locals started talking to her. Gordon Saunders, a widower who operated a local, rustic bed-and-breakfast called the Stonehouse Inn, hired her to help out with waitressing and cooking on the weekends. She also helped with the carpentry, and restored all the windows in the second storey, old stained-glass beauties with strap-iron hinges. She loved the texture of old wood, the blond, smooth shimmer when it was refinished.

One day she heard a big crash and she ran down the stairs. Gordon was lying at the bottom of the ladder. His first stroke. The cops came. They turned on their hi-lo siren and drove her to Kenora at one hundred miles an hour. On bumps, they were airborne. She kept giving Gordon mouth-to-mouth. She didn't have a clue what she was supposed to do.

At the hospital she spoke to Ray Morgan, the dark-eyed doctor with the Jesus beard who conducted clinics, sometimes in Minaki. He took charge of Gordon. He had nice black fur on his arms. All the local wives thought he was a hunk.

Somehow, after that, she became the person morally responsible for the Stonehouse Inn. Gordon, hospitalized in Toronto, would call and describe all the tasks "that we have to take care of this month." She felt like saying, "What's this 'we'?" On top of it, Gordon's slime-mould of a son somehow won power of attorney for his father's affairs and refused to send any more money. She didn't want to be paid, necessarily. She was willing to keep up minimal maintenance on the place as a favour to Gordon and a favour to the inn, but she'd be damned, damned, if she'd pay for repairs out of her own pocket and then be forced to listen to this briefcase-toting character from Toronto accuse her of embezzling money from his father.

Now she was getting upset again. She sat down, waited, stood up. Meet us at the railroad station, McNabb said. You can get Mike settled at the inn. Wonderful, she thought. There's nothing I'd rather do than act as a chauffeur for Mike Saunders. She slid her palms into the bum pockets of her jeans and paused to look down the road. Around the corner came Ben McNabb's brown van.

SAUNDERS SAW HER when they pulled into the station. He got out of the van and raised his hand. "Hello, Maggie."

"Hello."

McNabb waved. "Maggie . . . could you run Mike over to the hotel and show him around?"

She nodded.

"Mike," McNabb said, "I'll be back in the morning. We'll go over the place and work out those numbers as accurately as we can."

"Fine," Saunders said. "See you tomorrow, Ben."

He followed Maggie to her pick-up truck. Her big husky sat in the back. He had a head like a grizzly bear. Maggie turned on the ignition before Saunders had shut the door.

"Will you be staying all week?" she asked.

"Unfortunately no. I've only got a day or two."

"And you've definitely decided to sell?"

He nodded. "Yep. Why, do you know someone?"

Maggie backed out of the parking lot. "I know some people who might want to rent it."

"We already tried that. Several years ago my father rented the place to Joan Victoria. She's that feminist anti-smoking advocate? She tried to run it as a health retreat. It didn't work out."

"But these people are reliable."

"Who are they?"

"It's a bit complicated. I should really introduce you to them."

"When?"

"Tonight. Are you busy?"

After a weighty pause he said, "I guess not."

"Good," she said.

Maggie drove the big three-quarter-ton with deft authority, jamming the shifter through the gears and exchanging waves with other townspeople. The sleeve of her T-shirt rode up her arm, showing her plump deltoid muscle, her brown skin. At the outskirts of town they turned onto the Stonehouse road. The woods were cool and sun-dappled. A partridge skittered across the road. She parked the truck. "There it is."

Saunders stared at the tall weather-beaten inn, the crooked porch, the weed-tangled lawn. He had psyched himself up for this moment—seeing the hotel in daylight—but still, it looked pretty bad.

"Shall we?" Maggie said.

They walked around the side of the inn out onto the front lawn, past the wrought-iron bench where his mother used to sit out in the sun and write long letters to her sister back home in England. The lawn sloped downwards slightly toward the rustic cabins facing the water.

"So has your prospective tenant seen the place?" he asked.

"Oh yes. It's a local group."

"Sounds very mysterious."

"Not really."

"Whatever happens, I intend to square up with you on the work you've done so far."

"Sure."

"And I want to talk to you about the listing. It might be better if we let Ben handle it."

"Why? It's not the money, is it?"

"You'll be paid either way."

"Listen, I'm not concerned primarily about the crummy fifteen hundred dollars. Your dad asked me to look after the place. I want to help you find a tenant, that's all."

"Fair enough."

They came up to one of the small log buildings. Maggie produced a short length of hockey stick with a key attached. She unfastened the padlock and eased the door open. "This is a good cabin."

It was dark inside, full of the day's heat. Maggie went into the kitchen and unfastened the big plywood shutters. Sunshine and cool air gushed in. Saunders dumped his bag on the couch. "So when do I meet these tenants?"

She moved toward the door. "My place at seven?"

Saunders watched her go up the lawn to her pick-up. Strong legs, effortless stride. Nice lady, he thought. Even if she doesn't seem too impressed with me.

He hung up his clothes in the bedroom closet and peered out through the window and the interlaced branches to the blue glitter of water. Back home again. Home sweet home. He sat on the bed, a rickety old thing with a steel bedframe and a mattress that sagged like a hammock. In the kitchen, he found several unopened cans of beer in the fridge. The fridge was not plugged in and the beer was warm. He opened one and sat at the little wooden table.

He dug into his briefcase and tossed some magazines on the table: *Small Business, The Northern Ontario Real Estate Gazette, Penthouse.* Saunders opened up *Penthouse* and looked at the centre-fold. He looked at her right side up and he looked at her upside down, then laid the magazine on the table and took a long, slow swallow of warm beer. I'm supposed to feel overwrought, he thought, coming home. But it's not so bad. He lit up a smoke, his first of the day. All I have to do now is get through this. With any luck, two weeks from now this whole business will be resolved.

The wind rustled at the screens. Back in the woods a red squirrel chattered. Time for a swim, he decided. He hadn't brought a bathing suit, but he could get away with a skinny dip. He took off his shirt and pants and looked in the mirror. He patted his stomach with his hands, inhaled a bit, slipped on his shades and knotted a towel around his waist.

Outside, the long grass was tangled and unkempt, full of burrs that nipped at his bare feet. He walked down the rock stairway and out onto the warped planks of the dock. At the swimming ladder he dropped the shampoo and towel. Should he dive or cannonball? He used to be a pretty strong swimmer but he'd gotten away from it. The water was deep here, maybe ten feet. Green sunlight slanted down through it, then disappeared into the really deep purple zone where the shadowy leaves of cabbage weed moved with the tiny, needle-shaped minnows.

Maybe I'll just climb in, he decided. The ladder wobbled when he touched it. It was constructed of rotten two-by-fours and rusty nails. He could imagine the whole thing giving way just at the critical instant, dumping him into a watery grave. *Consultant Dies in Shampooing Attempt.* It was either that or go for it, dive, maybe hit his head on a timber, or get savagely attacked by the big muskie that used to live under this dock. Who needs it? He tossed the towel over his shoulder. Better to swim at the beach.

The beach was next door to the inn, in a secluded bay that belonged to the government. Saunders walked past the shuttered cabins, through the back lawns, the tall-standing daisies alive with bees, and finally came to the beach. He waded in up to his knees, feeling the corrugated sand underfoot, the frigid slap of waves. Soon the sand turned to muck interspersed with sharp stones and he hesitated with thoughts of yard-long bloodsuckers twining around his leg. Then he dove forward and swam hard in a wide circle. Surprising how you never lose some skills.

He swam until he was exhausted, then waded back to the beach, zipped open his overnight kit and lathered his face with shaving foam. Kneeling over his reflection by the water's edge, he shaved and wiped off his face. This place is like a paradise, he thought. Big trees, the sun going down. I never really appreciated it when I grew up.

Later, he strolled around the property, feeling like Mike the Innkeeper in his neat white denims and green Oxford cloth shirt. He peered through screens at the hotel verandah, shady under a log-timbered roof. Chairs and wicker couches were stacked against the wall and above them hung a moth-eaten bull moose with glass eyes. The door was locked. Everyone seemed to have access to the place but him. He only owned it.

Down in the boathouse he rummaged through the piles of equipment. A leather jacket from his teen-age years, wrinkled and dessicated. A hand-made paddle. His old fishing rod. A fifteen-foot cedar and canvas canoe he and his father had fixed up one winter. It was all patched and dried out, light as paper. He'd forgotten about most of this stuff, but now that he could lift it and look at it, its value returned. Whatever happened, he'd have to come back here with a U-Haul and clean out the place. He wasn't going to let some complete stranger take over two generations of family memorabilia.

It was almost time for the big meeting. He lifted the canoe off its rack and carried it out to the end of the dock, then slipped it into the water and climbed down the creaky ladder, which didn't give way, after all.

The craft teetered under him. He knelt on his leather jacket and gave a tentative stroke with the paddle. The canoe glided forward, light as dandelion fluff. He half-hoped Maggie had located a good tenant. Maybe there was a way to resolve this.

6

~

WHEN SAUNDERS WAS A KID THERE WERE THREE
ways of getting around this part of the country: by boat,
by car or by The Path. Mud-packed and overgrown
with foliage, The Path meandered like a deer trail
through the woods, with forks and junctions that
peeled off or rejoined the main trail without sign or
explanation. You had to know where you were going.

By car, you drove up the sandy Stonehouse Road to
the main highway. Saunders and his buddies used to
patrol the road with their slingshots. They built a
treehouse in the woods and kept a weather eye peeled
for bears. Eddy Grogan was in charge of shooting bears.
In those days nobody doubted that bears existed for the
purpose of being shot by Eddy Grogan. One of
Saunders' earliest memories was of riding down the
road on his father's shoulders and seeing, in the
undergrowth, a dead bear, ganged by flies. Another

time, years later, a car with fender skirts and a coon tail on the aerial rumbled down the road. Inside the car were Frankie Grogan, Eddy's greaser son, and half a dozen grinning teenagers. They stopped the car to talk to Saunders and urged him to try a puff of a cigarette. Then, of course, they all laughed hilariously as he coughed. It was the first time Saunders tasted tobacco. Now he went through a pack a day.

By water you had two choices: go west, away from town, leaving the cottages behind and travelling further into what eventually became a tangle of islands, inlets, wilderness. Or you could paddle south past the Stonehouse Bay, around Ferguson's Island to the entrance to Town Bay, where you could see the steel x's of the train bridge spanning the river, the spindle of the town's microwave tower and, on the shoreline going by, a parade of increasingly fancy cottages. The Grogan clan, being third-generation locals, owned a huge stretch of swampy land on the edge of town. And on Grogan's property, in a bay inhabited by herons and water lilies, Maggie's houseboat was anchored.

Saunders drifted quietly up to the houseboat. The water was a mirror. Dave Brubeck played softly. The dog lay out on the deck and thumped his tail as Saunders approached. Down here at water level Saunders could see that the houseboat was basically a small cottage built on a floating deck, with coarse, black steel pontoons underneath. The building itself was finished with cedar. Flowerpots hung beneath the windows. Maggie opened the door. Her thick ripply hair was clipped back and she had white flour all over her hands. "Hello."

"You saw me coming."

"From quite a ways off. Your canoe?"

Saunders nodded. "I came a bit early. I thought you might want to get a bite to eat somewhere."

"Come on in," she said. "I'll make you something."

Saunders tied the canoe onto the houseboat and climbed aboard. Maggie dabbed at her face with her hand, leaving a streak of flour on her cheek. "You're actually right on time because I'm making perogies. Our latest scheme is to have a series of ethnic dinners, every second Sunday night. Charge ten dollars per ticket, volunteer staff. Do you need a job?"

"Uh, no thanks," Saunders laughed. "Are you the chair of the fund-raising?"

"No, the mayor," Maggie said.

The inside of the houseboat was like Witch Hazel's hideout—hanging spider plants, candles, Victorian lace, an aquarium with tiny, darting fish, a huge bear skull, books, a crazy quilt on the bed. In the tiny kitchen half-made perogies sprawled on the pine cutting board. A large window looked out on lily pads and blue water. "Sit," she said. "Can I offer you a glass of wine?"

"Thank you, sure," said Saunders. He sat on an old overstuffed couch.

Maggie took down a frying pan and greased it, then laid half a dozen perogies in it. She pulled a wine bottle from the fridge and expertly popped the cork, poured two glasses and handed him one. "We have five minutes. Then we'll feed you and go."

"Where are we going?"

"To the town hall."

Saunders raised his glass. "I'm quite curious about these tenants."

Maggie bustled around the kitchen before she finally stopped for a glass of wine, leaning against the counter. Tendrils of fine hair escaped from an ivory barrette at her ear. Her eyes were sharp and intelligent. "So . . . ," she said.

"Are you really the mayor?" he asked.

"Sure am."

"How does one get to be the mayor?"

"Just bad luck, I guess. They needed someone and I was handy."

"Sounds like a good system."

"I think everyone does it sooner or later. How does one get to be a consultant?"

"I actually trained to be an artist."

"An artist?"

He nodded. "Fine Arts at UBC. I had the misfortune of striking up a friendship with Skip, who was flunking out of Commerce at the time. He moved to Winnipeg and started a consulting company. I graduated. Later, I ran into him and he hired me to do some design work. Some brochures and so on. One thing led to another. Pretty soon I was handling a lot of the research too. Then I took over half the company."

"Is it interesting?"

"It's more interesting than being broke, which is something I became familiar with when I was an artist."

"Your father said that he always wanted you to run the hotel."

"That's why I fled to the west coast."

"Have you thought of keeping the place? Just for yourself?"

"I can't afford it."

"So what are you going to do?"

He shook his head. "I don't know. I'll have a good look at it tomorrow. Make a list of the jobs that need to be done to put it in tip-top shape, then tally up the costs. If I can't afford it, I'll knock it down."

"May I come along? When you and Ben do your walk-through? There may be ways that you can do the repairs inexpensively, using local people."

"Great."

"I just want to make sure I get a chance to put in my two cents' worth before you make up your mind."

RAISED BY THE RIVER

"All right."

"Because I think a well-informed decision is one that considers all the options."

He smiled, lifting his wine glass. "I read you loud and clear."

"Anyway," Maggie said, "if you think the inn looks bad now, you should have seen it last year. First time I saw the place, it looked like a massive headache. All those crazy roof lines. Sagging foundation. Stained-glass windows . . . you ever try to weatherproof a leaded window? But your father needed the help so I pitched in. Once I invested some time in it I was hooked."

Saunders nodded. "So I've noticed."

Maggie stepped on a stool and reached high for one of the plates displayed above the cupboards. Her green shirt rose up, showing a flat stomach, a curve of a rib. I like this little floating house, Saunders thought. I like Maggie. She's a rebel. I could use a little of this action in my life.

They went to the meeting in Maggie's antique wooden boat. In an orange blaze of thunderheads, the sun sank in the west, and the lake was flat and lurid as paint. They tied the boat up to the public pier at the foot of the hill, and walked up through the town to the barn-sized community centre where the meeting was scheduled. Inside the hall was the standard cigarette-fouled assembly room, with twenty or thirty steel chairs and a plywood lectern set up at the front. They were a bit early. Mayor Maggie went into the kitchen and made coffee. Soon the audience began to filter in—a lot of new faces Saunders didn't recognize. Maggie introduced him to some of the councillors. One of the men present was Dr. Ray Morgan, who ran the local medical trailer. He shook Saunders' hand but only exchanged a wisecrack with Maggie. From their manner, conspiratorial and teasing, Saunders guessed that Maggie and the good doctor already knew each other. Some of the audience were old-timers who shook Saunders' hand and remarked on his success. "It's like having our own movie star," Eddy Grogan said, leering. A soggy cigarette dangled from his lips.

"Still shooting bears, Eddy?"

"They're down in numbers," he shook his head. "I don't know what happened to 'em all."

Children arrived too, an assortment of native and half-breed kids ranging in size from toddlers to teenagers. Soon there was a good-sized crowd in the hall. Maggie called the meeting to order and introduced Saunders, "a professional consultant from Toronto," who now owned the Stonehouse Inn.

A chubby woman with tightly curled hair and a faint moustache rose and introduced herself as the director of the Minaki Day Care Centre. She said that, first of all, she wanted to thank Mr. Saunders for offering the use of his hotel.

"Well, I don't really know if—"

Maggie elbowed him, whispered, "Just listen."

"We're in a real bind right now," the woman said. "And we're hoping that if we can set up a rental agreement with you, we can launch our new program for fall of next year."

"How would the children get to the inn?" Saunders asked. "That road is pretty tough in the winter."

The woman opened a file folder. "Can I show you ... our figures?" She came forward and handed him a photocopy of a Dodge Maxi-Van that a wealthy local cottage owner had donated to the community. "We have eighteen children," she said. "Right now. But we have to find a space that passes the Fire Marshall's inspection."

The woman gave him a bundle of financial projections and other data. Saunders flipped through the documents. They'd evidently applied to NEBLA for operational funding. "And your grant has been approved?" he asked.

"We're still waiting to hear about it."

The next presenter was an off-duty OPP officer who ran something called the Minaki Boys Club. "We'll volunteer to heat the place for free," he said, standing up self-consciously.

"How will you do that?"

"We cut wood every Saturday. Canadian Tire donated the chain-saw. Henry's Esso provides the gas. I supply the truck. Me and the kids," he said, pointing vaguely to a group of children in the row ahead of him, "we've been delivering free firewood to disadvantaged families in the community. And if you were to donate the space to the Day Care Centre, we'd commit to supplying half a cord of firewood every Saturday."

Donate?

"We've drawn up a letter of intent," the policeman continued, gesturing with a blue file folder. "Would you like to look at it?"

Others followed. Saunders collected all the submissions and Maggie moved the meeting along. Soon the focus of attention shifted onto other matters.

When the meeting finally broke up, Saunders discovered that he and Maggie, the twosome, had become a threesome. Accompanied by Dr. Morgan, they walked through the darkened streets back to her boat. Saunders was off balance. He hadn't realized Maggie had a boyfriend. It was no big thing but, combined with the meeting, he felt disappointed. All those eager tenants, none with his money. He knew that the world was a pathetic place. But every once in a while you get your nose rubbed in it.

Maggie drove the boat back to the inn. They dropped Saunders at the front dock. "Nice to meet you,

Raymond," he said as he climbed out. "See you tomorrow, Maggie."

He went up through the trees to the inn, past the white wrought-iron benches, the stone gardens with their knee-high weeds and dead flowers. He stopped to look up at the hotel's rounded stone battlements, socketed with dark windows. Suddenly, a shadow loomed out of the night.

"Michael." It was Maggie. "You forgot your canoe at the houseboat," she said. "Do you want to come and pick it up?"

"Oh . . . well, I'd rather do it tomorrow, actually. But thanks for reminding me."

A moment passed, neither of them speaking. Then, "You're disappointed in what happened at the meeting," she said.

He shrugged. "Everyone has good intentions. No one has any money."

"Skip told me you have lots of money."

Saunders chuckled. "Even if I did, I wouldn't have it for long if I started renting out buildings for free."

"You know what I think?"

He studied her for a moment. Far out on the lake, a loon called. "What?"

"I think you should spend a few days here. Walk around. Smell the flowers. You've got a very special inheritance in this building." She put out her hand. "I'm sure you'll do the right thing."

"Thanks. We'll see you tomorrow."

Saunders walked back to his cabin and went inside. He heard Maggie's boat leaving. He snapped on the reading light above the bed and sat on the mattress. When he was a kid, they sometimes lived in this cabin during the summer and rented out the large apartment on the third floor of the inn to guests. You couldn't have kids running around while guests were trying to sleep in. He remembered lying in the dark in this very bed, listening to the TV news from the other room. His father's rumbly voice, his mother's softer one. And Walter Cronkite interviewing some politician who talked as though he had a clothespin on his nose, John Fitzgerald Kennedy. On the door frame he could still see the faint pencil marks of his height on three successive summers: M.S.—'60, '61, '62.

He kicked off his shoes and unbuttoned his shirt. Maggie said she believed he would do the right thing. What gave her that idea? No matter what happened, it was going to be a difficult decision, and he had little faith in happy endings. People die. Marriages break up. And the finest hotels sink like the *Titanic*. There wasn't much you could do except make sure you didn't get dragged down too.

7

~~~
~~~

SAUNDERS WOKE EARLY AND WENT FOR A SWIM. HE WAS drying off when Maggie appeared, paddling the canoe. She pulled onto the beach. "Good morning."

"Hi," he said, steadying the canoe. "Thanks for returning it."

"No problem. I like an early morning paddle."

He held the canoe as she stood up. She wore leather sandals and khaki shorts. Her legs were tanned and muscular. A red scratch cut across one thigh. She adjusted the blue shoulder strap on her bathing suit and handed him a thermos. "Have you had your morning fix?"

They walked up to the inn and sat on a bench on the lawn while they shared coffee from the thermos cup. The grass was high and Saunders knocked an occasional insect off his bare legs. But the sun was pleasant and the weeds sparkled with dew.

"So," Maggie said, "did you look at those proposals from the meeting?"

He nodded. "Nice people. I'm sympathetic, believe me."

"But?"

He shrugged. "It all comes down to money. I'll write up a list of necessary repairs and get it to Skip and Neil, and they can tell me what it's going to cost to get the place in shape. There's no point in having meetings with tenants until I figure out whether the hotel is even repairable."

"It's not that bad."

"Well, you say one thing," Saunders replied. "My engineer tells me different."

A truck door slammed, and the chubby realtor came around the corner. "Good morning, people. Ready to go to work?"

Saunders stood up. "You bet." He loosened the padlock on the front door and wrestled it open. They all went inside through the verandah to the dank-smelling lounge. Fallen plaster had splattered the sagging linoleum floor and thick cobwebs hung on the partially boarded-up bay windows. There was a big stone fireplace along one wall.

Maggie folded her arms across her chest. It was chilly. She pointed up at the ceiling. "There's UFFI insulation up against those dormers," she said. "Your engineer said it would have to be removed."

"What does it cost to hire workers around here?"

"I could help," she replied. "Finding good trades people is sometimes a bit of a problem."

McNabb seemed nervous at any discussion of a long and inefficient renovation project. It would delay the sale of the property and complicate the prospect of getting a quick and neat commission. He edged out of the lounge area, tapping Saunders' arm. "The dining room area, as you can see, needs a fair amount of work too."

"I should write down the size of these rooms," Saunders said.

"And how big is this room?" Maggie asked.

"Um, twenty-two, I think," said McNabb. "No, wait."

"I'll get it," Maggie said, pacing the distance across the floor.

Saunders jotted down the dimensions of the room as Maggie called them out, and drew a floor plan with the location of doors and windows.

McNabb wandered into the kitchen. "And this is your kitchen area?" he asked. "All the appliances are here, but they're in pretty bad shape."

Maggie opened the door of the oven. "There's nothing much wrong with them. Look at the ornate grill-work on this old wood stove."

McNabb chuckled. "People are frightened off by old things. Believe me, Margaret. I see it every day."

Saunders pried open the door of the fuse box and glanced at the spaghetti of wires on the inside. He pulled open the door to the cellar and peered down a dark stairway. "God knows what's down there."

Maggie got a flashlight out of the cupboard and led them down the treacherous flight of stairs. The cellar was cool and damp, earth-smelling. A forest of teleposts held the ceiling up. Saunders looked at the furnace, a monstrous thing. When he was a kid, it had always reminded him of an enraged squid, or one of those fat-armed trees that is always hooting at lost children in fairy tales. Maggie poked at it while McNabb made clucking, disapproving noises. Saunders waited, feeling claustrophobic under these sagging beams and rusty pipes welded and conjoined by his dead father. Cardboard boxes full of anti-smoking literature were piled against one wall. A few old wooden signs. DON'T BE A SISSY CIG-SUCKER.

Maggie jammed her hands into her pockets and

looked at Saunders. "I don't care what anyone says. That's a good old furnace."

McNabb muttered, "Shall we carry on?"

They climbed up the steep stairs, passed through the kitchen and entered the main lounge. Maggie went into the manager's office, the cubbyhole under the stairs where Saunders had searched for his father's accounts. Dozens of keys hung on a punchboard on the wall. On the little desk were an old Philco radio and a black telephone. Maggie went through some of the drawers in the enamel-green desk. "Some of these papers would be a big help once the place was renovated. Mailing lists. Old booking sheets. You could contact all your old clientele."

Oh great, Saunders thought. First she's got me writing cheques. Now I'm operating a hotel.

"And here's your employee black book," Maggie said. She laid the book, which was red, on the stack of tattered paper on the desk top. "It's very straightforward, the books for a place like this. You see this? This is your opening inventory, right down to the last washcloth and packet of ketchup."

"Uh huh," said Saunders. McNabb wandered away. Too annoying for him.

"And receipts, warranties . . . and advertising stuff, price sheets. I'm sure that you'll want to look at all this material later."

"It's not really a big concern," said Saunders. "I can't see that I'll ever need any of this."

"Shall we have a look upstairs?" Maggie said. She'd taken charge.

The staircase rose in a steep L, with a roof low enough that Saunders still automatically ducked his head going up. At the top of the stairway stretched a narrow hallway. The floor was covered with red indoor-outdoor carpet. Vague sunlight slanted through the shutters. Three doors on the left and two on the right opened off the hall. Lumber and rusty water pipes were piled on the floor. "Your dad and I restored a lot of these windows," Maggie said. "We did the floors and stripped the walls. We were just starting to rewire when he got sick." Saunders was silent. "These, of course, are your guest rooms," she said, wrestling with a stubborn door, banging it open with her fist. "There's not much to see."

Saunders peeked into an unoccupied bedroom. There was a double bed, stripped of blankets, with an Africa-shaped urine stain on the mattress. Vermin had burrowed into the mattress and there was fluff all over the floor. A gang of cowboys thundered across the oil painting above the bed. A pair of French doors, painted green and hung with a set of chintzy curtains, led onto the balcony. Saunders nodded towards the French doors. "Do we still have a balcony out there?"

"Sure," Maggie said. "Have a look."

"I wouldn't stand on that balcony," McNabb cautioned.

Saunders jerked and yanked at the doors. Finally he got one open and he and Maggie went outside. The balcony was actually the roof of the verandah, surfaced with tar and gravel. There were a few rickety wooden chairs. Saunders walked down to the far end of the balcony and knocked his knuckles on the rotten wood. He gripped the railing and wiggled it back and forth. Place is falling apart, he thought. He looked out at the limbs of the massive red pines. What a bloody disaster. "How bad does the roof leak?" he said.

"I would think you'd want to reshingle," she said, her voice crisp and efficient. "While we're doing it, we can put in new insulation."

"We?" he said.

"Well . . . I assume you're going to need all the help you can get."

"To say the least."

"You're based in Toronto," she continued. "I'm sure you can't afford to take much time off work. You'll need a general contractor. Someone who can be on the site and watch over the jobs. Also you need someone who cares enough about the building to keep the trades people in line."

"Are you expensive?"

"Not really, I'll work for whatever you can afford. I assume you'll want to pay me something. Even if it's a token amount."

"Can I ask you something?"

She nodded.

"Why are you doing this?"

"I've always liked woodworking. And architecture. And apart from that, we've got a small community, and we can't afford to have buildings torn down and hotels closed."

"Uh huh."

"It's not as bad as you think. I'll spend a few hours a day keeping an eye on things, that's all. You sign the cheques. When you sell, you get the money back. This property will be worth twice as much with a functioning, cleaned-up building sitting on it."

"With all new plumbing?"

"Yes."

"Septic field?"

"You may not have to replace it."

"Oh really? That's good news." His voice was flat. He scribbled a list of calculations in his notepad. Finally, after a sigh of resignation, he thrust the pen back into his pocket and sat down. Across the yard, the pines swayed in the wind. The water sparkled. No matter what he did to deny it, this used to be his home.

"Should we go down?" McNabb inquired from inside.

"You go. We'll be there in a minute," Saunders

replied. He heard McNabb murmur something as he went downstairs. Saunders laced his fingers and said nothing.

Maggie looked at him. "So what do you think?"

"I'll have to talk to Skip."

"Is McNabb going to be angry if you decide to renovate?"

"He's the least of my worries," Saunders replied. "I just need to find the . . . energy, I suppose, to consider this." He felt overcome by nostalgia and sadness for his lost parents.

Maggie's voice had a hint of humorous consolation. "It won't be so bad."

8

At FOUR O'CLOCK THE NEXT AFTERNOON, SAUNDERS took a seat in the cocktail lounge of Winnipeg's International Airport. Skip's plane was late. Saunders drank a beer while he went over his notes from the inn. He wanted to get this matter settled.

He gazed out the big windows. Far away, past the tall, upright tail fins of the Air Canada clippers, the tarmac stretched out as flat as a painting, with dead autumn grass and runways the same cement-grey colour as the sky. A tiny spot approached, trailing black smoke, and a voice on the PA announced the imminent arrival of Skip's flight. Saunders quaffed his ale and signalled the waitress.

At the terminal gate, he heard a loud hoot and saw Skip coming down the escalator. "Michael! Hucka mucka loagy!" The people around him glanced uneasily at Skip, who strode off the escalator and whacked Saunders between the shoulder-blades. "Spikey Mikey! How are you, mate?"

"Fine."

"Man! What a trip! How are you, mate? Let's go grab my luggage. Did you bring my car?" Skip propped his sun-glasses up in his hair and looked at Saunders. "I met the most incredible woman down east, Mike. I'm totally in love."

"Good."

"She's unbelievable. She's, well, it'll take me a couple of hours to tell the story. Did you sort things out at the inn?"

"Not quite."

Skip cuffed him. "You fired the broad, though, right? Is it all taken care of?"

"It is . . . it was. I'll have to explain it to you. I've got some figures I want you to look at."

"Great. So listen, what's new? You're not going to believe this lady, Spike. She's the ultimate woman. Wait until you meet her. Listen, how's everything in Minaki?"

"Good."

The automatic doors swished open ahead of them and they walked outside. Raindrops, just beginning. The Buick was parked out front. The turn signal was blinking and there was a parking ticket under the wiper.

Skip put his bag in the trunk. "Mike, you won't believe this woman."

"Oh yeah?"

They got in and Saunders started the car. He turned on the wipers and the ticket fluttered away.

"So anyway Mikey, she's unbelievable."

"What's her name?"

Skip lit a cigarette with the dashboard lighter. "Giselle."

"French?"

"Italian," said Skip. "They make the best women."

"Where'd you meet her?"

Skip held his cigarette pointed slightly downward, Bogart style. "Mike . . . I always knew that one day I'd be standing there, bored at a social gathering or on a crowded commuter train, and I'd look over and I'd see her standing there. I've always known it."

"Yeah."

"My mind wasn't even on a woman that night. Chief Leo and I were at a cocktail party, the opening of that new shopping mall in Ottawa. I'm standing there with a drink in my hand, spearing melon globes, and I look over suddenly and there she is, the *vision* of my *dreams*. About five ten, long wavy auburn hair, beautiful Parisian dress, gorgeous face. I swear, I almost had a heart attack."

"Uh huh," Saunders said.

"So I stood there, wondering, what can I do? What can I say to her? I was tongue-tied."

"That doesn't sound like you."

"Yeah, but this was different. This wasn't a pick-up in a singles bar. This was—"

"Different." Here we go again, Saunders thought.

"Wait'll you meet her. You'll understand."

"So what did you do?"

"Nothing, Mike. I stood there with my knees knocking. I watched her put on her coat and head for the door, by herself, and I thought to myself, you wimp, are you going to let the girl of your dreams walk right out of your life without even saying a word? What if she's *single*? So I followed her out the door onto the street and I said, 'Excuse me . . .' And she turned around and she was so beautiful, in that romantic night, that I almost started babbling. I said, 'Excuse me, excuse me.' "

Saunders chuckled.

"Hey, I didn't know what to say. I said, 'Excuse me but I have to say that you are the most beautiful woman I have ever seen in my life.' And do you know what she did?"

"Hollered for a cop."

"No."

"Walked up and grabbed you by the honker."

"No."

"What did she do?"

"She *blushed* . . . just like a school girl. Can you believe that? Here's the most beautiful girl in eastern Canada and she's *embarrassed* because some hick thinks she's pretty."

Skip opened the window and threw out his cigarette. They were driving east on Wellington Crescent, a winding asphalt road slathered with fallen leaves and lined with mansions. He said, "So as soon as I saw that I said, 'Can't we please talk for a few minutes?' She shook her head, 'No. I have to go.' I said to her, 'Can I walk you to your car?' And she was getting a bit uncomfortable by now, because there were people walking by, you know, listening to all of this, so she started half walking away, sort of backwards, sideways, saying, 'No thank you.' And of course by now I'm getting the bit in my teeth and I'm walking alongside her saying, 'Oh pul-lease couldn't I call sometime? Couldn't I pul-lease?' "

"Skip, the man with no shame."

"Darn right. So half-way down the street she stops beside this gleaming black Lamborghini and slides the key into the lock, gives me this slow, reluctant, big-eyed look and says, 'I shouldn't do this, but I suppose we could go get coffee.' "

"Yahoo."

"So we went for coffee. I really laid on the sincerity. Then we walked along the canal. She told me all about herself. She's a Montreal fashion designer and a model. She told me about her family, her friends. I said I'm a consultant in the real-estate development business. She said that was a coincidence because all her relatives were in real estate too. I told her Chief Leo's joke about consultants. You know, how can you tell the difference between a consultant and a rattlesnake?"

"How?"

"Stretch 'em out on the highway and leave them there for an hour? When you come back, the rattlesnake will be the one with the skid marks in front of it?"

"Right."

"She thought I was hilarious. Meanwhile we're strolling, arm in arm. She's telling me how much she admires my self-confidence. My willingness to risk making a fool of myself. She stops and looks at me with her eyes all sparkly in the moonlight, and says, 'It's funny but I can't help thinking, is there such a thing as love at first sight?' "

"Get serious."

Skip slapped the dashboard. "I *swear* to god, that's what she said."

Saunders laughed.

"No, I'm serious," Skip protested.

"Listen Skip, go easy on the love stuff. I believed everything else. Like, I went for the opening, and your establishment of the setting. The part about the Lamborghini was a bit hard to swallow; maybe you'd be better off having her drive a 944 or something. But don't ruin the story by seducing her in one night. I think it would be better if—"

"Mike, it's not a story! It's the gospel truth. You haven't even heard the good part yet!"

"What's the good part?"

"We're not even close to the good part. But there's a part about her modelling career, like, modelling swim-suits and lingerie. Also, she wants to start a modelling school. She's got students already. She's practically famous. Have you ever heard of Angelique sleepwear?"

"No."

"You haven't seen those billboards in Montreal? With the gorgeous wild-haired girl in the naughty underwear? The one that causes all the car accidents?"

"No."

"Look, can you imagine one of these shots, blown up to thirty-six feet high beside the DeCarie expressway?" Skip dug through his briefcase and came up with a glossy clothing catalogue. "Turn to page fifteen."

Saunders absentmindedly swerved to avoid a bicyclist. He turned to page fifteen with his free hand and looked at the colour photograph—a beautiful girl stretched out in the desert sand. Her hair was like a lion's, her bathing suit as green and shiny as mamba skin. "Maybe I have seen the ads."

Skip turned the page before Saunders could get a good look. "This is her in Mexico," Skip said. "Did I tell you about her luxury villa down in Manzanillo?"

"No."

"And this is her family. Society page in the Toronto newspaper."

"Who is this guy?"

"Her uncle."

"I think I've seen him before."

"You have," Skip said. "Look at these."

The next picture showed the same woman, this time wading up out of the surf in a black bikini. A red Mexican sunset raged in the distance.

Saunders pulled the catalogue away. "Let me have a look."

"You're driving," Skip said. "You'll kill us both."

"Where do I know her from?" Saunders mumbled.

"Hucka mucka loagy. I'm not telling."

"Who is she?"

"I haven't told you the good part. The unbelievable part."

Saunders flipped through the catalogue, driving

with one hand. Here was the same woman coiled on the bed in one of those lace nothings, her eyes closed in voluptuous contemplation of who . . . Skip Carter? Are you kidding? Saunders closed the catalogue. "Where did you say you ran into her?"

"At the mall opening."

"I must have met her at a party or something."

"It's not her you recognize. It's her uncle."

"Who is he?"

"I'll give you a hint," Skip said. "Our company may soon experience very rapid growth."

"Eh?"

"I mean this could be the big break. The *big* one, Mikey. Think."

"I give up," he said, pulling into the parking lot.

"One more guess," Skip said. He was like a five-year-old.

Saunders unsnapped his seat-belt and got out of the car. He unlocked the trunk lid and handed Skip his suitcase.

"Think real-estate developers," Skip said. "Look . . . did you ever see this guy?" He waved a newspaper under Saunders' nose.

Saunders studied the face of the man in the photo. He was surrounded by women, an old bull with his harem. Were they Italian? Yes, he was one of those *capos*, old-guard Toronto hoods. What was his name? DePaulo? Wasn't he the guy who kicked Sheila MacVicar's cameraman in the nuts? And the motorcycle cops just stood there laughing? "I've seen him on the news," Saunders said.

Skip nodded. "Uncle Vince, they call him."

"So who's the beauty?"

"Uncle Vince's niece, Giselle DeFranco."

DRESSED IN BOXER SHORTS, Skip leaned into the dressing-room mirror, putting the finishing touches on an extravagant beard of white foam. He tipped his head first one way, then another, solemnly studying the clownish mask for imperfections. Saunders leaned against the door, holding a brown envelope.

Skip ran hot water over his gold razor and tested the temperature of the metal against the side of his wrist. He unhinged his jaw and turned his head slightly, shaving foam from the jawline below the sideburn. He studied the swath of exposed skin and grunted in approval. "I don't even think that the DeFrancos are much involved in the real hard-core stuff anymore. I mean the drugs, the loan-sharking, and so on. In Toronto the Asian gangs control all that now. And they're much tougher than the Italians. I mean, Uncle Vince, come on, he's a *gentleman*. Can you see these old Italians in their seven-hundred-dollar shoes, trying to give meeting with some fourteen-year-old Vietnamese kid with an Uzi under his jacket? It doesn't jibe. Anyway, all the old Italian war-horses are dead. Paul Castellano, shot dead on Fifth Avenue in New York a few years back, right in front of all the shoppers. The Violi brothers. Dominic Racco . . . he was Rocky DeFranco's best man at his wedding. They found him on the railway tracks north of Toronto. And poor old Paul Volpe, Uncle Paul, stuck in the trunk of that car at Pearson International, stinking to high heaven. Giselle told me that Paul Volpe was the nicest man she ever knew. She said she can't walk through the parking garage at Terminal 2 without getting queasy. So that's the deal. Mostly they're into real-estate development now. And if this thing works out for Giselle and me, the New Age Associates may have access to some fairly awesome contracts."

"Well, good."

Skip shot him a look. "Good? It's like winning the lottery, man."

"Great."

"So what's the deal on the inn? Did you sell it?"

"That's still up in the air. Maggie seems to think I can spruce it up now, get it in shape and sell the whole package for a good buck later." Saunders opened the envelope and shook out a sheaf of papers. "I brought along a long list of repairs. I thought we'd price it out."

Skip looked at the floor and shook his head. "Oh boy, I knew this would happen."

"What do you mean?"

"So now what, you're going to waste more time dicking around with this thing? Wandering off to Minaki? Sitting on the verandah of the old family inn, reminiscing?" He slung the towel around his neck and shouldered past Saunders into the living room. "You're nuts."

Saunders followed him. "I am not nuts. What do you mean? I'm trying to pick the best option, that's all."

Skip sat in the black leather recliner and propped his feet up on the glass coffee-table. "Listen, we're partners. I hate to say it, Mike. But you're neglecting your work."

"I am not."

"I hate to put things in a framework of dollars and cents," Skip said. "But that's reality. We've got an inside track now with Vince DeFranco, if my friendship with Giselle works out. Do you have any idea where we could be a year from now, if we play our cards right? We have to *focus*, Mike. We have to get this company up onto the next plateau. Do you want to still be sitting in some rat-ass hotel in Kapuskasing when you're fifty-six years old, mumbling into a tape recorder?"

"No."

Skip shrugged. "Well, that's reality. We can't afford to send anyone else on the road, so who's going to do it? We have to double or triple in annual sales, then we'll hire some underlings and let them do the work. Then we can just sit back and answer our mail. Renovating the Stonehouse Inn? That's the *last* thing you should be investing two months of your time in."

Saunders frowned.

"We need to go after some new business," Skip said. "I'm going to have you sitting around a big dinner table with Vince DeFranco before this quarter is out. You wait and see."

"That's fine. But if I renovate, Maggie will be the general contractor. I won't even have to be there. She'll supervise the job."

"And you'd cut the cheques."

Saunders nodded. "I trust her." As soon as he'd said it, he knew he shouldn't have.

Skip paused, fingers frozen above a cut glass bowl of cigarettes. "You what?"

"I said I think she's trustworthy."

"You're banging her."

Saunders was calm. "No. She has a boyfriend. He's a doctor."

"You'd like to bang her."

"What's that got to do with it? I think she's trustworthy. She's not out to take my money. If she wants to help out, what's wrong with that?"

"So you're banging her," Skip repeated.

Saunders didn't reply. He sort of enjoyed hearing Skip say it.

Skip lit a cigarette with a block of green jade. "Pussy," he said.

"Will you let up?"

"No, it all makes sense to me now. It's pussy. The whole thing's pussy. You go to Minaki to sell the property. You come back, you've changed your mind. All this talk about responsibility. It's pussy. You're starting to listen to this broad. You're starting to take her seriously."

"Don't be ridiculous."

"No listen, who's running the show here, your brain or your crotch? You think that Maggie knows more about the construction business than you do? Or Neil? Or me? You're nuts." Skip shook his head in disgust. "And I suppose you'd renovate the place with your own money, right?"

"That's right."

"Well, you're going to bankrupt yourself. And you know why you're doing it? For pussy." Skip snorted in laughter. "But that's not the funny part. You know what the funny part is? This gal, this Maggie, is bored with her boyfriend, the doc, right? He's probably been playing it cool. Won't 'commit.' Et cetera et cetera. She wants to get the relationship wrapped up and he won't budge. Am I right?"

Saunders lit a cigarette and hissed out a thin, angry stream of smoke. "I don't even think they're seriously involved."

"Believe me, they are."

"So what if they are?"

"This woman, this lady you 'trust.' You know what she's using you for?"

"Because she cares about the hotel."

"Come on," Skip said. "She's trying to make her boyfriend jealous. And she'll give you some nookie, now and then, just to get the point across. But you'd better hope he's not a hothead."

"Why?"

"Because what do you think he's going to do when he finds out you're banging his girlfriend?"

"He's not going to find out."

"Of course he's going to find out! She *wants* him to find out! That's the whole purpose of it."

Saunders' jaw muscle twitched.

"So am I wrong? Or what?"

Anger boiled inside Saunders. He shoved the papers at Skip. "This is a list of repairs that are required to get the place ship-shape. I need you and Neil to tally it for me."

"Is that all you've got to say?"

"I know you think I'm a moron, that's fine. I can live with that. But let me tell you something. This whole issue has nothing to do with Maggie. It's a matter of principle. I owe something to that place. My father spent his whole life working at it. Do you think I'm looking forward to tearing it down? You want to help, do something specific? Give me a number on those. You think I'm twelve years old? I need your advice on women? Just give me a number." Long silence, a stand-off. "If it's clearly a waste of money," Saunders added, "I'm not going to do it. You should know me well enough by now."

Skip took out a calculator and put on his eyeglasses. He tapped out a series of numbers and paused, drew on his cigarette. The air was tense. Fifteen minutes passed while he wrote down numbers and calculations. Finally, he said, "Have a look at this." He showed Saunders a page of pencilled notations, numbers, mysterious algebraic symbols. "You follow?"

"Yeah," Saunders lied. He wasn't good with numbers.

"The hotel only has value as a hotel. You fix it up, you sell it as a business, not as a piece of cottage real estate. What's it worth? Well, suppose you winterize, fill it with ski people in the winter, on the weekends, and run mid-week conferences. In the summer you work the fishermen and the families. Seventy-five bucks a night, sixty percent occupancy. You access NEBLA funding for the renovations and keep everything on the cheap side. You'll have a minimum fix-up cost. You see this?"

Saunders nodded.

"Have a look at this," Skip said, producing a second sheet of notations. It was similarly infested with wavering columns of numbers, boxes, arrows and equals signs. "See what it adds up to?"

"Not really."

"The bottom line is, you spend one hundred and twenty thousand dollars fixing the place up, and eventually sell it for two hundred and change. Do you get your money back?"

Saunders waited.

"You lose forty, maybe fifty thousand of the money you spent on renovations. Also, you tie up three months' time. Plus you screw things up at the office because you're always baby-sitting the project. Have you forgotten about the Hi-way Inn? We went crazy over that job and we didn't even care about it."

"But we made a good buck. That's what we're in business for, right? I want to do the same with the Stonehouse."

Skip chuckled. "You're a great research man, Mike. But a lousy accountant. What do you think would have happened to the Stonehouse Inn if your father had survived?"

"He was trying to find another tenant, the last time we discussed it."

"Sure. What does that tell you? He was trying to get out of it, get rid of the place. He knew, Mike. He knew that the building was finished. Maggie is just a ditzy little chick who got drawn into the romance of the project. What did she do? Scrape a little wallpaper? What does she know about construction?"

"I have no idea."

"Nothing, is what she knows." Skip stubbed out his cigarette and went into the bathroom.

"So you're saying I should sell it as is," Saunders called after him. "And failing that, demolish it."

Skip was brushing his teeth in the bathroom. He peered out the door. White foam bubbled on his lips. "I'm not saying anything, partner. You're a big boy. You decide."

Saunders stood up, picked up the papers and went out onto the balcony. My buddies are all assholes, he thought. Well, I guess that really settles it. If I fix it up, I'm probably going to lose my shirt. And what's the point? Maybe whoever buys it will rip it down anyway. It's a free country. I can't force someone to keep the building if they don't want to.

To hell with it.

He crumpled the papers up into a fist-sized ball and aimed for the dumpster in the parking lot. It was twelve storeys down. The wind caught the paper and it bumped lazily against the building, coasted sideways and drifted down into the riverbank woods.

9

So THE NEXT STEP WAS, DO IT.

Saunders called McNabb the day after and left a message on his machine. It was mid-afternoon when McNabb called back, interrupting the quarterly meeting of New Age Associates. For once, Neil Olson, Skip, the Brain and Chief Leo were all there. Iris, the secretary for New Age, high-signed Saunders when McNabb's call came in.

Saunders left the meeting. He walked down the hall and closed the door of the Brain's empty office. For a moment he sat with the message light blinking on the phone. Do I really want to do this? he wondered. Out the window, the fire escapes and warehouses were gloomy under a dark sky. "Hello," he said finally into the phone. "Mike Saunders."

"Mike, it's Ben!"

"Yeah, I've been trying to get hold of you."

"Have you reached a decision?"

"I can't see any way we can afford to renovate," Saunders said. "I think we'll just have to list it as is, and if that doesn't work, demolish it and sell the cleaned-off property as a cottage site."

McNabb's voice was garbled. He was calling from his cheap car phone. "I couldn't agree more."

"What are you listing it at?"

"Eighty-five thou."

"Let's advertise it with the buildings included for a month or two," Saunders said. "Or maybe ninety days, if we can manage. I've got some business to catch up on in Toronto, but as soon as I'm free, I'll clean my personal belongings out of the building."

"Would you like me to run ads in the *Globe and Mail*?"

"Sure. Let's move on this as quickly as possible. I'd like you to orchestrate things. Deduct your fee from the proceeds. . . ." Saunders paused while McNabb scribbled instructions. "Deduct your fee from the proceeds," he continued, "and send the balance to my broker at Midland Doherty. If you need me, I can be reached at the following phone numbers in Toronto."

So back to Toronto, accompanied by Skip and Chief Leo. Chief Leo wore the plumed cowboy hat that you could see from anywhere in the 737. He and Skip were looking forward to an introduction to Vince DeFranco, courtesy of Giselle, and they were pumped. Vince DeFranco was doing a series of strip-mall projects and Skip's plan was to get New Age Associates to offer their services as general contractor. Chief Leo didn't bring much in the way of city-planning expertise but he could write one hell of a START application. Skip and Chief Leo went over their proposal, and ordered miniature bottles of Chablis every time the stewardess walked by. Three rows behind them Saunders stared out the window at the fading evening light. Thirty thousand feet below was the north Ontario bush country—lakes, forest. One of those tiny lights was probably Maggie's houseboat. He'd not had the guts to call her.

When they landed in Toronto they rented a powder blue Lincoln Town Car from Budget. Chief Leo and Skip needed a car for their meeting with Uncle Vince and the clerk persuaded them that they were the kind of cool hombres who needed one with a telephone. The night was black and hot. With Skip at the wheel, the Lincoln swayed and floated at eighty miles per hour through the soup of steamy, monoxide-stinking air. They swept east on a sixteen-lane river of traffic, past the industrial wastelands, the empty, impersonal arc-lit parking lots and sidings and railyards and warehouses and billboards and clotted ugliness of outlying Toronto. Chief Leo amused himself by phoning his cousins back on the reserve.

Skip took the off ramp and booted east on College, jumping the yellow light with his window rolled down and his elbow hanging out, slapping the steering wheel in time to the music. In Little Italy, men in tight pants hung out in crowds on the street corners, and cops in yellow cruisers drove by slowly, eyeballing the citizens. A right turn down to Dundas and then east into Chinatown, the smell of garbage coming in the window, the swirling neon lights and rampant dragons advertising Chinese Freemasons and Dart Coon Club. Skip did a slow crawl down Yonge Street to make sure that Toronto's drug addicts and transvestites were still on the job, then cruised down to the harbour and Saunders' apartment.

At the apartment Saunders checked to see how long he'd been away. He could tell by the number of plants that had died and the viscosity of the milk in the refrigerator. Skip and Chief Leo erected their campsite in his living room. They wanted Saunders to draft some

materials for the meeting with Vince DeFranco the day
after tomorrow, but he wasn't in the mood. He just said
good night. "I am going to bed for three days."

In the middle of the night he woke up to pee. He
looked at himself in the bathroom mirror, evaluating
the wrinkles around his eyes. Wrinkles were caused by
a loss of elasticity in the collagen of the skin. It was
horrible. You get old and die. I've made a decision, he
realized, that I'll have to live with for a long time.

He shut off the bathroom light and crossed the
sleeping consultants. The balcony sliders were open.
Raining now. Cooling down at last. Drops of
sulphur-dioxide-scented rain blowing in off the lake.
He could imagine a loon call crossing the darkened
lake, looping through Maggie's screen window, a
thousand miles northwest of here.

Next morning, back to work. Back to the little office
in the Federation building on Queen Street East with
the lunch room down the hall and the glazed
doughnuts—probably the same ones—sitting by the
coffee machine. Back to pink messages with his name
on them. Back to a two-hour lunch with a prospective
client. Back to returning to his office at two-fifteen just
a little bit pissed, propping his feet up on the desk and
looking out at the industrial heartland of Toronto, the
swarming freeway, the rain on the Dirty Don.

Meanwhile, Skip and Chief Leo stayed at home in
his apartment, gearing up for their audience with
Vince DeFranco. Saunders stayed that night with
Deborah, then sped back to his apartment the next
morning. He discovered reams of computer print-out
on the living room floor and a photographer taking
shots of Chief Leo out on the balcony. In his bedroom
a printer chattered. Skip and Chief Leo were away
from home and were conducting themselves
accordingly, deftly cleaning out his dope supply and

liquor cabinet and playing his Sinatra records without bothering to put the platters back into their sleeves.

"You're destroying this place," Saunders accused.

"Now now," Skip said. "Don't act out."

"What the hell have you done to this kitchen?"

"He's pretending he's mad," whispered Chief Leo. "He's shy about showing us his love."

"You assholes."

"Did you call McNabb, dear?"

"Why?"

Skip handed him a slip of paper, arching his eyebrows lasciviously. "Says he's got a hot prospect, Mikey."

Saunders went into the bedroom and called McNabb. A lawyer from Kenora, a retired widower, wanted to make an offer on the property. "Great," Saunders said. "What's he offering?"

"Seventy-nine five."

"Sold."

"But he wants to make it subject to you removing the main building and the boathouse from the site. He wants to build his own place."

Saunders grimaced. So it was true. Nobody wanted an old log and stone inn.

"He'd like to get the demolition done in the next couple of days. He wants to get his house started before the cold weather."

"Well, I can't tear it down until maybe next month. I just got back."

McNabb groaned and whined that if they didn't move right away they might lose the customer.

"Let me get back to you," Saunders said. "I have to reconsider my schedule."

McNabb said he'd hold the guy off for twenty-four hours. Saunders was half-tempted to just write off the hotel's personal belongings and make a clean break of it. He wouldn't miss most of it and he had nowhere to put it. What was he going to do with a canvas fifteen-foot canoe?

That night he went out for a drink with Chief Leo and Skip. Not even a trio of foxy secretaries in spike heels could cheer him up. They met the women in the night club of the Royal York hotel. Up on the stage Kris Kristofferson was mumbling into a microphone. Saunders kept whispering to Skip. "Maybe I'm selling it too low."

"Eh?"

"The guy grabbed it as soon as it hit the market. Maybe I should raise the price twenty grand."

The women at the next table glanced at Saunders. "Ssh," one of them whispered.

"Hush to you too," Saunders remarked. Chief Leo chuckled. The unlit cigar bobbed in his mouth.

Kristofferson directed a dark glance towards Saunders.

One of the women leaned forward. "Do you mind? That's Kris Kristofferson up there."

"Oh really?" Skip said. "Well, this is Mikey Saunders down here and he's trying to give meeting."

"That's right," Saunders said. "Do you girls want to buy some cottage property?"

The girls must have found Saunders and Skip and Chief Leo amusing because an hour later they were all cruising around Rosedale in the rented Lincoln, looking for the address of a rumoured party.

Saunders was trying to rewrite his ad. "Like, I wonder if I should stonewall this guy and relist the property at a better price."

"Who knows?" said Chief Leo.

"Who cares?" said one of the girls.

"Is this the street?" Skip said. He was driving with his arm around the woman squashed between him and Chief Leo.

"What's the wise choice, though? To sell now, or hold out for more money? It's a risk, either way. I don't know."

"Go left here," Chief Leo said. He turned a piece of paper right-side up and upside down, trying to decipher the map to the party. His eagle feather was bent against the roof of the car. "You know what? I don't get this map."

Saunders was sitting forward, his hands on his knees. "Skip, I'm serious. I need to get this thing sold."

"Then bulldoze it," Skip said. "A good man with a Drott Cruz-Air could turn that sucker to kindling in ninety minutes."

"But what do you think of the price?"

"Let the schmuck pay," Skip said. "Sell it now. Take the money and run."

"But am I selling it too low?"

"Nope. You're robbing the guy."

"Is this the street?" Chief Leo said, studying the map.

"But I can't decide whether to go and retrieve my stuff."

"What?" Skip said. "Is this the street?"

Chief Leo studied the map. "Go straight."

Skip was driving too fast. The car humped up and down like a stampeding buffalo. The cute redhead with Skip gave a cowgirl gee-haw. The other two girls laughed and toasted drinks. They were having a grand old time, Thursday night out.

"Was that the street?" Skip exclaimed, stabbing the brakes.

"No no, keep going. Hang a left here. Jesus," Chief Leo exclaimed. "You drive like an old woman."

Saunders reached over the front seat to retrieve the cellular phone. He leaned back in the soft velvet seat and tapped out McNabb's number. It was a good phone. A thousand miles away, McNabb's phone rang as clearly as a bell.

"Ben, I've made a decision," Saunders said,

clamping a hand over his ear. "Can you hear me? I'm coming out to Minaki as soon as possible. I'll try to leave tomorrow. I want you to tell the guy I accept his offer. Can you hear?"

McNabb said he could.

"And I want you to arrange a meeting with some contractor—" The car hit a row of bumps and bottomed out spectacularly three times in a row. Female whoops erupted inside the car and orange sparks blew past the window. "A *contractor*," Saunders repeated. "Someone who knows how to demolish a building."

10

By MID-AFTERNOON THE NEXT DAY SAUNDERS WAS caught up in twenty-four lanes of traffic, heading out of Toronto. The back seat of his BMW was piled with various tools, leather gauntlets and new work boots from the Red Wing store. Waggling behind the BMW, hooked to a new trailer hitch, was a boxy yellow U-Haul trailer. Do it right, he thought. It's your hotel. Drive out there and see it through to its conclusion. He wished there was some way to set the big hotel adrift, watch it blaze, a Viking burial. But gradually his initial euphoria turned to depression. This was a sad task, going off to retrieve the odds and ends of his family home.

The afternoon wore on. Radio stations criss-crossed and faded. By evening the crew-cut autumn fields had yielded to dark pre-Cambrian forest. A trio of deer tail-flagged across the highway. Through the window he could smell the lakes and evergreen forest of Shield country. By midnight, he rolled into Sault Ste. Marie, home of Phil Esposito, and booked a room across from the rumbling paper mill. Next day he drove over the north shore of the lake, Gitcha Goomie, hoping to hear "The Edmund Fitzgerald" on the car radio. He had been in Duluth, waylaid in a hotel above the lake, when the big taconite boat sank in a November snowstorm many years ago. That disaster had barely rated an item on the national news. None of these events is in itself remarkable until some folksinger gets it on the pop charts.

Thunder Bay. Coffee and lemon pie at a roadstop, then out into the night. Friday night. A sex therapist was on the radio. Saunders listened to a progression of sad stories about eros and love. All over the continent, he realized, people, right now, tonight, were trying to connect unmatching genitalia. The sex therapist was patient. Have you checked your vacuum lines? Your pressure plate? Your rear bushing? Nobody wants to consider the possibility that love is a bird that alights for a moment, then goes.

So the night wore on. Long hills. Big Macks and Peterbilts going by. Swirls of leaves blowing across the road. Then another motel, this one with varnished log walls and stuffed fish in the coffee shop. The night clerk was a pretty redhead, freckle-nosed and small-town friendly, who wanted to know where Saunders was going. He told her about his family resort. He told her about his mother and father, and the Stonehouse Inn, built painstakingly, piece by piece, each granite slab chipped and hammered by his parents. He told her about the big white pine beams in the lounge, the square-hewn posts in the walls of the dining room, the verandah overlooking the lake. He didn't tell her he was on his way to tear it down.

Next morning, the last leg of the trip, was real primal wilderness—muskeg swamps and monstrous, misty, unending forest. Saunders was starting to get that feeling again: I'm coming home. Occasionally he stopped to urinate by the deserted roadside. He stood atop the only object that links east and west—the concept of Canada reduced to a thirty-foot-wide strip of asphalt. This was what it would be like after the nuclear holocaust. No people. Just an occasional raven, broken trees. Skip blew a tire along this stretch, a few years back, and the tire iron grunted and squealed as he loosened the lug nuts. It was moose rutting season, and the noises apparently were mistaken for cries of love by a very large and very ugly (according to Skip) bull moose, who swaggered out of the bush, spied Skip and decided that if he couldn't make love he'd make war. (Or maybe he wanted to make love, who knows?) Saunders could imagine Skip in his mauve disco suit, gold chains and platform shoes, skidding frantically on the gravel as the moose chased him around the car.

When Saunders got to Kenora it was noon, a cold, blustery, autumn day. He phoned McNabb and set up a meeting, then buttoned his jacket and went across the shopping centre to get some French fries at the chip wagon. He was eating the fries, guzzling a magnum of hot coffee while leaning against the cold fender of his faithful BMW, when McNabb walked up. In his camel three-quarter-length, he looked like a white-haired gnome.

"Michael," he said, sounding concerned, extending his hand. "How was your trip?"

"Fine," Saunders said. "I brought a trailer."

"I can see that."

"So what's the story, did you locate a wrecking crew?"

McNabb nodded. "Well . . . yes and no. I wasn't able to get bids from several contractors, as you suggested, because most of the companies have their heavy equipment tied up on the west bypass right now."

"So where does that leave us?"

"I found one very good local fellow with a machine who has a few days off."

Saunders nodded. "How much?"

"Five thousand."

"That's ridiculous."

McNabb shrugged. "This machinery costs a lot of money."

"Whatever happened to crowbars and minimum wage? Never mind. Tell him to come on out in the morning." Saunders glanced at his watch. "If I'm going to get that building cleaned out tonight, I'd better go get started."

SAUNDERS BACKED THE TRAILER against the inn's front door. The ivy-garlanded stone battlements seemed cold and forsaken. He walked down to the boathouse and looked through its shelves and cupboards. There wasn't much here worth saving. His old leather jacket. A couple of fishing rods. Tools. He boosted the canoe overhead, surprised at how light it felt, and walked up to the car. He went back for the tools, the paddles and the other things, then closed the door of the boathouse. This time tomorrow there'd be nothing here but a patch of scarred shoreline.

The interior of the hotel didn't have much in the way of valuables. He took apart an old bed on the third floor and carried it down to the yard where he loaded it in pieces into the U-Haul. A china cabinet of his mother's received similar treatment. With cardboard boxes he'd found in the basement, he went through the dining room, packing plates, photographs and silverware. He worked all afternoon, choosing anything that seemed to have sentimental value. The more careful he was, the less difficult it would be to finally drive away.

At six o'clock dusk was falling, and the job was done. He rewarded himself with a fat glass of warm whisky, chased with a couple of Rothman's. Outside, he leaned against the car and turned his collar up. The wind ripped sparks off the cigarette. What about the canoe? He couldn't lash it to the top of the trailer. And there was no room inside. Anyway, what was he going to do with a canoe in downtown Toronto?

Give it to Maggie.

It wasn't much of a peace offering. But he knew she'd take this news badly. Maybe a heart-to-heart conversation would help her to understand why he'd done this.

He pulled on his new Red Wing boots, tightened the stiff leather laces, then stuffed a tiny survival flashlight in his pocket and hefted the canoe onto his head. In the gathering darkness the lake was charcoal-grey, shot through with fading light, wrinkled with waves under a stiff northern breeze. Should I tie it onto the car? he pondered. To hell with it. It's a light canoe. I'll just carry it.

He manoeuvred the little Tekna-light out of his pocket, clenched it in his teeth and followed its bouncing beam into the woods. Up above, the wind ghosted in the trees. He always found that a walk in these woods was a humbling experience. He might be a know-it-all consultant, but these trees, this wind, had a knack of reminding him that the total significance of his life, in the long term, was nothing.

After a while he crossed the railway tracks and gained the road. Bits of rain rattled against his coat. The headlights of an approaching car swam along the face of the rock cut. Saunders walked down the shoulder. Mister Canoe-Head. At Maggie's road he shut off the flashlight. The lights were off in her houseboat. He lowered the canoe onto the ground and called out, "Hello?" No answer. He walked up the gangplank and knocked on the houseboat door. The building stirred slightly as the wind nudged against it. He opened the door. "Maggie?"

Silence. He waited a moment, then stepped inside. A kerosene lamp burned dimly on the table. It was so nice and quiet in here, warm, smelling of spices and feminine clothing. He took a pen from his pocket and found paper in a notebook on the shelf. He scanned the books and photos. There was a picture of Maggie on a bicycle, smiling, with a group of Asian people. A backdrop of jagged mountains. Thailand? China? Another picture of Maggie with a bear cub. She was just a pretty young woman, a teenager, and she was carrying the bear like a human infant.

Saunders sat down and thought for a while. Finally, he began to write:

Dear Maggie:

I would like you to have this canoe.

As you may know, I have decided against renovating the Stonehouse Inn. I simply cannot afford to spend the money to fix it, and I've had offers from individuals who are interested in purchasing the property, but not with the hotel on it.

My father spent two winters restoring this canoe, and I hope it will be of some use to you. Please take it as a token of my admiration. I know we didn't "click" when we first met, but under different circumstances I think we might have become friends.

Do you ever get to Toronto? I'm attaching a business card, and would be only too glad to buy you dinner if you ever feel like a visit to the big city.

All the best,

Michael G. Saunders

He drummed the pen on the desk, half-hoping Maggie would arrive and catch him in her house. He wanted to talk to her. Life is mean, the way you meet people, then never see them again.

He walked back to the hotel and, because the beds were taken apart and packed in the trailer, decided the most comfortable place to sleep would be right in the car, with the seat folded back. He unpacked his Woods sleeping robe and arranged it on the passenger seat. It was a cold night, very still, with the metallic scent of winter in the air.

He slept fitfully. A strange wind prowled under the car. At first light he was drawn up in a foetal ball, with the sleeping bag over his head like a burial shroud. He was aware of two things immediately: the bits of rain ticking against the glass and the windshield, and the intense cold. He wasn't sure if it was the cold or the rain, clickety-clacking on the windows, that woke him. Or the snorting of the heavy tractor coming towards him as if it meant to crush his car.

He pulled the sleeping bag away from his face and looked out the side window. A big Drott Cruz-Air growled and blew a gust of blue smoke as it backed into place by the parking lot. The yard was white. The evergreens along the driveway swayed and twisted in a screen of flying snow. Sleet and ice particles rattled on the windshield. It wasn't rain, it was snow.

Winter.

11

~~~~~~~~
~~~~~~~~

SAUNDERS DRESSED HURRIEDLY, THEN CLIMBED OUT OF
the car and walked towards the hotel. Sleet blew across
the yard, biting into his eyes.

He stopped.

The canoe was propped against the side of the
building, with a note pinned to the gunwale. He tore
off the sheet and read it.

> *Mr. Saunders:*
>
> *It was late when I got home but nevertheless I
> thought it best to return the canoe immediately. I
> thank you for the gift but you have no reason to give
> me anything. I was very disappointed to discover that
> you will be tearing down the inn and you'll forgive
> me if I say that you're making the wrong choice.*
>
> *Perhaps you can sell the canoe in Kenora.*
>
> > *Best of luck,*
> >
> > > *Maggie Chavez*

Saunders read the note several times. Snow whirled around his head. He balled the paper up angrily. *I guess she thinks her little itty-bitty regrets over losing the inn are more important than my own.* He stomped the snow off his feet and went into the building. McNabb was showing the demolition team around the place.

"Ah, there he is," McNabb exclaimed. He was dressed in a fashionable Eskimo parka, with big mitts on his hands. His spectacles were frosty and he tripped over a chunk of plaster as he moved towards Saunders.

"Hi Ben," said Saunders, extending his hand. McNabb was always lunging for someone's hand.

"This is Frank Ross," said McNabb, indicating a large, bovine-looking individual in coveralls and a hard hat.

"I need a cheque before I start work," Frank Ross said bluntly. "A certified cheque for half. You can hold back fifty percent for after clean-up." He removed a mitt and thoughtfully wiped a drip of snot from his nose. "I can't start until I get a cheque."

Saunders could hear boisterous laughter in the next room, and boot steps going up the stairs to the second floor. "What are they doing upstairs?" he demanded.

McNabb shrugged. "They have to determine the best way to knock the building down, right Frank?"

"I need a certified cheque before I start work," Frank Ross repeated. "I'll clean her right off to your satisfaction, Mr. Saunders, but we don't work for free."

Saunders laid his briefcase on the table. "Okay, I'll have to go into Kenora and get a cheque certified. What are you going to do in the meantime? Wait around? It's an hour and a half, round trip."

"We'll get started, no problem," Frank Ross said. He pointed a fat finger at Saunders. "But we want her certified, okay? Square deal?"

"Did you get everything out of the building yet?" McNabb inquired.

"Yeah, but . . . "

An enormous crash, like a dresser being tipped over, sounded upstairs. "What the hell are they doing up there?" Saunders asked again.

"Maybe getting started," Frank Ross replied. "My boys like to work."

"And you'll clean off the site?"

Frank Ross spat on the floor. "Clean as a whistle. We'll knock her down and truck her to the dump. Just need a cheque."

Saunders hurriedly looked around at the kitchen, its hand-made shelves, its cupboards. The leaded windows, cracked, clotted with blowing snow. I hate this, he thought. Everything I'm looking at, I'll never see again.

McNabb patted him on the back. "So you'd better get going to the bank, Mikey boy. It's a long drive."

Saunders nodded. He went outside. The Drott Cruz-Air was idling in the driveway. It looked like a soot-covered brontosaurus. Frank Ross clomped down the stairs. "She's in your way. I'll move her."

Saunders got into his BMW and started the engine. The Drott snorted, belched smoke and backed out of his way. It backed all the way across the lawn and hit the rotted old pine pole that supported the inn's martin house. The pole tipped over and fell. The Drott's huge back tire passed over the martin house, which crumpled like a house of cardboard. Saunders sat in the car, shivering. The Drott continued on for several feet, then stopped.

Saunders knew he had to shift the car into gear now and move forward. He knew he was supposed to drive past the tractor, continue on up the road and go to Kenora to get his cheque certified. When he returned, all he needed to do was pay the contractor, hitch up to the U-Haul and head back to Toronto. In a few weeks McNabb would send him the cheque and that would be the end of it. The easiest eighty thousand bucks he ever made.

But he didn't move the shift lever.

He stared at the multi-coloured swatch of wood embossed on the snow, marked by the tractor's tread. His father loved birds. He knew the names of all the bird species, and he even memorized their whistling calls before he became too hard of hearing. He'd spent maybe a month building that martin house. He got the design from *Woodworker's Digest*, and took great pride in painting it. Saunders was a little kid the day it went up. He recalled his father pouring the cement footing, and making an elaborate hinge for the base of the pole so that the house could be taken down and cleaned every spring. Cleaning the bird house. Can you imagine that? As if there weren't enough chores to do around here. Gordon had to provide hotel accommodation for the birds too.

The pathetic part of the whole story was that the martins never used it. Even the grubby starlings never used it. Every spring, Gordon would clean and paint the bird house, and every summer the birds would ignore it. Now here it was, thirty years later, smashed to kindling.

Saunders put the car in gear and rolled past the tractor. He drove up the slope, past the snow-clotted spruces. When he came back, the inn would look like the martin house. It was so pathetic. The goddamned selfish birds never even used the place.

He jammed his foot on the brake and stopped the car, then got out and walked back down the road to the inn. McNabb was gesticulating beside the tractor, pointing the best way for Frank Ross to get around to the back of the building. Maybe all the debate, all the arguing with Skip, with Neil, with Deborah, all the driving back and forth, writing notes, biting his nails, was just a process of getting ready for what he knew he was going to do in the first place.

"Shut it off," said Saunders.

His voice startled McNabb. "What's that, Mike?" he asked, smiling.

"Get these assholes off my property," Saunders said, hooking his thumb over his shoulder. "I'm not going to permit this."

12

NOW WHAT?

After McNabb and his wrecking crew vacated the inn, Saunders went into the hotel and sat on a turned-over Pepsi crate. Snow fell obliquely past the window. It was silent. He could see the exhalations of his breath.

He would obviously have to stay here for several weeks. Draw some money from his savings and hire some people to get the inn shipshape. He'd have to keep an eye on the project. And what about food? Warmth? Could he get the old furnace going?

There was only one solution to half these problems. Eddy Grogan.

Saunders drove over to Grogan's Supply and parked the BMW in front of the office. A young man told him that Eddy was in the back. Saunders walked around through the yard. The snow drove sideways through the openings between the mountains of piled lumber. Eddy was having a smoke break with a crew of shifty-looking helpers. Scrap lumber burned in an oil drum. A big truck was half-loaded nearby.

"Hi Eddy," Saunders said.

Eddy wasn't the hardest-working man in his brother's contracting and lumber business, but everyone liked him. Saunders explained that he wanted Eddy to work for him.

"What do you need?"

"I guess, just for starters, I'd like you to get the place liveable. Then I'll probably have some real renovation work for you."

Eddy spat on the snow. "You need your water lines done, if you're going to live here in this weather."

"Oh yeah? What's wrong with the water lines?"

"The way it is, she's gonna freeze up on you." Inside the cab of the nearby truck, Eddy's helpers were shoving each other.

"Maybe you could fix it, then. I'd like it done properly."

Eddy shook his head. "I'd wait until spring."

"I need it done now," Saunders insisted.

"Expensive," Eddy smiled.

Saunders scowled at the snow-blurred outline of the saw house. "How much would it cost to fix the plumbing for winter? Properly."

"Properly," Eddy said. He scratched his chin. The inevitable saliva-blackened cigarette butt hung from the side of his mouth. "Properly, eh . . . well, I don't know. Eight thousand bucks."

"Good," Saunders said. "Can you start next week?"

Eddy carefully pinched his nostrils between thumb and forefinger and blew a stream of snot downwind. He repositioned the cigarette butt and nodded. "Nine thousand," he said. "Maybe ten."

Saunders nodded.

"Twelve."

Saunders looked at him.

Eddy grinned. "Just kidding."

Saunders went back to the inn and cut enough firewood to get him through the night.

Evening came, darkness. Inside the storm-besieged inn he cleaned and swept, scrubbed out cupboards, filled dozens of garbage bags with trash and anti-smoking literature. Mouse nests and dead baby mice were everywhere. If he stopped for even a minute the sound of the storm moaning and bumping against the walls made him feel so chilled and lonely he wondered if he were having some kind of mental breakdown. Now you've done it, he kept thinking.

That night he slept on the couch with a fire going and half a dozen quilts piled up to stave off the cold. In the morning the snow had stopped and the yard was sunny and cold.

Over the next couple of days Eddy Grogan's brother-in-law Dwayne McCafferty set up shop in front of the Stonehouse Inn. His immense backhoe turned the entire yard into an open-pit mining operation. It was odd to see that soft earth piled up and steaming in the bitter cold. Saunders phoned Skip that night, and listened in silence while Skip ranted and raved about Saunders' irresponsibility.

Deborah wasn't any happier. She told Saunders to do whatever he wanted, but "don't call me when you're broke."

To get the wiring in the inn upgraded, Saunders needed extensive electrical work on the inside and two extra poles on the outside. He kept running into nice little surprises, like finding out that the hydro line also required upgrading and would cost eleven thousand dollars. Considered individually, the costs didn't seem insurmountable, but gathered together, they scared him. The whole project was a high-wire act, and if anything really nasty happened he didn't have a net.

Eddy's workers used a frequent expression—"shit happens"—and Saunders began to think of it as an accurate description of his work site.

Because of a small problem in the site survey, he had to jack up one of the cabins. It took them two days to get it on skids and move it. It was horribly cold with the wind knifing in off the bay. They had to keep running up to the inn to warm their aching hands. The cabin's new site was on a steep slope. The back side of the cabin rested on low concrete pads and the front side on a high network of criss-crossed beams.

When it was all done, Saunders got the bright idea of moving the Caterpillar out of the way. He forgot to unhook the chain that was attached to the foundation of the cabin. The cat scrabbled forward. The chain jerked tight. The cabin shimmied sideways, then with ponderous dignity tipped forward and tumbled down the hill, up and over, settling with a cacophonous crash onto the ice lining the shore.

It was one of those incidents that's so unexpected and savage there isn't much to say. Saunders was dumbfounded. He looked at Eddy, who stood in the ice fog in a dark blue, grease-smudged Ocean Pacific windbreaker and, of course, his favourite baseball hat. INSTANT ASSHOLE—JUST ADD LIQUOR. Eddy peered down at the ruined cabin on the ice, then shrugged and lifted an evil eyebrow. "Well, Mikey, at least nobody got killed."

The cabin was ruined. It took another day to demolish it. They salvaged what they could and burned the rest. One of the crew hinted that Saunders' big construction project was becoming quite popular as a topic of coffee-break conversation among the locals. He could just hear them—"Yeah . . . I guess they're having quite a time over there at the inn. Young Mikey there, he's 'improving' the inn, you see. Ho ho. Finishing off the job he started long ago, you might say."

To appease Skip, Saunders bought a FAX machine in Kenora and tried to keep enough correspondence going back and forth from Winnipeg to Toronto via his cubbyhole office under the stairs to make it seem he was hard at work here in Minaki, dreaming up new schemes, greasing current clients and just generally keeping up the flow of paper. But it was hard to glue together convincing letters when all his crib files were in Toronto. And, no matter how much correspondence sailed through, Skip knew Saunders was faking. "I'm concerned about Deborah," he said one night, after tearing Saunders from sleep with a midnight phone call. "I saw her with Elwood, that guy who's been chasing her around the racquet club."

"I can't stop Deborah from going out at night," Saunders said. "I have to do this. Just give me three weeks."

A few nights later a snowstorm knocked down the power lines and Saunders awoke to a frigid bedroom. Shivering in bed, he saw weak daylight filtering through French windows, and trees weeping in the snow. He went into the kitchen, where he noticed he'd left the cap off the peanut butter jar the night before. He turned on the gas under the kettle, made some toast and stuck a knife into the peanut butter. A small grey creature ran up the knife and half-way up his arm. He screamed and flung the jar across the kitchen, and clutched his wrist as if he'd been bitten by a snake. On top of all the job disasters, the unexpected cost overruns, the new worries about Deborah and the consulting business, this was the last straw. He was sick of eating food embedded with mouse excrement.

"Get out," he yelled. "I can't stand it." The mouse, dazed, crouched in a corner.

Saunders put on a couple of sweaters and locked up the inn, then slung his duffle bag over his shoulder and hiked out through the blowing snow to the car. The wind was wild. A real blizzard. The sleet and wet snow drove horizontally across the evergreen-bordered yard. The little green BMW was forlorn under a thickening pelt of snow. He just wanted out.

He cleaned the window with a cassette box. Inside the car, he pumped the accelerator. His breath hung frosty in front of him. He popped the car into gear and moved forward. The wheels dug and spun. He shifted back into reverse and pressed the accelerator. The car wallowed backwards with a wail from the differential. Right. He sure needed to get stuck here.

Finally he developed some back-and-forth momentum. He charged forward and ploughed through the drift of snow that the wind had built around the car, shifted into second gear and rounded the corner. Free at last. In an hour, he told himself, I'll be drinking hot soup.

The car slid off the road about half-way out to the highway. One minute everything was fine; the next minute the road shrugged, a queer animal motion, and PLOP, it was like falling into a feather bed. He couldn't get the door open. He climbed out the window and surveyed the damage.

He opened the trunk and looked for a shovel. He knew he didn't have a shovel. There was, however, a hub-cap, which he used to scoop at the compacted snow for several minutes. Holding the hub-cap in both hands, he fired the snow backwards between his legs like a dog. When he paused to rest, his back creaking, he was perspiring. All he had to do now was get good and wet, walk up the road for a while, get cold and disoriented, then fall down and die. It happened all the time in these parts, especially to people who thought they could dig a car out with a hub-cap.

After digging for a while, he got back in the car and tried it, but one drive wheel spun freely. He was high-centred. He climbed back out of the car and searched around. Was there anything else he could use? He snugged on his gloves and walked up the road, tapping the hub-cap against his leg, surveying the ditch for traction materials.

Here in the shelter of the forest the storm seemed to abate. The snow fell thick and feathery around him and he could hear the wind in the high spruce tops overhead. At the top of the ridge the bare vertebrae of the road surfaced through the snow. Further along was a valley, and he kneed down through deeper snow. He would never get the car through this stuff. He scooped angrily at the snow with the hub-cap, working his way down through twenty feet of snow-clogged road, then paused and straightened with his heart banging in his chest and tears in his eyes.

Dammit. He threw the hub-cap down the hill. It soared down into an evergreen and fluttered out of sight. That was smart, he thought. Now I'll have to buy another one.

Wading downhill through the deep snow, he searched the heavy drifts for the hub-cap. It was nowhere in sight. He growled like a dog and sank into a sitting position in the snow, catatonic with frustration and sorrow. The valley stretched out forever. Large, wet snowflakes fell with an audible rustle in the trees around him. At the bottom of the valley the creek flowed in patches of olive-coloured water where the ice hadn't formed yet. Thickets of red willow lined the sides of the creek, and on one of the willow wands a magpie teetered, dipping its bill in the water.

Saunders stared forlornly at the bird. A cold drop of water snaked down his neck. I'm going back to Toronto, he thought. Deborah has forgotten me, the company is going down the tubes. I must have been crazy to think I could stay here.

I hate this place.

The magpie cocked its head, as if listening to Saunders talk to himself, then sprang into the air and flew down the ravine, disappearing into the veil of falling snow. A moment later he heard the dull, arguing sound of an approaching vehicle.

Saunders got up and waded toward the road. A large, four-wheel-drive pick-up truck appeared, bulling through the snow. It was coming his way. At the bottom of the valley the wheels bounced like soccer balls in the potholes and the big all-terrain tires spat a cascade of mud and stones.

Saunders watched the truck slew and claw up the hill towards him; blue smoke belched from its exhaust pipes as it skidded to a stop. There was a lone person inside, someone in a hooded parka and scarf. The window rolled down. "Hi there," she said.

He stepped forward. "Maggie?"

"SO THEN WHAT HAPPENED?"

Maggie was full of questions. Saunders blew on the hot spoonful of consommé soup and mouthed it tentatively. He got in another spoonful before answering. Hot soup for an aching soul. This is fate for you—one minute you're thigh-deep in wet snow, whipped, beat, disheartened, the next minute you're sitting with a pretty woman in the BoBo Cafe drinking hot soup and waiting for your prawns to arrive.

"How is the project going, in general?"

"In general," Saunders said, "I'm running short of cash and patience."

"Maybe I could help?"

"I appreciate the offer," he said. "But I think this project is beginning to shape up as a disaster. Nobody should be trying to renovate a building in the winter, in this country." Saunders paused for a mouthful of soup. "You can't even drive the roads."

"I could swap vehicles with you," she said. "My truck has four-wheel drive."

"Or else I could just go back to Toronto. Where I belong. And that would solve everything."

She smiled.

"Hey," he said. "Why don't I just sell the hotel to you? You're its guardian angel."

"I don't have any money."

"Surprise me, why don't you. How come people with principles are always broke?"

She shrugged. "I'm not really broke. I just don't have a hundred thousand dollars in my savings account."

"Well, in any case, I think I'll put it off until the weather gets a little more cooperative. Skip is mad at me anyway."

She nodded. "Whatever you decide, let me know if I can help."

When they finished their soup, they went outside and got into the truck. Maggie drove it out of Kenora. The road was wet and black. Snow cannoned sideways into the headlights. The wipers clapped rhythmically and the heater poured warmth.

As they turned onto the Stonehouse Inn road, Saunders laid his arm along the back of the seat and watched the headlights rake through the snow-laden spruces. It seemed a long time since that summer day when he and Skip had first come to visit the inn and pick up his dad's papers.

Maggie dropped the truck into second gear. She hit the wiper switch and squirted cleaning fluid on the windshield. The wipers cleaned away the clotted slush, revealing a pristine white road winding through the forest.

"It looks great when you're snug and warm inside the truck," Saunders said. They passed the BMW, swamped in a white blanket that came almost to its headlights. "Do you have a chain?"

"Let's do it in the morning," Maggie said. "It's too late for you to leave tonight anyway."

"You're probably right."

When they arrived at the inn, Saunders invited Maggie inside and showed her all the work they'd done. The plumbing worked. Hot water steamed out of the taps in the kitchen. The floors were all swept, the windows sheathed with plastic vapour-guard. The power was back on.

He knocked on the walls. "You see this here? New plumbing. You can't see it, but these walls contain a couple of hundred feet of shiny new copper pipe."

"Really?"

"Yep. You never really appreciate a simple thing like hot and cold running water until you rebuild an entire system."

Maggie chuckled.

"No really!" he said. "This is a miraculous thing. You've got a frozen lake out there and in here," he leaned forward and touched a pair of stainless steel faucets, "you've got a state-of-the-art walk-in bath tub. You turn on a tap and this whole wonderful arterial system springs to life.... And presto, my Jacuzzi runneth over."

She smiled. "I'm impressed."

He took her upstairs and showed her his bedroom. "And these are all the temporary storage rooms." He led Maggie into a room full of junk, boxes and furniture. He cut open a box to show her a pamphlet—a caricature of a man with his lips pursed hungrily for a cigarette. The man wore baby clothes and looked as if he were going to burst into tears. ARE YOU A CISSY CIG-SUCKER?

"Our former tenant," Saunders said.

He led her down to the second floor to show her the guest rooms and the south wing. "You should sleep in here," Maggie said.

"I was going to paint it, strip the wood," he said. "I don't like the smell."

They went downstairs. Now that the power was back on Saunders felt guilty about decamping. Outside, snow twirled around them but the storm was ebbing. They walked to Maggie's truck and stood for a moment, looking at the hotel. The roof was cloaked in a blanket of Christmasy snow. The windows shone yellow and bright. Maggie got into the truck. It was one of those moments of poignant silence: much being considered; little being said.

"Would you like to go out for a drink sometime?" he asked.

"A drink?"

"Yeah. You know, a date. Maybe a movie?"

Maggie sat behind the wheel of the truck. She thought for a long moment. Her eyes were steady. "Thank you for the offer."

He smiled. Never be afraid to ask for the sale.

"I think I'd better not."

"Why? We could talk about the hotel. I know you're already involved, but so am I. What's wrong with a little date?"

"Listen, Mr. Saunders," she said. "You're an interesting fellow. But I think we should stick to the subject."

"And what's that?"

"If you have to leave, why don't you reconsider my original offer? I'll babysit the project for you. We can have the renovation finished in a month. I'm accustomed to dealing with local people, the roads, all that. Once you get used to winter, you hardly notice it."

Saunders nodded. "Well . . . let me have a few days to consider things."

She started the engine. "Will you be all right now?"

"Oh yeah. I just needed a hot meal and a chance to bitch to somebody."

THE NEXT DAY, THE STORM TRAVELLED in a northeasterly path and blew itself out. A northerly flow came sweeping in behind it, and the air soon turned sharp and brutally cold. By late afternoon the temperature fell to twenty-eight degrees below zero. Saunders decided he'd spend Christmas in Toronto and take a break from the project. He set the thermostat on low and got Eddy to fill the heating oil tank with a month's worth. Eddy's three-ton fuel truck pulled the BMW free of the snowdrift and by suppertime, Saunders was eastbound on Highway 17, heading home.

Meanwhile, the Stonehouse Inn stood desolate and deserted in the blue winter twilight. Out of the tall chimney twisted a thin scarf of smoke. The yard was scalloped with deep white snowdrifts, the stairs and sidewalks unmarked by human tracks. In the evening, when the western sky was still stained with a broad wash of dying day, a ruffled grouse flew out of the dark evergreens, glided across the yard and landed on the branch of a crab-apple tree.

In winter storms, many small creatures take cover and avoid movement until the weather clears. This particular grouse—a dapper creature, with a barred breast and a wide fan-shaped tail—had spent the storm snuggled deep in a snowdrift along the same road where Saunders had ditched his car. Now the day was getting late and the grouse was feeding energetically, making up for lost time. He hopped clumsily from branch to branch and pecked at the tiny frozen crab-apples.

In mid-winter, wild fruits and berries are frozen on the branch and certain weather conditions allow the fruit to ferment and turn alcoholic. It's not uncommon to see grouse wheeling drunkenly in the woods like small airplanes with defective engines, clipping branches and crashing into the undergrowth. In the crab-apple tree in the front yard, the handsome eighteen-month-old bird was doing quite well, considering that it was quite drunk. The bird clambered from branch to branch and gave each apple a slightly wobbly, cross-eyed look of edification before taking it in his beak and gulping it down. Finally he paused and shuffled his feathers.

He looked across the white yard. The red stain of the winter sunset, etched by black spruces, was reflected prettily on the bay window of the inn. The day was over. It was time to find shelter for the night.

The grouse launched itself from the tree and flew with quick-whirring wings across the yard. Like a two-pound brick wrapped in feathers, he disappeared with a crash into the sunset on the window.

13

~~~~

ON CHRISTMAS EVE, SAUNDERS AND DEBORAH WENT TO midnight mass, complete with a candlelight procession and a thundering choir, at a cathedral in north Toronto, Deborah's family parish. A horn section almost blew the roof off on "Hark, the Herald Angels Sing," and then the lights went out and a lone violinist played "Stille Nacht." There was a vast silence in the church. The minister raised his hands and said, "Do not be afraid. For unto you is born this day in the city of David a saviour who is Christ the Lord."

After the service, everyone went out into the softly falling snow. The bells pealed out overhead. Deborah and Saunders hugged each other. Saunders had forgotten how beautiful life in the city could be. People were coming out of the church laughing, watery-eyed from the violin solo.

Christmas Day they had dinner at Deborah's

parents' home. On Boxing Day, at seven o'clock in the morning, the telephone rang in Deborah's bedroom, interrupting a heated argument on the subject of the Stonehouse Inn. "I'm sick and tired of this," Deborah was saying. "Are you telling me you're leaving again?"

"I *have* to," Saunders said. "It's almost finished."

"I thought you were going to wait for spring."

"I can't afford to sit around for six months. I have to sell it and get my money out."

"You're broke."

"No." In the background, the phone was ringing.

"Then why is it such an emergency?"

"I have to do this. I'm almost *finished*, for pete's sake."

Deborah pulled away from him. "I knew this would happen."

She answered the phone and gestured to Saunders. He legged out of bed and she handed him the phone, giving him a dour look. He put the receiver against his ear. The voice at the other end was tinny and faint.

"Mikey!"

"Hello."

"Spikey Mikey."

"Hello."

" 'Get me a ticket for an aero-plane. Ain't got time to take no fast train . . .' "

"What's up, Skip?"

Across the room, Deborah was stepping into her panties.

Skip answered, singing, " 'Lonely days are gone, Ah'm a goin' home' . . . hey Mikey, are you there?"

Saunders cupped the phone, looking at Deborah. "Should I tell him to call back?"

"I don't care."

"Oh come on, baby."

"Don't call me that." Looking like a topless dancer, Deborah walked out of the bedroom. Nobody's baby.

Saunders shook his head, watching her departing physique, nice broad shoulders narrowing down to the smooth muscles of her sacral curve, plump bum. Gorgeous woman. Isn't Deborah what every man wants? A beautiful woman with her own income?

Saunders could hear Skip's voice fluttering under his hand. He put the receiver back to his ear. "Skip, I have to see you."

"And I you," Skip replied. "Don't you ever answer your FAXes? Christ, your clients are all over me."

"No they're not. I've been meeting with every single one of them, these last few days. If I take any more meetings my ass is going to seize up. Where are you?"

"Right here, Toronto. I'm at Air Canada, downtown."

"Where are you going?"

"To beautiful, fashionable *magnifique* Montreal. Do you want to come?"

"No."

"Mike . . . I talked it over with Giselle. She wants both of us to come down and meet the family. I want you to come and give meeting with Uncle Vince."

"I'm going back to Minaki. I've got a resort to renovate, remember?"

"Hey," Skip said. "The place has been there for a hundred years. It's going to be there when you get back."

"I can't afford to go to Montreal."

"Think of it as a business investment. Wait'll you get friendly with Uncle Vince. I mean, we're talking private jets, condos in Mexico, Bahamian bank accounts. You can touch him for a loan; your troubles will be over."

"Sure. I'll end up wearing concrete overshoes." Saunders could hear the shower thundering from down the hall. "Skip, I'm not going to Montreal. But listen, I have to see you."

"Why?"

"I'll explain when you get here."

"This better be money-related."

"It is."

Saunders went into the kitchen and made coffee. Deborah had a low-impact stretch and strength class most mornings. There were a few young ones at Hollywood's, but mostly her clients were middle-aged. Whenever Saunders dropped in, he saw them lying on the mat grunting and groaning to Rod Stewart. A lot of them had tried this surgical procedure called liposuction. Apparently the surgeon incises the patient's immense buttock and sucks out all the fat with a high-power vacuum. Two years later, hooked on chocolates and two-hour lunches, they're back for more of the same. Juxtapose such individuals with a group of Ethiopian stick-babies.

Deborah's voice came from the bathroom. "Tell me something, Michael. Do you have another girlfriend?"

Saunders paused, wincing. "I don't know what you're talking about."

"What about this person, Maggie?"

Saunders was quiet for a moment. "Her? I barely know her."

"But you've had dinner with her?"

"As a friend."

"I don't buy this friendship stuff," Deborah said, her voice flat. "Men and women are not friends."

"She's got a boyfriend, some doctor."

"Well, that's never stopped you before, has it? I think I was engaged to be married when you met me."

A few minutes later there was a loud knock at the back door. Saunders opened it. Skip was standing there. "I can only stay a few minutes."

"Come on in," Saunders said. "Coffee?"

"You said you needed to see me. What's up?"

"Hey, it's been a long time since we talked. That's all. Come in."

Skip kicked the snow off his shoes. "How's the renovation going?"

"Fine," Saunders replied. "It's going very well."

"It's a total disaster, in other words."

Saunders poured him a coffee. "Not at all. I'm almost finished."

"Well, I'm glad we're on the subject," Skip said, "because the company's feeling your absence. Keenly."

Saunders sat down, stirred sugar into his own coffee and nodded sympathetically as Skip listed their woes: New Age Associates was doing practically zero in the way of new business. With Saunders gone and himself spending so much time in the east, nobody was moving the ball. While they talked, Deborah drifted in and out in a belted bathrobe that barely covered her behind.

Skip got up and refilled his coffee. He planted his hand on Deborah's hip. "So when are we all going to see Mikey's new improved hotel?"

"I don't think we ever will. I keep hearing about this place. But I'm beginning to wonder if it even exists."

"You're permanently invited," Saunders said. "You should all come out for New Year's. Giselle too."

"Right on," said Skip. "Maybe after I'm in Montreal."

"I'm not coming," Deborah said. "And you better not spend New Year's there."

Saunders ignored this. He looked at Skip. "Why are you going to Montreal?"

"Meet Giselle's family," Skip said, not removing his hand from Deborah's hip. "It's a big deal in these Italian families when the guy comes to meet the relatives."

"Tell me," Deborah said sceptically, "what is so wonderful about this woman."

"She's perfect," Skip said.

"What do you mean?"

"I mean she's flawless. She's smart. She's kind. She's rich. And above all, she's unbelievably gorgeous."

Deborah lifted an eyebrow. "Oh really?"

Skip quaffed his coffee. "Let me put it this way, Deborah. She's exactly like you. Except she's a redhead."

"I'm not rich," Deborah said. "When did you meet her?"

Skip retold the story of meeting Giselle at the wine and cheese party in Ottawa. The winter morning was bright in Deborah's kitchen windows. A tractor banged somewhere out on the street. The sunlight arrowed in through the kitchen and bathed Skip's haggard face in light. He was worn out; too much running around.

Deborah sipped her coffee. "You might be in big trouble here, Skip."

"I know."

"You may have met your match."

"I know." He looked at his watch. "Anyway, I gotta go. What's next, Mike? Are you serious about having us up to the inn?"

"Of course," Saunders replied. "But I have to sweet-talk Deborah."

Deborah lifted an eyebrow. "I can hardly wait."

Saunders slipped on his camel overcoat. He followed Skip outside to his car. Their breath billowed in the sharp cold. "I need a favour," Saunders said.

Skip brushed snow off the windshield. "What?"

"I think you know."

"You're getting stretched for funds, right?"

"That's the general idea."

"Come and see Uncle Vince. Maybe he'd throw in some venture capital."

"I need to borrow twenty grand. Or ten, at least."

"I know. But Uncle Vince has all the money you'll ever need."

"I don't feel right about dealing with him. You just lend me the ten kay, and I'll be fine. I need to spend about twenty more, to get it shipshape. And I'm about ten shy."

"But you should talk to Uncle Vince, really."

"Fine, maybe later. But you just spot me the ten, I'll be able to keep things going."

"I don't have it."

"Yeah sure."

Skip climbed into his U-Drive. The engine was running. White smoke throbbed out its tailpipes. He regarded Saunders through an opening in the window. "I don't have it."

"Are you kidding me?"

Skip pushed in the lighter and withdrew a pack of cigarettes from his pocket. He shook his head slowly. "I don't know, Mike. It's like I told you. You're gone. I'm on the road all the time. There's nobody running the store."

"I thought you were making money hand over fist. That's what you told me."

"I was counting on things that never materialized. We need you in the office. Not your voice on the phone. Toronto division is Mike Saunders, plain and simple. And now you're leaving again." When Saunders didn't say anything, Skip went on. "Talk to Neil," he said. "He might be your best bet. You know, construction guy. Christ, he's got little revenue properties stashed all over the place. Me . . . I don't know where I'm going to be six months from now. Suppose things work out with Giselle." He shrugged. "I'll be living in Montreal or California probably."

Saunders looked at him. "How much do you have?"

"Five, maybe."

"Lend me seventy-five hundred."

Skip shook his head. "I can't."

"Six."

"Five," Skip said.

You couldn't horse trade with Skip. "Okay, give me the five."

Skip wrote out a cheque and handed it to Saunders through the window.

"All right," Saunders said. He slapped the door of the car and straightened up. "Well okay. You say hello to Giselle for me."

"You should look for financial backers. Whatever you think it will take to finish it, it's guaranteed to cost more."

"Yeah yeah."

"But do it."

"Goodbye Skip."

Saunders watched the car go off down the street. He went back inside, hands in his pockets. At the kitchen table he finished his cold coffee and studied the cheque. When he got back to Minaki he was going to have to deal with the brute fact that the cash supply was almost gone. He needed to finish fixing the place and sell it, pronto.

He lifted his head. He could hear Deborah puttering in the bathroom. "Deborah," he called.

Eventually she came out, wearing her spandex gym suit. "If you're going to tell me that you want to borrow some money . . . to fix that dump," she said, knotting her belt, "I'm going to hit you."

14

SKIP CARTER COULD BE A PRINCE OF MEN WHEN IT CAME to rustling through his closet and giving away all sorts of expensive clothes. But never let it be said that he was a man easily separated from his folding money. Saunders was reminded of that fact when he waltzed into the TD bank at Dundas and Spadina and tried to convert Skip's cheque into five thousand dollars cash. "I'm sorry, sir," the teller said. "There are insufficient funds in that account."

Saunders was taken aback. "Pardon?"

The teller repeated the news, wearing a thin smile that hinted that the amount in the account wasn't even close. Like, it had four dollars in it. Or it was overdrawn. Saunders stomped out.

The snow of mid-winter Toronto drizzled down on his unprotected head as he waded through the slop along Spadina, fuming. Why does he do this to me? Is he a sadist? He *knew* there was no money in that account! Doesn't he realize that this is much worse than just saying no? Now what am I going to do?

This time, on his way back to the Stonehouse Inn, Saunders drove the south route through the States. He'd decided it was time for desperate measures. He'd already discovered that the quickest way to manufacture large sums of cash was to provide pointless information to the government. Therefore, he was going to get back into consulting. In his car he carried a new improved portable office in the form of a nine-pound Hewlett-Packard lap-top with miniature colour printer, modem and disc library containing four years of New Age back files, correspondence and PPCS outlines for sixty or seventy assorted projects. His money factory.

He drove to Winnipeg before reaching Minaki, hoping to confront Skip with his rubber cheque. Who did he think he was, anyway? Skip's Wildcat was parked behind the New Age office. Saunders took the back stairs and walked into the office. "Hi Iris. Is Skip here?"

Iris cooed her usual greeting. Skip was at a meeting. Saunders walked down the hall and checked Skip's office, just in case. Maybe Iris was covering for him. No coat, no briefcase. I'll choke him with my bare hands, he thought. No, what I'll do is turn him upside down and shake him until the spare change falls out.

He sat down at Skip's desk and waited and waited. An hour passed. No more Mr. Nice Guy, he thought. My line of credit at the bank is blown to the limit. I owe money all over Minaki. I can't go on this way.

Neil poked his head in the door. "Mike, what are you doing in town?"

"I'm looking for Skip."

Neil came forward and put out his hand. "Happy New Year. How are you making out?"

"I've been better," Saunders said.

Neil hooked a thumb. "Come in my office. I'll buy you a coffee."

In Neil's office, Saunders pulled up a chair while Neil hung up his parka, sat down and put his cowboy boots up on the desk. "So how goes it?"

"With what, life?"

"Who gives a shit about life? How's the reno project?"

"Things are tight. I'm underfinanced, Neil. I should have hired a consultant."

"Why do you want Skip?"

"He bounced a cheque on me. As if I don't have enough troubles."

Neil looked at his watch. "He won't be in again. It's getting on to three."

"He told Iris he'd be back."

"This is Skip we're talking about."

Saunders nodded. Christ, what a fiasco. "Listen Neil, while I'm here, can you come out sometime and look at the inn? Tell me if there are any inexpensive methods I can use, finishing the job?"

"I didn't know you were nearly finished."

"I shouldn't say finished. It'll never be finished. I just want it to be in good enough shape that whoever buys it won't tear it down."

Neil stuck a toothpick in his mouth. "When do you want me to come out?"

Saunders shrugged. "Any time it's convenient for you. Tomorrow?"

Neil chewed thoughtfully on the toothpick. "If we gotta do it, what the hell. Let's drive out there right now."

Saunders and Neil gassed up and drove out of town, Neil following Saunders in a big yellow crew cab. It was nothing for Neil, the country boy, to take a little drive in the afternoon, put four hundred miles on his truck. They had cellular phones in their vehicles to keep in touch. Saunders found CBC's classical music station on the Blaupunkt and sped east across the rippled white prairie. He balanced the heater, reclined the seat back a notch and contemplated what was becoming a familiar scroll of scenery. Flat and barren, frozen lake-bed left over from the ice age. East of the city the road climbed up a series of beach ridges and entered the scrub forest, black spruce and bare rock of the pre-Cambrian Shield. The afternoon sky flamed like Gomorrah in the rear-view mirror.

At Prawda they stopped at the Shell for dinner. On a table napkin Saunders drew some sketches of the Stonehouse Inn. If he was the guy who bought the place, he'd spend about two hundred thousand more and turn it into the Stonehouse Resort and Conference Centre. Split level decks. Ski trails. The new cabins would have the same lines as the inn. After a hundred years, the place would still be standing. He scratched in some feathery pines and a sea-gull sailing over the roof. The waitress stole a glance, impressed. "Oh my, an artist."

Neil peered at Saunders' design and chuckled. They paid the waitress and went out into the darkness and bitter cold. The highway was black and scabbed with ice. Neil took the lead in his four-wheel drive. His tail-lights soon faded from sight. At the green Minaki Tourist Area sign, Saunders caught up to Neil's truck stopped on the shoulder with a turn signal blinking. Saunders tapped the horn and made the corner, and Neil pulled out and followed him. Twenty minutes later they were at the turn-off to the inn. Saunders noticed with some pleasure that the Ministry of Transport had finally put up the new sign he'd asked for: STONEHOUSE INN—AHEAD.

The road into the inn was unploughed so Neil's big truck went ahead to break trail. Still, the BMW dragged its belly in the deep spots and Saunders was glad Neil was here to pull him out if he got stuck.

At the Stonehouse Inn Neil did a few loop-the-loops in the parking lot to knock the snow down. Saunders parked behind him, then popped open the trunk to get his boots. He shivered, "Man, is it getting cold or what?"

"Yep, she's a cool one." Neil lit up a cigarette. His parka hung open. Maybe his thick sideburns and burly hairy chest kept him warm.

It was early yet, only about eight o'clock, but the night was already violently cold. On the radio Saunders had heard something about it going down to thirty-five below zero. He tossed Neil the keys. "Go ahead," he said. "Light switch is on your right."

Neil crunched off through the snow.

Saunders kicked off his shoes and squeezed into his frozen workboots, wincing. Where's Maggie? he thought. I get here, first thing I want to do is see her. He put his boot up on the BMW's bumper and tied the frozen laces, then pulled on his heavy garbage mitts. He slapped his hands together, slammed the car's door and clambered through the snow, following Neil's trail. The lights blinked on in the kitchen, then the dining room. Saunders climbed up the back stairs and went in, expecting to feel that nice gush of warmth when he stepped into the kitchen.

The heat was off!

The hotel was all bright and lit up but as cold as a walk-in freezer. His breath steamed as he walked into the frozen kitchen. He was stunned. The linoleum was slippery. Spikes of ice drooled from the faucets. The new copper pipes were split, ice everywhere. In the dining room the window was smashed, as if someone had thrown a brick through it. Snow covered the floor. "Burglars?" Saunders muttered.

Neil didn't answer. He knelt down in the darkened lounge to study a piece of evidence. Saunders was stupefied by the extent of the damage. The staircase was a frozen waterfall, each freshly refinished oak riser covered with ice. This wood may be permanently ruined, he thought frantically. What am I going to do?

"Here's your burglar," Neil said. He walked up carrying a dead scruffy-looking thing.

"What is it?"

"Chicken."

"Nobody has chickens here."

"No no, bush chicken. Partridge."

Saunders took the frozen bird and turned it over in his hand. He shook his head. "I don't know why the heat's not on, though."

"Bird broke the window. Cold air got in. Thermostat clicked on. Furnace blazed wide open until it ran out of fuel. You're lucky the place didn't burn down."

"So the furnace burned up a month's worth of oil in a week."

Neil nodded.

Saunders wagged his head. "God, I can't take this."

Neil patted him on the shoulder. "Look on the bright side. You've got a partridge for supper."

15

IN THE COFFEE SHOP OF KENORA'S BAYVIEW HOTEL, THE weak winter light leaked through hoar-frosted windows. Trucks snorted past outside. Disembodied heads of pedestrians floated on billows of ice fog. Saunders sipped at his breakfast coffee and watched McNabb fill out an appraisal form. As of right now, the Stonehouse property was for sale. Half-renovated or half-demolished. Whichever way you preferred to see it.

McNabb punched the button of his pen. "I'll have these ready by tomorrow then, Mike." He slid the papers into his briefcase. "And then I'll come out and get a sign up. Probably tomorrow afternoon."

"Okay." Saunders paused. "I just can't go on, Ben. I thought I could do it, but . . ." He shook his head.

McNabb held up his hand. "Mike, you did your best. You did as well as any son could do."

Saunders was quiet. He felt lousy.

McNabb said, "I can't guarantee that our first party, Mr. Simkins, will still stand by his offer, but I'll let him know the property's for sale again."

"And do you think we still have to tear it down?"

McNabb shrugged. "You've got a half-renovated building there, with a lot of work left to go. The yard's all dug up. The plumbing is ruined. The property is probably less desirable now than when you started. I don't see that there's much choice."

"And what about that contractor, what's his name—"

"Frank Ross," McNabb shook his head. "He doesn't want to have anything to do with you, I'm afraid."

"Is there anyone else?"

McNabb snapped his briefcase shut. "Leave it to me, Mike. I'm sure we haven't crossed all our bridges yet."

On Friday, McNabb came by and once again erected the For Sale sign in the bulldozed earth of the front yard. The following day, a mild Saturday, Saunders poked around the inn, cleaning up and packing things for the trip home. Why did he ever do this? He'd spent forty thousand dollars cash and there was nothing to show. Nothing. The ice had melted in the walls and the floors slopped with water. Around mid-morning he heard a truck pull into the driveway. It was Neil Olson, accompanied by five of his brothers and cousins. Neil was driving the big three-quarter-ton. Its box was loaded with copper pipe and drywall.

"What are you doing here?" Saunders asked.

Neil climbed out. "We're here to fix the plumbing."

Saunders pointed to the sign. "I just put the place back on the market."

"Don't be a wimp," Neil remarked, lighting an Export A. "You want us to fix the joint or not?"

Saunders nodded quickly.

"I have one request," Neil said.

"Anything."

"Keep out of our way."

The Olson boys rampaged through the hotel with nail-pullers, tearing out walls, throwing things over their shoulders, yelling at each other. Saunders kept them supplied with truckloads of copper pipe and drywall and lumber, not to mention sandwiches and beer. At the end of the day the job was completed. Except for the horrific mess on the floor, the building looked more or less the same as it did before the partridge flew through the window. Saunders walked Neil to the truck. "You did two weeks' work in twelve hours."

Neil nodded, "Yep."

"I want to pay you."

"Nope."

Saunders stood still. Neil was in the truck, the window half cranked open. It was evening, a mild winter dusk. Saunders looked at Neil and all his kin. "I don't know how to thank you, you guys."

Neil pointed across the yard. "Just take down that sign."

MCNABB WAS AGHAST when Saunders showed up at his office the next morning and told him he'd decided not to sell. "I just put an ad in the newspaper."

Saunders shrugged. "I guess I made a hasty decision. I'm sorry."

"But you've done this to me three times now."

"Believe me," Saunders said. "I am going to sell the place. And when I do, I'll make sure you get the listing." McNabb turned red. Saunders could tell he was almost ready to say, Take your goddamn hotel and . . .

Saunders carried on with the work, concentrating on jobs that required manpower more than cash. He built a scaffold inside the main lounge and started scraping the foam insulation from the ceiling. Like a grim Michelangelo, he lay on his back all day, wearing a surgical mask, scraping at the wooden ceiling planks as the eggy folds of UFFI peeled off. He started at the bottom and worked towards the top, doing one row of boards per day. Terrible work. But the pine logs and roof planking under the foam were blond and solid. When he finished each row he sanded the pine until it was clean and pale, then painted the exposed wood with glossy Varathane. At the end of each day he climbed down off the scaffold to admire his work. Above his head, the rows of gleaming pine were a preview of what the entire roof would become.

For the next few weeks, Saunders would usually get up and work in the morning for three or four hours on New Age Associates current projects, FAXing materials back and forth to Toronto and Winnipeg, making phone calls to clients, writing letters. At noon he would break for lunch. Skip had taken off to Montreal. Saunders knew Skip was busy romancing Giselle, but he resented the fact that Skip never bothered to call. And he was still mad about the rubber cheque.

After lunch he would go to work on the ceiling. It was slow work, and when Maggie showed up one day, volunteering to help for a few hours, he no longer had the willpower to resist. Maggie was a good worker. She had the v-shaped upper body of a power swimmer and, with her hair tied back, her sleeves rolled up, she climbed around in the scaffolding as if she'd been doing it all her life. She was also a good cook. Saunders was not a helpless male who needed a woman to show him how to make an omelette or iron a wrinkled cotton shirt. He could do housework as well as any woman. Let the editors of *Cosmopolitan* scream all they wanted; he was different. But when it came to cooking, he had to admit that Maggie was talented. Her food was tasty. She made odd-looking things that were consistently delicious. His own recipes often turned out soggy or soot-blackened.

In the ten days or so that Maggie helped him with the ceiling, they usually broke for dinner about seven o'clock. Maggie would wash up and start dinner. Saunders would put away the tools and roll up the extension cords. Wood scraps would go into the fireplace. He'd sweep the scraped-off piles of UFFI foam into orange garbage bags and carry them out through the crisp winter darkness to the bed of Maggie's pick-up truck. The garbage dump had a special section reserved for the Stonehouse Inn, these days. Then back into the homey warmth of the kitchen, where Maggie would be stir-frying Chinese vegetables for their dinner. She'd hand him a half-tumbler of Ballantine's on ice and give him the weary smile of a partner on a tough job. The scraps of two-by-four spruce and old shattered moulding would be snapping in the fireplace when supper was finally ready, and they'd carry their plates into the lounge, sit on a couple of old, tasselled, Oriental cushions on the hardwood floor in front of the fire, and dig in.

One night the telephone rang half-way through dinner. It was a long call, and Maggie was bringing in the coffee by the time he was finished. "Creditors?" she said.

"Actually, it was Deborah. You know who my friend Deborah is?"

Maggie sat on the floor and arranged the coffee in front of them. "Is she the one who owns the fitness studio?"

Saunders nodded. "The one who thinks I've lost my marbles."

"So what's new with Deborah?"

"She was talking to Skip, and I guess they've all decided to come for a visit."

"They?"

"Deborah, Skip and Skip's new flame."

Maggie said, "They're coming to check up on you."

"Whatever they're doing, I hope I get some work out of them. With three more people working, we could get this place finished."

She smiled. "In a weekend?"

"Well, maybe not. But it's amazing how much more you can take on with a team. Look at the work we've done. Since you showed up, we've accomplished more in a week than I could have done in a whole month."

"These places are meant to be operated by a couple," she said. "You can't do it alone."

Maggie's hair was cinched by a red cowgirl bandanna that was knotted into two bunny ears above her head. A tendril had escaped and hung askew across her cheek. She blew it away as she drank her coffee. She was too exhausted to keep up appearances.

Saunders felt it would be the most natural thing to reach across and brush the hair from her eye, knead the muscles at the back of her neck, give her a kiss. When they worked at a difficult task, leaning into the scaffold together to move it sideways, he liked her smell. What would it be like to kiss her? When he lay in bed at night, feeling that lonesome tingling in his groin, it was not Deborah he imagined climbing under the covers next to him, but Maggie. He knew Maggie was a principled type, and wouldn't entertain any romantic activities outside her relationship with Raymond. But still, he liked the feeling of sitting here beside her. Raymond was off doing his night shift at the hospital. Deborah was scissor-jumping inside the mirrored walls of Hollywood's. And they didn't have to apologize to anyone for being together.

"More coffee?" Maggie asked.

"Sure."

She poured coffee into his cup. "Are you tired?"

"Well . . . not really."

"You're usually more talkative."

"Am I?"

She smiled. A long moment of silence passed, then Maggie finally spoke. "So tell me about these people who are coming. Tell me about Deborah."

DEBORAH CLARKSON.

Saunders had had a dream several years ago. He was standing on a dark cliff above the moon-bright sea. He had a wet, rough, hairy rope around his neck, and was getting ready to plunge off the cliff and hang. A woman in a dark cloak came and lifted the rope off his neck. She took his hand and led him up to the high grass, and made love to him. It was a deeply affecting dream. He couldn't concentrate on his work for days afterward. He thought it was a sign. Someone was coming.

A month later he was on his way home after a business trip to Sudbury. He was going through a lonely phase. Too many nights on the road. He pulled into the parking lot and got out of the car, exhausted. Skip was using his apartment. And when Saunders looked up at the high tower, there were lights on in the windows and dark silhouettes of people on the balcony. Skip was having a party. Saunders locked the car and went up. An attractive blonde woman in a black raincoat stood by the door of the apartment. Saunders nodded. "Hello there."

"Hello there yourself."

He put out his hand. "Mike Saunders."

"Deborah Clarkson."

"Are you coming in?"

"I'm just leaving," she said. "Nice meeting you."

Saunders went into the party and had a Scotch. The blonde didn't leave. She kept her coat on while she sat on the couch talking to Chief Leo. Skip told Saunders she owned a fitness studio here in Toronto. She was thinking of hiring New Age Associates to do a market study. Skip was trying to butter her up, along with some other clients.

With her hair tied back in a bun, Deborah Clarkson looked like the cool, prim ballet-school type. She had a crinkle around her eyes that made her seem slightly concerned. She looked as if she'd spent at least a little bit of time thinking about the plight of the homeless. Saunders was starting to feel better with two drinks under his belt, and wanted to get something straight. He sat down beside her. "Excuse me Deborah, but I'm an optometrist. And I couldn't help noticing. Are your eyes bothering you?"

For just a moment she didn't react. "No, not really."

"Well, they're bothering me. They're beautiful."

She stood up. "Now it really is time to go."

About an hour later the party moved onto the balcony. Deborah still hadn't found the front door. It was lightly raining and they were standing out of the drizzle. A garbage dumpster was burning down on John Street. The red lights of the fire trucks splashed on the wall of a parking garage. Skip was singing a Frank Sinatra song, trying to get people to join in. Deborah Clarkson wasn't singing. She was as quiet as a statue. Saunders went up to her. "I'm determined to make small talk with you."

She smiled and touched his arm. "Drive me home."

They dated for a long time, maybe two months, before they made love. Saunders had the impression that Deborah would have thought it was fine, just fine, if they never moved beyond the stage of exchanging comradely hugs at the doorstep. Saunders was a man of base appetites and he wouldn't have bothered with her if she weren't such good company. They'd sit in restaurants drinking coffee and laughing until closing time. They had so much in common and looked so good together that Saunders was prepared to overlook the fact that there wasn't much in the way of fireworks in their love life.

He didn't know if the lack of passion was due to some kind of dysfunction, or whether it was just a reflection of their chemistry. Every time you join a man and a woman you get a new world. But he liked Deborah. He respected her business acumen. And when Skip's gargantuan, low-slung Buick wheeled into the driveway of the inn on that blizzardy Friday afternoon, heralded by a flurry of honking, he hurried outside to give Deborah a squeeze and a kiss to show his gratitude that she'd come all this way.

"Mikey!" Skip exclaimed. "How is it?"

A woman in a lynx coat got out of the Buick. She had auburn hair, pancaked cheeks and a beauty spot at the corner of her mouth. Her loose breasts jiggled inside a black turtleneck. She wore a pair of somewhat gaudy knee-high hooker boots.

"And you must be Giselle," Saunders said.

She offered a limp hand. "Hello Michael." Her breath was all whispery.

"Hello hello," Saunders smiled. He gave a theatrical shiver. It was snowing hard. There was a storm warning again. More pleasant weather. "How was your drive?"

"Piece of cake," Skip said.

Deborah crinkled her eyebrows. "He nearly killed us about three times."

"I need a drink," Skip said.

"Let's get you all settled inside."

They hauled luggage into the hotel. Saunders had decided to install Deborah and himself in the lakeshore cabin, so that Giselle and Skip would have the use of the two renovated bedrooms inside the hotel. He didn't know if Giselle and Skip were sleeping together yet, so it was best to be diplomatic. He conducted the grand tour of the building, showing them all the work he'd done so far and all the work that needed to be done, and when Deborah remarked on the beauty of the log ceiling he felt she really meant it. She wasn't just being polite.

"Are those real logs?" Giselle said.

"Oh yes," he nodded. "It's not finished yet. I still have to do the top."

"Skip didn't tell me it was so beautiful."

"Depends what you call beautiful," Skip said. "You should have seen what a dump it was the last time I was here." Giselle ran her fingers down the brawny logs. "We gotta get Uncle Vince out here," Skip said. "Take him fishing. Can you fish through the ice, Mike?"

"If you're very well dressed and slightly retarded."

"Uncle Vince is a fanatical fisherman."

Giselle made a face. "Don't bring my relatives here. They'll try to buy it from you."

"Good," Saunders said. "First cheerful thing I've heard today."

"But they'll only give you half its value."

"Sold. When do I get the cheque?"

"And Uncle Vince will put statues all over the place," Skip said. "Statues of Caesar Augustus. From the K-Mart garden centre."

Saunders didn't reply. He avoided talking to people who went around giving out rubber cheques.

If Skip knew Saunders was mad at him, he gave no sign of concern. "Mikey, you done good work."

"What time is dinner?" Deborah said. "Are we going out?"

Saunders hooked a finger through Deborah's belt loop. "Yeah. We're going out. But can we have a little nap first?"

16

~

AFTER SAUNDERS GOT DEBORAH SETTLED IN THE CABIN, they made love and then lay cozily under the blankets, talking. Deborah held Saunders' head and doodled through his hair with her fingers. "Don't worry," she murmured. "We'll sit down with Skipper and sort the whole thing out."

"He does this to me over and over again. I'm just not going to put up with it anymore."

"What are you going to do?"

"I've taken my last rubber cheque. I'm going to make him chew on it. And swallow it. Without a glass of water."

"Now now," she soothed.

Saunders could feel gloom coming on. Deborah was always patient with his moods. She usually became quite maternal after their love-making. He was her little boy, with squalid appetites that needed satisfying. Now that she'd gotten it over with, she was blissfully content.

"I probably would have had the place sold by now," he said, "if it wasn't for him." A soft ripping snore told him that Deborah was asleep. He lay awake, thinking of the overloaded camel that was his life.

When it grew dark, he got up and put on a pair of freshly laundered jeans. A bit loose around the waist. He was getting trimmed right down to fighting weight by all this prolonged hardship.

Deborah stirred. "Dinner time?"

"Yep."

"I'll be there in just one more minute, okay?"

He pulled on a red turtleneck and a grey wool sweater, and straightened his hair by hand. He'd stopped combing his hair too. Let it blow wild, like Whitman's grass, the uncut hair of graves. "I'll see you up there," he said. He went outside. The wind roared in off the frozen lake, driving the snow into pagoda-shaped snowdrifts.

Finding the rock staircase was blind man's work. He groped forward, afraid of stepping off the steep stairs and wrenching his ankle. The big Buick was in the driveway, headlights burning. Skip was inside, revving the engine. He flicked the lights at Saunders.

Saunders climbed in. "What's up?"

"Well, you made dinner reservations for six-thirty, right? That's ten minutes ago."

"Where's Giselle?"

"Painting her face."

Saunders nodded. He sat in silence for a few minutes. "Your cheque bounced."

Skip paused. "What cheque?"

Saunders took out his wallet and handed Skip the cheque. He stared at it as if it were written in Martian. Saunders propped his arm along the back of the seat and watched the twin headlights funnelling out into the storm. "I owe money to my workers. It's no joke."

"I'll write you another one."

"Great. And it'll bounce too?"

"Don't tell Giselle, all right? I'll get the money to you as soon—"

Saunders looked at him. "Shut up. I thought you wanted to help me. What am I, a client? To be treated like a moron?"

Skip put his head down and cradled it in his hands. Finally he looked back at Saunders. "I totally forgot that I'd moved the money out of there."

"Sure."

"There's a chequebook in my other jacket."

"I don't want another cheque."

Skip sawed at his finger. "I'm going to give you my diamond ring right now. Five thousand bucks. If I don't give you the money the day after tomorrow, the ring's yours." Saunders shook his head in disgust. "No, I'm serious," Skip said. "I want to get this straightened out. I mean, you're my best buddy. And I don't want this to affect—"

"Shut up, will you?"

Skip yanked at his finger. "No, I'm serious. The ring's worth ten grand. It's yours, the day after tomorrow, so help me God, if I don't get your money."

"Skip, I believe you."

Skip raised a hand. "Nope, it's gone too far. I want to get this out of the way. I don't want this harming our friendship. I don't want—"

Saunders jumped across the seat and jokingly throttled him.

Skip chuckled and fought Saunders off. "Hucka mucka loagy!" he shouted.

Saunders punched in the dashboard lighter to light a cigarette. He looked at Skip. "I oughta get my head examined, associating with you."

Skip lit a cigarette of his own and the two men

smoked in silence. Then Skip said, "So what do you think, buddy?"

"About what?"

"About Giselle."

Saunders said, "Well . . . she's very nice."

Skip was wary. "What do you mean, 'nice'?"

"I mean nice. You know, friendly. Decent. Polite."

"Yeah, but what do you think, do you think she's perfectly gorgeous?"

"Sure, I think 'gorgeous' is a fair term."

"What do you mean?"

"Skip, she's the Playmate of the Month, all right?"

Skip tapped his cigarette on the rim of the ashtray. "Well, I think she's mighty gaw-damned purty."

Saunders nodded. "Yes, she is."

Skip adjusted the JESUS baseball cap he wore on the back of his head. "Well, I think I could be down for the count this time. Like, I think I'm totally in love."

"Good," said Saunders.

"No, but I mean seriously."

"Good," Saunders said again.

"Like, she says to me, 'Skip, I think I want to spend the rest of my life with you.' And I feel like saying to her, 'Giselle sweetheart, I want to spend the rest of my life with *you*.' "

Saunders nodded. He'd heard Skip make these testimonials of undying devotion before.

"So we're madly in love, Mike. It's what I've waited for all these years. I walk around all day with this dazed smile on my face. All I want to do is look at Giselle, and be with her, and *talk* to her . . . it's crazy. It just keeps getting better and better. And we haven't even made love yet."

Saunders nodded again. No sign of Deborah. Should he go and get her?

"You know the only thing that worries me, though?"

"What's that?" Saunders said.

"What if she's not in love with the real me? What if it's just a fantasy thing? What if I give myself to her and she decides I'm different from what she expected?"

Saunders shrugged. "Then you're out of luck."

"Thanks for the encouragement."

"You're welcome."

Skip smoked his cigarette nervously. "But really, Mike, you're good at the old overview. You've met her. You've seen her. What do you think I should do? Stay cool? Beg her to marry me? What do you think?"

"Well, I suppose you have to pay your dollar and take your chances, just like you've always done. Look at it this way, what happened the last time we had this conversation?"

"Eh?"

"What happened last time, remember? You were dating that nice stewardess from Vancouver, and you decided you wanted her to 'bear your children.' She quit her job, moved to Winnipeg and did just about everything you wanted, and finally you decided you didn't want her. So when you talk about Giselle, just remember she's taking a chance too."

"Yeah, but the others weren't even in the same ballpark as Giselle. This is the *ultimate* woman."

"That's what you said about the stewardess."

Skip puffed on his cigarette for a while. "Well, maybe you're right. I don't know . . . I sure like her, though."

Saunders smiled. For all Skip's faults, he had a healthy respect for his own dishonesty. "And you still haven't slept together?"

"Are you kidding? Her family'd string me up by the thumbs. It's marriage or nothing. Her brother is a body-builder, got about fifteen assault convictions. He says to me one night . . . he grabs my face like this—" Skip seized a soft handful of Saunders' face and shook it with vigour. "Her brother always grabs you like this, like he's Kirk Douglas giving you the kiss of death or something. He grabs me and he says, 'Skip, you're a good guy. Anybody ever hurt Giselle I'd snap his neck like a twig.' "

Saunders chuckled.

"He would do it too," Skip continued. "He's a killer. He's one of these guys, you know, he reaches into the fruit bowl, takes a Delicious apple and *snap*, breaks it open just like that. Hands like a wrecking machine. Uncle Vince is tough too, although you'd never know it. He grew up on the street. He's killed people, probably. So no, I haven't pushed it. Giselle and I have been playing it straight."

"And you're going to sleep in the same bed with her tonight? And you're not going to do anything?"

Skip shook his head. "I'll be up all night, smoking butts, splashing cold water on my face. I can hardly wait until she goes back to Montreal. I'll be able to get some sleep."

A moment later Deborah and Giselle appeared. Saunders opened the door to let them in. "Your friend Maggie called," Deborah said.

"Oh really?"

"She and her boyfriend want to join us for dinner." Deborah smiled. "I'll get to meet this woman, finally."

THE STREETS OF KENORA were stormy and deserted. Snow sped diagonally through the high streetlights along First Avenue. At the main intersection the car ahead of them slowly turned sideways, floated gently as a curling rock down the road and caroomed violently against a curb. Skip was in his glory, driving his enormous doomed Buick. Nothing could stop him. More than once he rolled his window down and yelled greetings to strangers on the sidewalk. At the BoBo Cafe the proprietor was just hanging up the Closed sign when they pulled up. Deborah insisted on getting out of the car and talking to the man. Saunders and Skip and Giselle watched from the car. Saunders could see the Chinese man shaking his head. Deborah's posture was very erect and she snapped her feet in the snow little-boy-style as she walked.

"I feel a Bayview coming on," Saunders intoned.

Skip asked, "Is the food any good there?"

"Sure," replied Saunders. "If you have the gastrointestinal equipment of a German Shepherd."

They parked the car and climbed out into the teeth of the wind. Giselle held on to Skip, Deborah held on to Giselle and Saunders held on to his ears. Inside the Bayview, the Spanish Provincial dining room was empty but obviously open for business. The sudden warmth indoors, the glitter of silverware under the muted restaurant lights, the music from the cocktail lounge, the furry red wallpaper made Saunders feel light-headed. He wondered if he were getting sick. The waitress led them to a rectangular table in the centre of the room.

A few minutes later Maggie and Raymond showed up, Maggie rosy-cheeked and windblown, Raymond with his U-shaped sourdough beard and multi-pocketed mountaineering parka. "Mike, long time no see."

"Hi Raymond. Maggie."

Saunders introduced everyone. Deborah stepped forward and shook Maggie's hand. Both of them smiled sweetly, or so it seemed to Saunders, who wondered if he detected a slight competitiveness in the air.

Skip rubbed his hands together. "Well now, let's get down to some serious drinking."

During dinner Saunders felt that his tentative friendship with Maggie was out of order, with others present. His jokes fell flat. His references to various renovation chores went unnoticed. It felt odd to be in a social situation where they were both with other people. Raymond talked about health and fitness with Deborah. And Saunders gave up and talked to no one.

Afterwards, they returned to the inn. Abandoned by his two women, Saunders took solace in whisky. He decided he didn't give a damn. He sat with his stockinged feet up on the hassock and let the heat of the yellow flames warm his soles. The old wooden radio played beautiful Handel music, the music of winter, and the storm creaked and sighed against the inn's massive walls. Feminine voices and laughter echoed in the kitchen. Saunders closed his eyes. He didn't realize he'd fallen asleep until he heard whispering and chuckling around him.

"Oh brother," he said. "I dozed off."

Giselle patted his shoulder. "Poor Michael, I bet you were having a nice nap."

"I was. I guess I didn't get much sleep last night."

"It's this church music," Skip said. "It would put anyone into a coma." He snapped off the radio and put on a record of old teen-age dance hits, then pushed some furniture out of the way and started jiving with Giselle. "Come Along and Be My Party Doll." Skip was a good dancer, with almost as much grace as the average woman. Giselle's skirt swung as she pirouetted in his arms. Deborah and Raymond joined them for the next few songs. Raymond danced like Frankenstein, his forehead glossed with sweat and eyes rolled back. Skip did the frug. The swim. The slow jerk. "The dirty dog," said Skip, seizing Giselle by the hips.

Next, Roy Orbison sang "Leah." Skip showed Ray and Deborah the two options you had for waltzing in his neighbourhood. You were either a Dude or a Homo, according to how you cocked your wrist when you waltzed. It was turning into a boring night.

Saunders kicked his feet off the hassock and announced he was going to bed.

"What?" said Deborah. "I come all this way to visit? And you're going to bed?"

Saunders shrugged. "I'm tired."

Giselle put her hands on her hips. "Mich-ael! You haven't even touched your rum toddy."

"Oh, I didn't realize you made me one."

"Of course I made you one."

"Don't be a homo," said Skip.

"Still . . . I think I'll pack it in. You guys go right ahead and have a party."

"Giselle, dance with Mike," Skip commanded.

"I'll dance with him because I want to, not because *you* tell me to," she said, giving her hair a haughty swish.

"Give Mike a little kiss," Skip said, pushing Giselle forward.

Giselle said, "You think I have to be ordered?" She stepped forward and hesitated, then kissed Saunders on the side of the face. "Oh pul-lease stay up for a while, Mike." She reeked of perfume.

"All right, all right," Saunders grumbled. He sat down with his drink.

"I thought we were going skiing," said Maggie, sounding as cranky as Saunders.

"Shall we go for a ski?" said Deborah. She sat on the arm of Saunders' chair and ruffled his hair as if he were a spaniel.

"It's okay by me," said Skip. "Although I'd prefer to get stoned and party naked in the Jacuzzi."

It was dark on the lake and the wind was sharp as glass. They started in a group but soon were scattered by cold and the darkness. Saunders, alone, paused and felt the uneasy sensation of the ice tipping up underneath him. It was a trick played by the inner ear. He would ski hard for several hundred feet, then stop, lost in the no-sensation of bitter darkness and momentum, flailing out with his ski poles to keep his balance. He kept looking for Maggie but he couldn't see her. She was fast on cross-country skis and had disappeared.

Forty minutes later he came around the corner of the island and saw a fire through the trees. There was a warm-up shack here for skiers. Saunders paused, holding his side. He had a sore stomach, a muscle stitch. He skied up to where Skip, Raymond, Giselle and Deborah were standing around the bonfire. Deborah was putting on her skis.

"It's about time you showed up," she said. "We're ready to go already."

"So go."

"Now now, Mikey," Skip said. "Don't be grumpy."

Saunders kicked off his skies. "Did you warm up in the shack?"

"It's colder in there than it is out here," Deborah said.

Raymond spread his fingers over the bonfire. "Maggie's got a wood burner going inside."

Skip threw one last armload of spruce boughs onto the fire. Sparks and choking black smoke rolled up into their faces. "Nice work, Skip," Deborah said, fanning the smoke. She looked at Raymond. "Why does he keep doing that?"

Skip took a soggy marijuana cigarette out of his mouth and re-lit it. He inhaled deeply, paused, then tried to hand it to Saunders.

"No thanks," Saunders said.

"You want a hit, Ray? Oh shit, I just remembered you're a doctor."

Raymond chuckled. "So?"

"Okay, so you want a hit?"

"No thanks, Skip," Raymond said. He looked at Deborah and deadpanned, "I'm high on life."

"Try a hit, Mike," Skip said.

Saunders shook his head. "Sore stomach."

"Go ahead."

Saunders ignored him.

"Take a hit, Giselle," Skip said.

She looked at Skip in annoyance. "Will you stop sticking that thing in my face?"

Deborah said, "Well, Doctor Morgan, I'm leaving before I freeze."

Raymond stepped into his skis. "I'm with you."

Deborah spoke to Giselle. "We'll go back and get the hot chocolate started."

"We're outa here too," Skip said.

"I'll be along in a few minutes," Saunders said. He watched the others leave. Well, he thought, I guess this is my chance to have a three-minute conversation with Maggie. He stomped through the snow and entered the shack.

Maggie knelt in front of the wood heater, feeding splinters of wood in through the damper door. Her hair, cinched behind her head, was glossy and thick. She had pink cheeks. "Frozen?" she asked. She pushed a chair towards him. "Pull up a seat. I'm trying to get this wood going."

He ignored the chair and sat instead on a rough wooden bench near the fire. An oil lamp cast a gloomy light inside the shack. The fire clicked and murmured from the steel drum.

"Don't burn yourself," she said.

Saunders didn't say anything. He took out a bent cigarette and got it going on the stove's cherry-coloured backside. He shrugged off his jacket and rubbed the stitched muscle in his solar plexus. Felt himself thawing out.

"Can I offer you a rum toddy?" she asked.

"No thanks."

"Something wrong?"

"No."

Maggie stood up to take off her jacket. She unfastened her pony-tail and shook her hair down over a longjohn top, half unbuttoned. Her breasts moved like loose fruit.

Saunders winced, rubbing his stomach. Maybe he was getting ulcers. Twenty years he scrambled for a living in the city. Now he moved to the peace and quiet of the hinterland and his nerves were frying.

"Something wrong?" Maggie asked again.

"Why do you keep asking me that?"

"I'm a nurse."

"Well, that makes sense. You medical types stick together."

She sat on the bench beside him. "Yes," she said. "I'm Nurse Maggie. Look at me." She studied his eyes. "The eyes look all right. They look quite good, as a matter of fact." She put a hand on his forehead. "You don't seem to have a temperature."

"I don't."

She ran a hand lightly through his hair and kneaded the back of his neck. "There's a bit of tension back here."

"Yeah."

"But where is the pain?"

He rolled his shoulders. "First my stomach, now my shoulders."

"Ohh," she said in a soft voice. "Poor boy." She stood behind him and rubbed his shoulders. "Are you angry at me?"

"Not at all," Saunders answered. "It's just that I find the whole situation quite awkward."

"So do I," she said. After a moment she added, "But I didn't expect to."

Maggie got up and slid the bolt on the door. An old railway lantern hung from a coat hanger by the wood heater. She raised the chimney, pursed her lips and blew the flame out. The shack fell into darkness. Through the mouth of the stove, the fire threw dim orange shadows on the floor.

Saunders walked toward Maggie and put his hands on her waist. She lifted her chin and he kissed her on the mouth. They kissed for a long moment and then, sighing, he embraced her.

Her voice was husky. "Well, I see I've melted that icy demeanour of yours."

He muttered, "Yes, I'm cured." He kissed her again.

"I'm kind of surprised that we're doing this," she whispered.

"Didn't you ever wonder what it would be like?"

"Only recently, I've been wondering."

He nodded and brushed her face with his fingertips. "How do you feel?"

"Nice," she murmured, "but a bit sinful."

He pulled her tight. They kissed, open-mouthed. Saunders ran his hand inside her shirt, along her smooth back. Her soft hair brushed his face. He could feel the wild electric tickle of her tongue. His heart pounded. Oh Maggie, he thought. You own me.

17

~~~
~~~

SAUNDERS STOOD IN THE SNOW AND WAVED AS THE Wildcat slewed down the driveway.

Deborah, Giselle and Skip were gone at last. Finally he could enjoy a few minutes' peace. Deborah had chosen breakfast-time this morning to pour two cups of coffee, take him by the elbow and give him a free twenty-minute lecture. It was a very nice hotel, she said. But wasn't it time he stopped playing Junior Boy Scout and faced his responsibilities to his consulting partners?

At least their visit had produced a much-needed injection of cash, in the form of a cheque from Mr. Sydney L. Carter for the sum of five thousand bucks, delivered with much stuttering and apology from Skip, who wrote it out after Giselle found his chequebook and a pen.

Saunders deposited the cheque and paid off several thousand dollars in outstanding debts. Which still left him in hock to various local businesses but at least averted the immediate prospect of being taken to court. Once Joe's Meats or one of those little companies files notice of claim, it usually starts a stampede. Saunders had seen it happen over and over again. You pull out one piece, the whole project comes tumbling down.

He felt good. The snow was white and sparkly. His guests were gone. The inn was silent and heat purred out the register. Somewhere, far off in another room, the comradely voice of Max Ferguson introduced another Irish folk-song.

Saunders got to work on the ceiling. He took coffee breaks every hour or so, allowing himself to replay the scene of the night before—the fire's glow in the cabin, the shadows on Maggie's face, the touch of her hand, the taste of her mouth. He worked hard all afternoon and resisted the temptation to call her. The worst thing he could do, he knew, was to push things. He should let her have some time. She'd show up for work sometime after lunch on Monday, and he could wait until then.

But Monday came and went, with no visit from Maggie. And Tuesday passed without so much as a phone call. He finally saw her on Thursday night, grocery shopping in Kenora. It was a night of icy streets and softly falling diamond snow. He was crossing the Safeway parking lot with two full bags in each arm when he spotted her opening the door of her pick-up truck to let her big dog jump inside. Saunders skidded up. "Hi."

She turned around. For the briefest moment she seemed embarrassed. "I've been meaning to call you," she said.

"Yeah. I wondered if you were all right."

"I'm fine." She closed the door of the truck. "Just really busy. How's the work going?"

"Not bad." He shifted the bags onto the hood of the truck.

"And your friends are gone?"

"Oh yeah. Skip and Giselle are talking about going on vacation to Mexico."

"Mexico?"

He nodded. "Giselle's family apparently has a condo."

"Must be nice."

"Yes." Pause. He zipped his jacket. "Cold," he said.

"You're not kidding."

The dog woofed inside the truck. Maggie looked at him. She adjusted her mitts. Looked at Saunders again. Silence. She finally spoke. "I've been doing a lot of thinking."

"About what?"

"About what happened the other night."

"You mean in the ski shack?"

She smiled. "Yes."

"Listen," he said, "if you think the floor was a little hard, don't worry, I've ordered in some broadloom for our next date." She gave him an exasperated look. "Okay, sorry," he said. "You wanted to tell me something."

"Well . . ." She gazed across the parking lot. Tiny diamonds drifted past her eyes. She had dark eyelashes, and cheeks that always took on roses in the cold. "I've been thinking about what happened."

"Okay."

"And . . ."

Saunders could feel his heart sinking. "Listen, if you want to take some time . . ."

"No, that's not it."

"Just don't tell me what I think you're going to tell me."

"What?"

"You know."

She frowned. "Mike—"

A car rolled by. Rock music thundered from inside. Saunders knew what Maggie was about to say. He felt sick. He saw Maggie and himself as people in the car might see them: a man and a woman exchanging some snippet of trivial conversation under a streetlight. "Did you talk to Raymond?"

She nodded.

"When?"

"The next day. But that doesn't matter."

"What matters?"

"What matters is doing the right thing. God gave us a conscience. Let's use it. I don't want to proceed with a situation where someone is going to get hurt."

"Who will get hurt?"

"Maybe Raymond, maybe you." She paused. "Me."

"I'm hurt right now," he said.

"That's not what I wanted."

"I know," he said.

"I'd still like to help," she said, "whenever I can. With the inn."

"All right." His voice was flat. "And I still owe you that money. I'm hoping to sell the place in the next few weeks."

She looked away and then back at him. "Do you want to go somewhere and have a coffee?"

"If I understand you," he said, "there's not much point. I guess what you're telling me is, you're going to stick with Raymond."

She shrugged minutely. "I don't think that's the issue."

"But you're going to pursue, more or less, your relationship with Raymond?"

She nodded.

"Well, I feel kind of bad," he said. "I don't really care about drinking coffee."

She waited, giving Saunders the opportunity to decide when it was time. But he had nothing else to say. "I'm sorry," she said finally, turning away.

Saunders loaded his groceries into his car and

climbed in. He sat for a few minutes, pumping the accelerator and waiting for the windshield to defrost. Maggie's truck crept by. It was awkward, wondering if she would look at him. She didn't. They were no longer friends. How strange. She pulled out onto the street and the tail-lights of her truck faded with all the others.

18

By the end of the week the weather was once again a nightmare of snow and blizzardy winds. He'd spent all Skip's money already, unbelievable as that seemed, and though he had a good supply of building materials and food, he had no money to pay anyone to help him. His constant absence was kicking the hell out of their consulting business, and he couldn't expect any cheques from New Age Associates for weeks.

He was heating with firewood these days to save heating oil, and he spent Friday laying in a fresh supply of wood. Stormy winds raked down through the spruces, stinging his eyes as he sectioned fallen trees with the screaming chain-saw. He soothed the loss of Maggie by driving the saw blade deep into the log, squinting into the maelstrom of flying chips. Every day another wad of invoices arrived in the mail. He couldn't pay them.

He finally shut off the chain-saw and realized he couldn't go on. He couldn't stay here. It was time to go. It was time to go and hunt money. He was like a moose on the ice, surrounded by wolves, doomed. He moved through the inn, and shut down systems and emptied the water lines so he could turn the heat off. Then he got in the car and drove to Winnipeg, wondering what to do. Should he just face facts and admit he was beaten? He'd committed the dumbest mistake in the book, he'd under-financed. He'd let himself get spread out with one foot on the boat and one foot on the dock. Some consultant.

When he arrived in Winnipeg there was no place to stay. Skip had gone to Giselle's family condo down in Mexico for a few weeks and hadn't left a key. Saunders booked into a cheap hotel, the Royal Windsor Arms, and gave them his credit card. Luckily, they didn't run it through the computer.

His room had a single bed and a urine-scented sink on the wall. The Royal Windsor Arms was on its last legs. Saunders had half-heartedly watched it go up and down like a yo-yo since he first got involved in the consulting business. Back in those early days the hotel was saved from demolition because a young, good-looking Winnipeg man, a Member of Parliament, was appointed to a high place in the federal cabinet. Possibly for reasons having as much to do with his striking coiffure as his personal abilities, he was soon a powerful force in the government. It was a rare thing, a miracle almost. An important federal politician who wasn't in bed with the voters of southern Ontario or Quebec. This change in tradition had the sudden marvellous result of channelling a torrent of cash—cash that would normally be sprayed all over eastern Canada—onto the perplexed heads of downtown Winnipeggers. The Royal Windsor Arms, in fact, the whole downtown neighbourhood of

Winnipeg, enjoyed a sudden Roman spring of renewal.

Bright canvas awnings, candy-painted fire hydrants, neat cobblestone streets—the Core Area, as it was called, suddenly wasn't such a rotten apple after all. Fern bars and quiche restaurants opened where before there had only been gloomy, murderous beer parlours, dirty bookstores and Quik Cash shops. Baffled by the sudden proliferation of cute menus and four-dollar drinks, the neighbourhood's ragtag occupation of winos fell back, trailed by an army of young liberals—people who wore the same longish hair and ratty boots but were, in fact, doing quite well. Saunders was one of them. On a typical night in the summer, Curly Boy So-and-So and his blues band would burn the Royal Windsor to the ground, two hundred and fifty people jammed into the little lounge, and waiters ploughed through the thick smoke, holding aloft immense platters of beer. There was no point in attempting to carry on a conversation. Saunders would drink until his face got numb, then he'd watch the crowd. He was a scientist.

"You have to risk something," Skip would say. "You have to identify your target and go after her. Never be afraid to ask for the sale."

That was the 1970s. Coupling and uncoupling. Open Marriage. Esalen Institute. John Travolta, "How Deep Is Your Love?" Not very deep, actually. A lot of people looked upon the Disco era, the 'Me Decade,' as a hopeless time of superficiality and self-indulgence.

Saunders and Skip would go out at night and there'd be nothing but open-necked shirts, gold chains, lots of hugging. "Hey dude, how is it? You're looking great! Terrific! Let's do lunch!" Skip loved every minute of it and Saunders, truthfully, didn't mind it. Disco reintroduced dancing to the party scene. Saunders liked dancing. And he liked shallow people.

Then came the 1980s. The oil price collapse. The interest-rate spiral of '82. The herpes epidemic. The stock market crash. The first signs of approaching middle age. Heart palpitations. Wrinkles around the eyes and mouth. Thinning hair. And a horrible new disease—AIDS. Like something out of a science fiction novel, or the book of the Apocalypse. Ashes ashes, all fall down. Go home with somebody you met in a bar, wake up with night sweats six months later, develop weird bruises on your legs, cough blood and die.

The western world re-entered a conservative period. Best-selling books were written by Lee Ioccoca, Donald Trump and other individuals with thick necks, small brains and fat wallets. The Liberals were booted out of Ottawa and the glorious money pipeline into Winnipeg dried up. The fern bars and quiche restaurants went broke. The Core Area went back to its original proprietors, the winos. This was the situation when Saunders arrived back at the Royal Windsor Arms that dark winter night. And now he too was broke.

Well, he wasn't entirely broke. He had about twenty-five dollars' worth of fruit and cheese. And he had about twelve dollars' worth of gas in the BMW, and he had a book, a hardback copy of Henry Miller's *Black Spring*, purchased for two dollars and ninety-eight cents at Red River Books, up the street. That left about fourteen dollars of folding money and change between him and the pavement.

The days went by. He reminisced about his sexy minutes of necking with Maggie. He missed her in the morning, when the first thing he heard were toilets flushing and radiators hammering. He missed her at night, when his eyes were too tired to read and he had to fight the urge to get up and go down the hall to call her.

One morning, at the beginning of his second week, he went down to the hotel coffee shop and indulged in his big extravagance of the day: tea, toast and a tabloid. This particular morning there was a story in the paper about a guy who'd gone into the Oxford Hotel the night before, just down the street, and held up the beer vendor with a sawed-off shotgun. The yet unidentified white male then ran out the front door of the hotel and sprinted, WHAM, into the side of a passing police car. Saunders could imagine the conversation in the cop car going from take-home pay and little Tina's day care to holy suffering Jesus what's this?

According to the paper the robber ran north on Albert, past Saunders' hotel and into a back lane where the speeding police car caught up with him. The two constables jumped out and yelled at the man to stop, at which point, according to the newspaper report, he "made a threatening gesture" with the shotgun and the cops fired. It's not like in the movies. The cops were forty steps away and they emptied their guns, firing ten shots. All missed except one, which hit the robber in the forehead.

For some reason, Saunders read and re-read the story, finding it very depressing. Maybe because it happened just down the street. Maybe it was because the man was stealing money. Maybe he had too vivid an imagination. He could feel his feet slipping on the gritty ice underfoot. He could feel the shotgun in his hand, the bag of cash. How much of a threatening gesture do you have to make to get yourself shot? The cops were usually half-decent guys, Wally Cleaver types. There was no point in blaming them. But he was starting to find life in general very depressing.

He had to sell the BMW.

Later that afternoon, heavy with frustration, he called the newspaper and placed an advertisement in the Classified section. That night he sat up late with the dashboard of his car disassembled on his bed. He crossed his legs like an Indian fakir and rebuilt the odometer, turning the little numbered wheels until they suggested that the car, in human terms, was a mere adolescent. I can't believe what a scumbag I'm turning into, he thought, but carried on anyway. The next day the desk clerk knocked on Saunders' door about every ten minutes. You didn't get too many MINT 2002s in the paper, CHEAP!

Saunders sold the car late in the afternoon. A man and a woman, two psychologists on their way to California, gave him every penny of the forty-five hundred dollars he wanted. The guy had a beard, Hush Puppies and a bald head. His wife was pregnant. They were nice people. You'd think that psychologists wouldn't be so trusting, after all the time they spent studying the hominid species. Saunders stuffed the certified cheque in his pocket and patted the car goodbye. At least you're going where it's warm, faithful little pony.

He celebrated with a solitary dinner that night. He smoked a cigar and ordered a great variety of drinks and liqueurs. He had some walking-around money but another notch had slipped, another timber had cracked in the jackstraw tangle that kept him from sliding utterly down the hole.

After dinner, he walked down Portage and north on Notre Dame. The buildings were a wind tunnel and the blowing ice crystals savaged his face. After a short distance he stepped into the lee of a travel agent's doorway to look at the posters. Inside, the travel agents were still working. Booming business, this time of year.

Posters of Greece. Brazil. Jamaica. A woman who looked as if she were experiencing sexual ecstasy reclined with her eyes shut on a golden beach in Mexico. Saunders stood with a mitt clasped over his ear. A particularly nasty cannonade of snow raked his face. He burrowed into his upturned collar and thought of

Skip down in Mexico. Skip, Giselle and all her family relaxing on the beach. Uncle Vince the mobster would be down there.

Son of a bitch. Maybe it was time to go for broke, see if he could hack out a loan with Uncle Vince. He'd tried everything else. The money from selling his car would last another three or four weeks, then what? He had to come up with a long-term financing plan. Something that would give him enough to finish the renovation and cover maintenance expenses until he could sell it. Sell the accursed thing. And get back to a normal life.

He shivered and looked at the people inside the office. The trouble is, he thought, how can I set up an immediate meeting with Uncle Vince?

I'm sure as hell not going all the way to Mexico.

19

THE 737 WHINED TO A STOP. SAUNDERS ORGANIZED THE contents of his briefcase, walked to the doorway and squinted in the bright sun. In the distance were sharp green mountains. Several hundred yards away a row of scruffy palm trees fluttered lazily. A big airliner taxied by, its exhausts blurring like dragon breath in the heat. He paused, put on his sun-glasses and climbed down the stairs onto the soil of Mexico.

Manzanillo, to be exact. Eighty degrees. The air was thick and banana-scented. Heat like a hammer. When he reached the arrivals gate his shirt was soaked from sweat. Inside the terminal, he stood in line to go through Mexican customs. Hundreds of people bustled about with loads of luggage. A Mexican airport employee passed by, pushing a rubber-wheeled dolly. On the dolly, an American college kid sat on his haunches, whooping loudly and waving a can of beer. Saunders went outside and found a taxi.

They drove out to the highway and ten minutes later they were speeding down the coast. This was the Pan-American highway, the road to Central America. On the left side the land rose steeply up into jungle-covered green mountains. On the right side were bone-white resort hotels and open vistas of Pacific Ocean. Saunders was devastated by the sudden transition, the heat, the savage beauty of the tropics. When he left Winnipeg, it was twenty below zero.

The cab driver kept studying the little piece of paper with the address of Uncle Vince's condo. Finally the cab turned into a long driveway bordered by green lawns and Babylonian gardens. At the end of the driveway was a condominium complex with white walls and a high mosque-style roof. A plainclothes security guard beside a wrought-iron gate waved the cab to a stop.

The guard looked at Saunders curiously.

Saunders said, "Senor, uh ... Sidney Carter, *por favor*?"

"Sir, you don't have to speak Mexican here," said the guard. "Do you have your keyholder card?"

"I don't really belong here," Saunders replied. "I'm just looking for a fellow . . . uh, Sidney Carter. Skip? He's kind of—"

"I can't help you," the guard said. "If you don't have a keyholder card, I can't let you in." The guard nodded to the cab driver. "Away you go."

"I came all the way from Canada," Saunders protested.

"That's too bad," the guard said. He didn't sound sincere. He made a circling gesture with his finger in the air. "Come on, turn around. *Vamanos!*"

The driver turned the car around. Saunders swore under his breath and sank back in his seat. A white golf cart lurched out of the garden and crossed the road ahead. As the cab driver accelerated to pass it, Saunders sat upright in the back seat, staring at the trio of well-dressed golfers. "Hey!" he shouted. "Stop . . . *alto, alto!*" The cab driver hit the brakes. Saunders jumped out. Riding on the golf cart were Giselle, Uncle Vince and Skip.

THAT NIGHT THEY HAD SUPPER on a terrace overlooking the ocean. The dark sea wind clattered in the palms overhead. Candles flickered in little lanterns on the table. Uncle Vince, Giselle, Skip and a variety of DeFranco family members monopolized a long table at the end of the terrace. In the washroom, after dinner, Saunders peed alongside Skip.

Skip shook his head. "I still can't believe you're here."

"Neither can I."

"How are things in Minaki?"

"I'm broke," said Saunders.

"Gee, that's a surprise."

"And you were right about Maggie."

"What do you mean?"

Saunders shrugged. "We had one night of romance. And then she went and told Raymond."

Skip shook his head. "You didn't listen to the old Skipper, Mike. Why do you think I get paid for giving people advice?" Saunders was silent. "So you're here to run away from it all?"

"I didn't want to say anything before talking to you," Saunders said, "but I thought I'd approach Uncle Vince."

Skip shook off his weenie. "For what, a consulting project?"

"A loan to finish the inn."

Skip chuckled.

"You're the one," Saunders said, "who kept telling me to come and meet him. So don't start in with the laughing, you son of a bitch."

Skip slapped him on the shoulder. "Hey, relax. I think you did the right thing. We'll get you some dough, one way or the other. If not Uncle Vince, there's other people I can introduce you to."

"What's wrong with Uncle Vince?"

"Nothing, really."

"What do you mean?"

"Well, when you're rich, you develop all kinds of idiosyncrasies. Uncle Vince is one of these guys, hates to talk business when he's on vacation."

"Everybody is like that. But sooner or later they loosen up. I don't want to hold a meeting or anything. I just want to have a drink with him, tell him the history of the place."

Skip shook his head. "His bodyguards will break your nose if you even bring up the subject. He's made it clear to everyone that he's here to fish, period. He comes here to collect trophies. He takes it real seriously. Like some people collect stamps? Uncle Vince has stuffed fish and stuffed birds and you name it."

"So what am I supposed to do, just leave?"

"Talk to one of the younger guys."

"Like who?"

"Vinnie."

"Who's Vinnie?" asked Saunders. "All these people got the same first name?"

"Vinnie Martens. You just met him, for pete's sake. He's sitting next to Giselle's brother. The little guy in the yellow shirt? Squirms around a lot? He runs some of their venture capital. I met him in Montreal, that time Chief Leo and I were down there together. Did you bring a package?"

"Oh yeah."

" 'Cause you should just make a presentation to him, site plans and photographs and all that. He'll probably go for it."

Saunders washed his hands. "I don't know, Skip. I think I'd rather work with Uncle Vince."

"Why?"

"Because this other guy doesn't know me from a hole in the ground. What am I going to do for credentials?"

Skip combed his hair. "You don't need credentials. You're with me."

The next morning Saunders got up early—Giselle had put him into a nice room with red tile floors and a balcony overlooking the sea—and spread his documents on the bed. He broke open a new sheaf of white linen paper and sketched the Stonehouse Inn, what it would look like with the landscaping finished and the renovations done. He slipped everything into a professional-looking leather sleeve.

He went down to the beach for a swim, then ordered breakfast on the terrace. After a while Skip joined him. They drank freshly squeezed orange juice and watched the surf hit the beach. Skip had a little pair of binoculars that he used to appraise different women on the beach. Saunders told Skip about the progress of the hotel. "I can't walk away from it now, Skip. It's almost finished."

"Well, go and see Vinnie."

"I'd rather deal with the old man."

"Why? What difference does it make?"

"I already told you. This guy Vinnie is going to want to nail my ass to the wall, to protect himself."

"Mike, I know you want twenty thousand dollars. To you, it's a lot of money. To Vinnie, it's nothing. You know what? There's a lot of people around here, they make twenty thousand dollars in an hour. He'll look at your situation, he'll propose some terms, and you can take it or leave it. If you don't like his terms, walk away. If you like them, sign the papers, and you'll go home with your money."

"Why can't I do the same with Giselle's uncle?"

"Don't you ever listen to me? He's down here to gather fish for his trophy room. I'll get you your money. Uncle Vince doesn't want to know about no cock-eyed Stonehouse Inn."

Soon after, Giselle joined them. She wore a tiny blue bikini and a white beach kimono. Her eyes were painted and her toenails were crimson. She planted a good-morning kiss on Saunders' forehead. There was something quite asexual about Giselle. She could sit on Saunders' lap and massage his nuts and he'd feel like telling her about the amazing pelican he saw that morning.

"Here comes the gang," Skip said.

Saunders looked down the beach. A canopied white Jeep drove slowly along the surf line. Several men walked beside it. "Is Vinnie with them?"

"Yep," Skip said, studying the group with his binoculars. He gave them to Saunders. "He's the little guy in the white shorts. Got the hair all over his shoulders like an ape?"

Saunders studied the blurry group. Vinnie Martens and Giselle's brother Frank were walking ahead of the Jeep. They were laughing, hands moving rapidly as they talked. Several paces behind them, in the convertible Jeep, several old women hunkered down in dark shawls. Uncle Vince walked ten yards behind the Jeep, carrying a fishing rod. Behind him strolled two security men. Periodically, Vince stopped to cast a lure into the surf, and everyone in the procession watched and waited.

"I should just go down and talk to him," Saunders said.

"Talk to who?" Giselle said.

"Your uncle."

"Why?" Giselle's voice always dropped a semi-tone when her uncle's name was mentioned. She didn't seem overly fond of him.

Skip said, "Because he wants to beg for some money."

"Skip," Saunders interjected, with an angry look. "I'm offering an opportunity to invest in a wonderful place—"

"I'm *joking*. All right?"

"So when should I talk to him?"

"Don't ask me," Giselle said.

"Just be patient," Skip said. "Don't hassle him."

"I don't want to leave it too long."

"Why?" Skip said. "It's probably thirty degrees below zero in Minaki this morning. Roads closed. Blowing snow. You wouldn't be getting any work done anyway."

Saunders nodded. "You have a point." He had bought a seven-day charter fare, so he was pretty well stuck here for a week. He would bide his time and wait for the perfect moment when he could catch Uncle Vince alone.

MEANWHILE, GISELLE AND SKIP lay on the beach, suntanning. Skip referred to this as "doing the big zero." They would have stayed there all day, but Uncle Vince seemed to appear whenever Giselle and Skip were by themselves for longer than an hour, and it unnerved Skip. So Saunders found he could persuade them to undertake at least one activity a day, as long as it wasn't too strenuous. In the early afternoon, they'd go have a cool, shady lunch somewhere, or walk down to the market in Las Palmas and buy a T-shirt or pair of sandals, or hire a taxi and go for a shopping trip to Manzanillo. Even then Uncle Vince wanted to know their whereabouts.

One night they sat in the El Tigre lounge and watched a movie on Uncle Vince's wide-screen satellite TV. In the darkness, Saunders studied the old man's leonine head, wondering whether he'd ever get a chance to approach him. Saunders thought about his other life, the real one. He missed Maggie. He thought about her a lot. You didn't bounce back from a clear failure, at his age. Even if it was no big romance.

The movie was *Jaws IV*. Up on the screen, the familiar old dorsal fin cut through the water as pretty girls in bikinis issued great theatrical screams. The sheriff and citizens of Amity, New York, fought and bickered with one another and drew together, finally, to face the common threat. Everybody in the El Tigre clapped and hooted as the shark was blown into sandwich meat. The movie was terrible but it had a fish in it, so it was good stuff as far as Uncle Vince was concerned.

Just before the movie ended, Saunders got an idea and slipped out of the darkened lounge. He went down to the dining room and located his pal Ramone, the resort's concierge. After a few minutes of small talk he slipped Ramone a tightly folded American fifty-dollar bill and asked him for a little favour. When Uncle Vince and his entourage came out of the El Tigre lounge, intending to head back to their rooms and call it a night, Saunders was crossing the deck with a plastic pail full of raw chicken innards in one hand and a seven-foot-long Fenwick surf casting outfit in the other.

Uncle Vince paused. "Mr. Saunders."

Saunders stopped. "Yes sir. Mr. DeFranco."

Uncle Vince approached him. He smiled and held his huge cigar aloft like a harpoon. "Are you going fishing?" he asked, as if he could hardly believe it.

"Yes sir."

"What are you fishing for?"

"Sharks, sir."

Uncle Vince looked back at his group. His head, up close, was furred with tight curls like a Hereford bull. "Did you hear what this kid said?"

IN THE DARKNESS the ocean roared and the tiny lights of the hotel swam in the winds. Uncle Vince had changed his clothes and was following Saunders down to the beach, carrying a rod of his own. The security man from the front gate walked off to one side. He carried a plastic-stocked shotgun. Saunders had spent a couple of summers, as a teenager, working as a fishing guide at the Stonehouse Inn and he was feverishly trying to remember the lingo.

"Where do you think we should fish, Mike?"

"By the rip channel," Saunders replied. "I think that should be a good place to start. With this moon coming up, we should get a chance at some pelagic predators along there."

Uncle Vince nodded. "I myself have never thought of doing this. And I've been coming here for years."

Saunders hoisted the stinky pail full of meat and they moved on. When they got to the end of the beach they could see little figures moving in the water in the dark—Mexican kids, fishing for mullet. Mountainous waves crashed on the beach. Saunders stood at the end of the point and looked out into the rip. The choppy water in the channel appeared to be running landward into the lagoon, meaning the tide was rising.

He clipped a big single hook onto Uncle Vince's leader and reached into the pail. The meat was warm and slimy. He threaded a chunk of raw liver onto the shark hook and moved down towards the water. An enormous wave rushed onto the beach, black and ugly, and collapsed with a roar. He ran forwards as the wave sucked back. At the bottom of the slope, with a new wave building like a wall in front of him, he flung the hunk of liver as hard as he could, then turned and ran back up the beach. A volume of water the size of a dump truck pursued him.

Saunders speared the surf rod into the sand, took the other fishing rod from Uncle Vince and rigged it up. He waited for a pause in the surf, then ran down and chucked the other bait out. He sat down beside Uncle Vince in the sand. Piece of cake, he thought. Who said I never learned anything from all those fishing trips?

Uncle Vince produced his Zippo and attempted to light his cigar in the wind. "You've done that before."

"Not this exactly. But similar."

"They tell me you own a resort."

"Yes sir. I'm renovating it. It's our family place."

"Is there fishing there?"

"Oh yes. Bass, northern pike, muskie. We had a guest caught the world record muskie in 1955, right in front of the dock. Fifty-nine pounds. The record stood for, I don't know, four or five years. We've got the photograph by the fireplace."

"I'd like to get your brochure before you leave."

"Certainly."

"I need a muskie. A trophy-sized specimen, of course."

"Uh huh."

"How many days would it take to catch a muskie?"

"Hard to say. Maybe a week or so, serious fishing."

"Make sure you send me a brochure."

"Yes sir."

They were silent for a while. The security man was standing well off to one side, looking bored, smoking a thin cigarillo. The shotgun was propped on his foot. Saunders lit a cigarette, cupping the match against the wind. The waves roared in front of them.

Uncle Vince said, "Do you think we'll catch anything?"

"I don't know," Saunders said. "It's a beautiful night." You always emphasize the weather, he thought.

"All the years I've been coming here," Uncle Vince reiterated, "I've never tried this."

Saunders could see the little *muchachos* running back and forth like shorebirds, fishing for mullet in the dark. They didn't have expensive Penn and Fenwick combos; their reels were white plastic Javex bottles wrapped with string. But they caught lots of fish. Ten minutes of silence. When Uncle Vince glanced at his watch, Saunders decided to seize the moment.

"I'm hoping to have the resort finished and ready for business come spring," he said. "But I'm a bit bogged down right now. I under-financed. I'm looking for some venture capital."

There was another long silence. Uncle Vince puffed on his cigar. He didn't respond. I've crossed the line, Saunders feared. He's discovered my motives and he's trying to decide how angry he is.

"How much do you need to finish up?" Uncle Vince said. His voice was unconcerned.

"Twenty thousand."

"I'd look for forty if I were you," Uncle Vince said. "Don't make the same mistake you did when you started. Go big or go home."

"Yes sir."

"I'd help you myself but I'm out of that, these days. Horseshit investments, pardon my French. Anyway, I'm on vacation."

"I understand."

"Talk to Mr. Martens. He manages our venture capital."

"Yes sir."

"He may be able to help you out. I don't like to get involved."

Saunders nodded.

After a while Uncle Vince said, "You seem like a smart boy."

"Thank you, sir."

"I'm worried about Giselle."

"Oh?"

"This friend of yours, Sidney."

Saunders waited before answering. "Skip seems flighty at times, but I believe he wants to settle down. He's really devoted to Giselle. And he's quite a good businessman."

"He's a lazy boy."

Saunders nodded carefully. "He's lazy, yes. But his heart is in the right place."

"Heart?" Uncle Vince chuckled. "He has no heart at all. He's empty."

Saunders countered, "He has a sharp mind."

"He has no mind, either. Lots of sharp remarks, yes. But he's heard them all on TV. Giselle is just a child. It seems like a few weeks ago, she was sitting on my knee. I don't want her running away with some hustler."

Saunders wanted to explain what he himself admired in Skip. He thought Skip was funny, and there was lots of energy there, but those attributes seemed scarcely worth mentioning.

"Here he is," Uncle Vince said. His voice had a grim undertone.

Skip approached with Rocky DeFranco and Vinnie Martens. They had flashlights. "Catchin' anything?" Skip shouted.

"Nope," Saunders replied.

Vinnie propped his hands on his hips and eyed the sea. "Sharks? Chris-s-st. . . . You guys are nuts or something."

"Sharks," Rocky snorted. "Whose idea was this?"

"Let me try it," Skip said, reaching for Saunders' rod.

"Leave it," Saunders said. "There's nothing to try."

Skip ignored Saunders and pulled the rod out of the sand. "You just letting the bait sit there? No wonder you're not catching anything."

"Skip, would you leave it alone, you're just going to—"

"You have to twitch it," Skip said. "I watch the Babe Winkleman show."

Skip gave Saunders' rod a little yank. It jerked back and then bent violently. Skip staggered towards the water. His voice was thin and panicky. "Help! I've got something!"

AT BREAKFAST THE NEXT MORNING Saunders and Skip recounted the episode for Giselle—the twenty-minute struggle, the crowd scene with Uncle Vince and Saunders and Rocky DeFranco and Vinnie Martens and about twenty children jumping around in the dark, shouting advice while Skip staggered back and forth, fighting the fish.

"Uncle Vince was even excited," Skip said.

Saunders said, "Excited? What about the security guard?"

"What an asshole," Skip said, shaking his head. "He blasted my fish."

Giselle said, "He shot your fish?"

Skip nodded. They were sitting under palm fronds, on a terrace over the ocean. It was early morning. Skip thumbed the wet side of the orange juice glass. "Just as the fish was almost at the beach he runs into the water and starts *blasting* with his shotgun. Orange flames shooting out of the gun, kids screaming and running, water exploding—"

"Oh no," Giselle said.

"Yeah, what is the story on all the guns around here?" Saunders said. "Like this Vinnie character, has he always got that little silver pistol in his belt?"

"You're starting to notice, are you?" Giselle said.

Saunders said, "But doesn't it bother you?"

"What choice do I have?" Giselle replied.

"I think it's kind of cool," Skip said. "I've got nothing against a little firepower. Like, you have to remember where we are. There's banditos around here. Vinnie has a business to run. Supposing he needs to feed somebody to the hog."

"To the what?"

"Feed somebody to the hog," Skip repeated. "It's what Vinnie does to clients who don't pay back their debts."

"Oh, what a lot of silliness," Giselle said.

"Skip," Saunders intoned. "Don't start up."

"No really. Vinnie has this six-hundred-pound hog, locked up in a pen somewhere? And when somebody doesn't pay him back, Vinnie starves the hog for a while and then puts the guy in the pen. And the guy yells at the hog and the hog grunts and runs away to the corner of the pen. And they sit there, looking at each other. And eventually, after one day, or two days, the guy drops off to sleep. And the hog, crazy with hunger, tippy-toes over and takes a bite out of the guy. And the guy yells and the hog runs away. And it goes on like this for a while. Vinnie doesn't know the details because he's off taking care of business. All he knows is that when he comes back later there's just a big red stain on the ground where his client used to be."

"That's silly nonsense," Giselle said. "I don't know why men tell such stories. Is it supposed to be funny?"

"But all things being considered, he shouldn't have shot my fish. This bodyguard is a loser," Skip said. "Can't you get him fired? I can't believe he did that. I was going to start my own trophy collection. I was going to have it mounted."

"You don't mount a *skate*," Saunders sniffed.

"Oh yeah? Well, maybe I could have it made into a coffee-table."

Saunders shook his head. Skip's fish had been an odd-looking thing, flat as a frisbee, with a long whippy tail. Overturned, it had a pale belly and a sad U-shaped mouth. The security guard had blasted it with several rounds of heavy buckshot and the pale belly was patterned like Swiss cheese. After the crowd had stared at it for several minutes in the glare of the flashlight, they released the corpse to the surf. All in all, not a scene that would have pleased Jacques Cousteau.

But Uncle Vince liked it well enough. He ended the evening by tapping Vinnie Martens on the shoulder as they all walked back to the condo, and telling him to have a look at Saunders' proposal. "Mr. Saunders has another fishing place I want to try," he said. "But he has to get the property cleaned up first."

Vinnie Martens gave Saunders a sharp look. After a moment or two he shrugged, as if Uncle Vince's word was law.

"You two gentlemen can find a moment to discuss this?"

"Yes sir. Thank you," Saunders said.

Vinnie Martens nodded.

Uncle Vince took Saunders aside for just a moment and offered his hand. "I understand that you're leaving in a day or two."

"Yes sir."

"I'm concerned about Giselle," he said. "I'd like you to keep an eye on Sidney for me. I'll leave a number you can call if there is any problem." Saunders didn't answer. Uncle Vince was holding his hand. The hand was large, hard, firm and polite. "Don't think of her as just another one of Sidney's girlfriends. She's Vincent DeFranco's niece. Do I make myself clear?"

EARLY IN THE MORNING a single flamboyant rooster strutted in the driveway as Skip helped Saunders load his bags into the taxi. The air smelled of salty ocean and of the purple bougainvillaea that clung to the white garden walls beside the entrance gate. Saunders had been looking forward to leaving all week, but now that it was time he no longer wanted to go. It was easy here in the warmth of summer.

Skip and Giselle accompanied him in the taxi. They kept whispering to each other, smiling, deep in that annoying, conspiratorial world of lovers. Saunders studied the sprinklers looping silver spray across the golf course, the palm trees, the deep green tropical vegetation glittering in the early sun. The cab driver's radio played loud, festive Mexican songs.

"So when are you returning to work?" Saunders asked, using the opportunity to bug Skip, for once, about ignoring responsibilities.

"What's that, Mike?" Skip said. Giselle was tickling him.

"I say, when are you returning to—" Giselle shrieked as Skip squeezed her knee. Saunders shook his head.

At the airport Saunders climbed out and unloaded his bags. It was hot already. He could see the tall tail fin of his wide-body jet above the terminal. Skip and Giselle whispered to each other inside the taxi. Saunders thought it was nice that they were madly in love, but this was really a bit rude.

Skip got out and held the door for Giselle. "Mike," he said, "we've come to a decision."

Saunders hefted a bag. "About what?"

"We haven't told a living soul," Skip said. "But we're getting married. Will you be our best man?"

20

EVEN WITH UNCLE VINCE'S FIRST CHEQUE FOR $13,333.00 stashed safely away in his briefcase, Saunders' wintry gloom returned as the jet thundered northward. New Mexico, Colorado, Nebraska and South Dakota flickered beneath the wing as he ingested half a dozen variations of raw stimulant and watched darkness come to the United States of America. Back to reality, he thought.

Whether he liked it or not, he was now an employee of Vince DeFranco. His job was to spy on Skip. Giselle's family didn't want her getting hurt. Saunders didn't want her to get hurt, either. And he would have done his best, in any case, to persuade Skip to make the right choices. But he felt very uncomfortable with this money being involved. Three cheques over three months, repayable at thirteen percent over two years or following the sale of the property. Whichever came first. He had asked Vinnie Martens what they wanted in the way of security and Vinnie just laughed. Very funny. Giselle's brother Rocky was there and he said, "You know those Makita portable drills? You oughta see what they do to a guy's kneecaps."

Upon landing in Bismark to drop off a squad of sombrero-laden farmers, the pilot cheerfully announced that the temperature outside was twenty-two degrees below zero. Volleys of snow ripped across the runway. An hour later, at seven o'clock, the plane touched down in Winnipeg. After a particularly long process through Canada Customs, Saunders walked outside and inhaled the lung-burning night air. Unbelievably, Skip had left the Buick plugged in and it started without too much coaxing; the rich stink of exhaust filled the interior as Saunders pumped it to life.

And so with a sunburned face and Pacific seacoast sand in his shoes he drove through the foggy city. The streets were black and slippery as ebony. What now ... back to the Royal Windsor? At least he could afford a better hotel now. What he should probably do is just go over to Skip's apartment and get a good night's sleep.

But he didn't have a key. He kept driving. An hour later he walked into a Shell gas station on the highway sixty miles east of Winnipeg. He sat on a stool at the curved counter and ordered a coffee, yawned, stretched his arms. The plate glass window reflected his spooked eyes and tired face. He needed to go home.

Saunders poured another forty dollars' worth of gas into the Wildcat, then pulled out onto the highway and pushed on towards Minaki. Ten o'clock at night. The time didn't mean much at this point. When he got to the inn he'd rig up a baseboard heater and sleep beside it. The hotel would be uninhabitable, frozen and dark. He didn't care where he slept, as long as he got home.

At the Ontario border the highway choked down to two snow-packed lanes, and the oncoming semi-trailers, big as houses, roared past towing mini-blizzards in their wakes. Every time a truck passed his foot hovered near the brake. Fifty miles an hour and he couldn't see a thing. It was precisely the sort of stupid situation to get you a little notice in the newspaper: *Single Vehicle Accident Claims Toronto Man.* Skip would be sitting on the beach when he got the news. A long-distance call from Canada. Your buddy Mike was hamburgered in a car accident. Your Buick sustained a few dents. Skip would manage a joke or two at the funeral. Deborah would be all right. If nothing else, it would give her an opportunity to express her grief in a healthy, adult manner. Maggie would swear and throw the hammer. I should have taken Mikey while I had the chance. Now he's embossed on the front of a semi.

For the last thirty miles his progress was slow and nerve-racking. The glazed highway was so slippery that even at half speed the Buick slewed its tail like a shark. To complicate matters, he could feel the engine beginning to sag whenever he accelerated. The fuel line was icing up. For two bucks he could have bought a little bottle of methyl hydrate at the last truck stop but he was too cheap—false economy if he ended up stalling and freezing his fingers off.

At the Minaki-Kenora junction he debated whether he should just pack it in, go straight to Kenora and check into the Bayview, or gamble, head up the last few miles of desolate ice-blackened highway to Minaki and the frozen halls of the Stonehouse.

At the Minaki sign he slowed down. What the hell. He hit the turn signal and drove toward Minaki. Climbing the first hill, the Buick sagged and bucked under acceleration. Ten miles further on the motor just quit; the car glided to a stop. When he turned the key the engine gave a dying grunt. No horn, no lights. The battery dead. Wrong choice.

Saunders buttoned his coat, put on his mitts and got out. Minaki was eight or nine miles distant. Before he had gone a hundred yards, his nose and face began to freeze. He turned around and walked backwards. Terrific. Just terrific. It would be about ten-thirty or eleven by now and it was entirely possible there would be no more cars along this road tonight.

Cue the wolves. He wasn't afraid of wolves but you might as well cue them anyway. Lots of times when they were kids, hitch-hiking home from a movie in Kenora, they'd missed the last car of the night and ended up walking all the way with the mist in the woods and the moon paving the deserted road. But this was hardly the night you wanted to take a twenty-mile walk. Cold enough to freeze you to death or take your ears and fingers as a keepsake.

He walked backwards into the jagged wind, holding his mitts across one ear and then the other. The road was like a skating rink and he moved with clownish caution. The wind needled in through the seams of his coat. He looked up at the star-spattered sky, which was devoid of gods or else he'd send up a request.

A mile further on his left ear froze. He stood still, holding his bare hand on the living thing that was now as solid as wood. Trouble was, this left his hands unprotected and he was starting to lose the sensation in his fingertips. The thought occurred to him that he might make it into the Toronto *Star* after all. He dropped his shoulder bag onto the highway and waded through thigh-deep snow down into the ditch, where he broke branches from a dead spruce. When he had a good pile of deadwood he fumbled for his lighter. It fell into the snow. His fingers just weren't working. He could see the lighter but his fingers wouldn't close on it. He used his hands like a scoop and picked the lighter up, held it in his teeth while he tried to stuff his hands into the folds of his flowered tropical shirt. He was standing there with the Bic protruding from his teeth, when the headlights of a car flooded the black woods in a soft brightening glow. It was headed the wrong way, towards Kenora, but at this point he wasn't fussy.

Saunders clambered towards the road but the snow was deep and the car sped past. God, they didn't see me, he despaired. But then, he heard the engine sigh and saw the brake lights go on. He scrambled up onto the road. The car was a Chevy Blazer, one of those pale brown government vehicles. It accelerated in reverse towards him, then slowed down and stopped. The letters on the car door said Health and Social Services. The driver leaned over and pushed open the passenger door. "Hey there buddy, are you all right?"

Saunders got in and pulled the door shut with his frozen claw of a hand. "I never thought I'd be so glad to see you, Raymond."

Saunders spent the first five minutes in the car in silence while Raymond got his bag. He was thinking about how to describe his condition to Raymond, but it would have necessitated buying ten separate Mastercraft bench vises and having Raymond attach each one to his fingertips. And then tightening each vise until the pain was almost unbearable.

After he had held his hands in front of the heater vent for a good long while, Saunders ventured to speak. "My hands are thawing."

Raymond reached over and rubbed Saunders' fingers, then squeezed them gently. "Does that hurt?"

"No. They hurt on the inside. Like they're hot."

"You'll be all right. Good thing you weren't out there long. Dressed like that."

"Yeah."

Raymond himself was dressed in knee-high mukluks and a shaggy Icelandic sweater. His winter parka was piled on the console between them. A pretentious bandanna was knotted at his throat. God's gift to women. I'm in the wrong line of work, Saunders thought.

Raymond wanted to know all about Mexico. "Maggie and I could use a break like that. Did you take some pictures?"

"No," Saunders replied. He didn't feel like discussing Raymond's vacation plans. But he felt that he should be polite, since Raymond had probably saved his life. "So how's work?" Saunders finally asked.

"Too busy," Raymond replied. "I made one of those deals, you know, where you sign up to work in a remote area for two years in return for a sweetheart student loan? So my term's up in June. Looking forward to getting back to civilization."

"You don't like working here?"

"It's not very challenging, frankly. I get all the standard complaints, colicky babies, ingrown toenails, sore throats, but there isn't much chance for professional improvement. I'd like to move closer to a big centre, maybe go back to school for a while."

"Do you mind if I smoke?" Saunders asked.

"Go ahead."

Saunders pushed in the dashboard lighter.

"Anyway," Raymond said, "I was talking to Maggie the other night, and I think we resolved a few things."

Saunders blew a plume of smoke. "Good."

"And it involves you. But I told Maggie I'd let her be the one to discuss it with you."

"Discuss what?"

"Maggie will probably want to tell you herself. By the way—are you okay sleeping on my pull-out couch tonight? I'm going back to Minaki in the morning."

"Sure. If you're generous enough to offer."

In Kenora they drove down a winding residential street and parked in front of an old three-storey house.

It was a triplex and Raymond lived in the upper suite. Raymond plugged in the truck and Saunders hefted his bag. The air was dark, cold, cruel. They crunched across the snowy yard and mounted the steps. Saunders had no idea what time it was.

Inside, the house was warm. A radio played softly in the kitchen. Raymond flicked on the light and Saunders sat heavily on the couch without even taking his coat off while Raymond bustled around the kitchen, talking in a pleasant singsong voice about some provincial political story that Saunders was too tired to follow.

Raymond came out of the kitchen, ferrying two glasses of Scotch. "Nightcap?"

"All right."

Raymond handed him a glass and sat on the chair opposite the couch.

Saunders took a sip. "So you were saying, you and Maggie resolved something?"

"I should really let her be the one to break the news."

"Just cut the shit and tell me," Saunders replied. "I'm past the point of caring."

Raymond smiled. He leaned back in his chair and crossed his legs. "Well, I guess we're going to join forces. We're going to live together."

Saunders nodded. "Congratulations."

Raymond took a drink, relishing the taste. "Thank you."

"Where will you live?"

"As I said, somewhere down east, most likely. In the Toronto area, perhaps. Or Hamilton. I went to McMaster, so that would be a good neighbourhood."

"Well," Saunders answered half-heartedly, "how about that."

Raymond drummed the barrel of his glass. "I should also tell you. Maggie told me about the night in the ski shack."

Saunders feigned ignorance. "She did?"

"But I don't hold a grudge. Sometimes a relationship needs a push, just to get it straightened out. I think you and Maggie have a lot of respect for each other. I know she's very fond of you."

"Just as a friend."

"Oh come on. Let's not be cute. You know what a romantic she is. She loves that broken-down old lodge. She imagines weeding the garden when she's sixty years old. She imagines canoeing down the shoreline in front of the lodge. It's a silly fantasy, sure, but people need the idea of a better life somewhere ahead. Maggie needs that. And I haven't been giving it to her. I should almost thank you for kicking my butt and making me realize what I was doing."

"Well, you're welcome."

"You look tired," Raymond said.

"I am."

"Just one thing I'm not too clear on. Did you and Maggie actually, you know, do it?"

Saunders shook his head.

"Because I didn't really want to ask for the gory details."

"It was never even close."

"It'll be very good for Maggie too, to move down east. She's in a bit of a rut here. And she'll be able to meet you once in a while for lunch. After all, we'll be neighbours." Raymond paused and thought for a minute. "Let's see now, any more good news?"

"This is the nice thing about coming back from a trip," Saunders said. "There's never any shortage of good news."

21

〰️
〰️

DEER GRAZE ALL SUMMER. COME AUTUMN, WITH THE first snowfall, they switch over to "browse," above-ground vegetation—twigs, leaves, bark. Browse isn't particularly nutritious, so from that point on they begin to lose weight. They begin to die. For some animals, spring's crop of new grass and melting snow is a cruel irony. They've starved for too long, and no matter how easy it is to stay alive, it's easier still to continue dying.

Saunders remembered that. He recalled the nature lore his father used to tell him and he was still a bit disbelieving that the worst was finally over. The weather broke several days after he got back from Mexico, and the countryside was flooded with warm winds, melting snow and the radiance of the late winter sun. Saunders encountered Maggie at the grocery store and took her for coffee at the gas station.

Bending over the sink to splash water on his face in the filling station's malodorous latrine, he was appalled by his tired and worn-out face. When he returned to the restaurant, Maggie didn't look much better. She waited for him at a table by the window, with her parka shucked off and her hair in a ratty-looking bun. They ordered coffee and stared out the window at the sloppy road, the blue sky. He knew she was moving in with Raymond, but after thinking about it, he'd decided that maybe it was for the best. He'd lost a chance at romance, but gained a confidante. Maggie was the only one who sympathized with his current problems.

"Who do you owe?"

"Everybody. Bob's Sand and Gravel. Northern Meats. Ontario Hydro. It's five hundred here and a thousand there. But it all adds up. People have been extending me credit without any complaints all winter."

Maggie sat pensively with her coffee cup raised. The nuclear-bright sun pierced the blue cigarette smoke in the coffee shop. "So what will you do?" she asked.

"I guess my first priority is to finish the hotel and sell it, and then maybe pay everyone off with the proceeds. Hopefully it will be finished in a couple of weeks."

"Just in time for tourist season."

He nodded. "Couldn't have picked a better time to put it on the market. By the way, did you hear that Skip is getting married?"

"Yes. Raymond mentioned it."

"I'm his best man."

She managed a faint smile. "My sympathies to Giselle."

"I've been instructed to keep an eye on Skip. It's one of the terms of my loan."

"Do you think he'll go through with it?"

"Well, he'd better. Or I'll shoot him."

"Then afterwards, will you still work together?"

Saunders thought about that. "I don't know. . . ."

"I suppose you'd miss the money. And the locker room banter."

"I'll miss this more."

"What?"

"Oh . . . having someone to actually talk to."

"You and Skip talk for hours."

"Yeah," Saunders agreed, "but that's shop talk. This is honest dialogue. And you're a woman."

"You aren't used to speaking honestly with women?"

He shrugged. "All that courtship stuff is inherently pretty phoney. You and I have moved past that. So now we can speak our minds."

She lifted an eyebrow. "No more flattery?"

"Nope."

"But we'll still be nice to each other?"

"Probably nicer. Men and women do things to each other all the time. Things you'd never let a friend get away with."

"Does this mean you're going to be nice to Raymond?"

Saunders grinned. "I had to be nice to him before. Now I can advise you frankly that I think he's a dork."

She made a face. "I liked you better when you were a phoney."

Saunders laughed out loud.

"So tell me," Maggie said, "what jobs are left to do at the inn?"

"Just the roof, the yard landscaping, the ceiling. Wallpaper upstairs. Cash flow, that's the main problem. I get a hit from Uncle Vince in another couple of weeks. But that's all spoken for."

"Well, should you get to work then?"

Saunders nodded and gulped the last of his coffee. He went outside while Maggie paid the bill. On her way to the car, she stopped to chat with an old lady in the parking lot. It was a warm day, the road glistening with meltwater, the sky blue and mild. Icicles on the roof of the restaurant trickled water into the snow. Saunders waited in the truck. Maggie climbed in, backed out, then stopped. She stared at the old woman, who was fumbling with her keys at the door of a VW van. "You see that woman?" Maggie asked. "I heard her talking to the waitress inside, asking about the Stonehouse Inn. So I spoke with her. She says that she's an artist, and she's looking for a hotel room."

"Well, she's going to have a hard time finding one this time of year."

Maggie didn't answer. Instead, she turned off the truck and jumped out. She hurried across the slush and talked to the old woman. When she returned, she was laughing. "Let's go," she chuckled.

"What's going on?"

"You own a hotel," she said. "And I just secured your first reservation."

"Well, I can't help her. I don't have any rooms."

"Sure you do."

"They're disaster areas. You've seen them."

"Then rent her a cabin."

"I only have one cabin that's suitable. And I'm living in it."

She squeezed his knee. Her voice was a patient whisper. "Then move out of it. Don't you want some income?"

He thought about this for a moment. "Maybe you're right."

Maggie drove the truck rapidly down the winding road to the inn and they hurried inside. Saunders ran down to the cabin and started cleaning away the piles of empty beer cans, unmade bedding and half-finished paperwork. He raced up the hill, arms full, and encountered Maggie coming down. She'd located some clean sheets and towels. "Can you vacuum the main lodge?" she asked.

"When is she coming?"

"She said she has to stop and pick up some things at the store. She's a bit grouchy, so we'll make the place double-tidy."

"Oh brother," Saunders said. He hurried into the inn and was vacuuming the floor when he heard a car door slam. He slipped into the office. The verandah opened, then the main door, then heels clicked across the hardwood floor. A moment of silence . . . then a *ping* from the silver bell on the front desk.

He inhaled and stepped out. "Yes?"

The same elderly lady stood at the desk—a ruddy face, blurry spectacles and a bristling white thatch of dandelion hair. "I want to rent a cabin for a *month*," she said, as if she'd already explained this to him. "Is there a vacancy?"

"Hmm," Saunders said. "Let's have a look. Do you want American Plan or light housekeeping?"

"American Plan," she said. "I *hate* cooking."

He pulled the register out and flipped through it carefully. The pages were as clean as blown snow. He selected a page at random and scowled. "Yes . . . I think we can give you Cabin 3 for a month, it's very nice."

"Is there a view of the *river?*"

"Yes, ma'am."

"Is there still a good restaurant?"

"Oh yes, ma'am," he said, pointing at the dining room. "Newly renovated."

"It's very pretty here." She scrawled her name on the register. Mrs. Jean Froelich, Oak Park, Illinois. "I always used to come in the *spring*," she emphasized. "For forty-three years, except for the last four years when I was in *Scotland*."

Saunders nodded. "I see."

"I paint the birds *mating*."

"Oh, that's interesting."

She gave him a suspicious look. "Are you new?"

Saunders ducked under the counter and surfaced with her room key. "Let me run out and get your luggage."

"You look a bit like Gordon Saunders' boy."

"I am."

Saunders accompanied Mrs. Froelich down to the cabin. He met Maggie coming up. She gave him a secretive okay signal. He winked and rubbed his palm to indicate money. "Are you going?"

"I have work to do."

"Okay, I'll call you later."

She waved, and Saunders and Mrs. Froelich went down the hill to the cabin. At the door Saunders paused to look up at Maggie's departing figure. She wore a grey hooded sweatshirt, gumboots and faded jeans. Nice ass. Even for a platonic buddy.

"Hey Mags."

She stopped.

"Thanks."

SAUNDERS WORKED ALL AFTERNOON in the little office under the stairs. His desk was piled with mountains of unanswered mail, bills, ripped envelopes and FAXes from clients and fellow consultants. He usually got at least one threatening FAX a day from his partners. MIKE: WHERE IS THE GODDAMN PPCS FOR THE ANICINABE HEALING CENTRE? NEIL.

There'd even been some rumbles lately about his partners buying him out. He felt guilty about his job performance. The last thing on earth he wanted was to damage the company. The only answer was to work harder at both jobs. And he was doing just that, writing a letter to a client, when Mrs. Froelich appeared at the door of his office.

"It's fifteen minutes of six," she said.

He nodded. "Uh huh."

"Is the dining room open?"

He clapped a hand to his forehead. "Oh Jeez."

"Jesus has nothing to do with it."

"No, I mean I'm sorry . . . I forgot that the dining room is supposed to be open." He stood up and snapped off the gooseneck lamp. "I'll get things going right away."

"When I used to stay here, Gordon Saunders always opened the dining room promptly at *five*," she said. "I don't know why you've changed it."

He went into the dining room and turned on the light above the big oak dining room table. "Just make yourself comfortable, ma'am," he said. He pulled out a chair for her to sit on. "Can I get you something from the bar?"

"I don't *drink*," she replied. "What's your name again anyway? Are you qualified?"

"Yes, ma'am. I'll get your menu right away."

He went into the kitchen. Menu, menu. He opened the fridge and scanned it, top to bottom. A quart of sour milk. Three eggs. An almost empty tub of margarine. What he needed was a woman's touch around here. Maggie, save me. He went down into the dark basement and switched on the light. The naked light bulb in the rafters flickered. Bad wiring. No end to the jobs that had to be done around here. He peered inside the freezer.

Empty.

He was still disorganized from having gone to Mexico. Searching through the pile of crumpled-up newspapers and freezer wrap, he found one small package of frozen side bacon. Bacon and eggs?

He returned to the kitchen, put the bacon on the counter and went into the dining room. "We have a special tonight," he said to Mrs. Froelich. "Ouevos revueltos."

"What's that?"

"It's very delicious," Saunders said. "Sort of a ranch omelette, very fluffy and light. . . ." His hands circled half-heartedly in the air, as if he weren't quite able to describe it.

"All right," Mrs. Froelich agreed.

In the kitchen, Saunders put a cast-iron frying pan on the new Jenn-Air range and turned on the element. He got out some dishes and cutlery and hustled into the dining room. "We'll set a nice place for you," he said, "and soon your dinner will be ready."

"Are you not going to light the *fireplace?* Gordon Saunders always lit the *fireplace.*"

"Of course I'm going to light the fireplace," Saunders replied. "I was just going to light the fireplace."

He hurried back into the kitchen and tore the wrapper off the frozen bacon. He turned the heat down slightly on the stove and tried to pry a couple of discs of bacon from the slab. No dice. Jamming the knife in, he hammered the rock-hard slab against the counter, then gave up and threw the bacon into the frying pan. He skidded it around before he raced back to the dining room to light the fireplace.

The wood box was empty except for a few mossy, broken twigs. "Shit," he whispered.

Mrs. Froelich cupped a hand over her ear. "You'll have to speak up, young man."

"Yes, ma'am. I'll be right back. I have to get some firewood."

Saunders went outside. It was windy and growing dark. The sky above the river was the colour of rose-tinted glass. Saunders walked around the back and looked for firewood. With all the other chores, he hadn't had time to fix the chain-saw. An old chair leaned against the rear wall of the building, a chair he'd used as a paint stand. He gave it a boot that knocked two rungs off. Then he jumped and stomped on it until it was smashed to fragments. Probably a priceless antique. He filled his arms and went back into the hotel, just in time to hear the wild hissing of bacon burning in the pan. He dumped the wood on the floor and pulled the pan off the element, burning his hand. With the flipper, he poked at the half-burned, half-frozen meat. Just enough for an omelette.

Once he extinguished the bacon, he gathered up the smashed chair from the floor and returned to the dining room, where he balled up some old pieces of newspaper and lit a fire in the stone hearth. Back to the kitchen. After filling the kettle, he got the three eggs out of the fridge and cracked them on the edge of the pan. Good. They weren't rotten. He gave the eggs a desultory stir with the flipper and ladled liquid bacon fat over them. This is what professional chefs do, he told himself. It reduces the amount of phlegm. He sliced up the bacon and sprinkled it onto the eggs, and had just folded the omelette when Mrs. Froelich screamed in the other room.

Saunders rushed into the dining room, right into a thick haze of acrid smoke. "Forgot to open the damper," he muttered. "Sorry about that."

He fanned with his hand and flipped the damper open. Smoke from the burning chair slowly drew up into the hearth. Mrs. Froelich was coughing and sneezing and chirping in violent discomfort in her chair. Saunders went back into the kitchen for her dinner and walked into the dining room with a napkin draped grand hotel-style over his forearm. He presented her meal.

Mrs. Froelich stood up. "It's so *smoky!*" she exclaimed.

Saunders fanned the air with a plastic table mat.

"Where's the *door?*"

He guided her through the kitchen to the back door and out onto the deck. A couple of garbage bags were in the way—he swept them aside with his foot.

Darkness was falling on the yard. The air was edged with the scent of garbage, woodsmoke, evergreens. Far away a loon moaned—the first loon of spring. A single bird, probably, that had claimed the open patch of water on the river.

The loon's sad call drifted up again. Mrs. Froelich issued a hearty sigh of satisfaction. "That's a Common Loon," she muttered.

"The first one of the year."

"Aren't you the boy who sketches?"

"You remember, do you?"

"Oh yes," she nodded. She made a sweeping gesture to take in the yard. "What is it, what are you *doing* here?"

"You mean the property?" She nodded again. Saunders hooked his thumbs in his pockets. "Well, I inherited it from my father. I want to restore it, bring it back to its original condition, then I'm going to, uh . . . "

What *am* I going to do?

The loon's call curved in off the lake. The big trees ticked audibly in the dark yard. Sap quickening. The air was musty with the open ground of spring.

"I'm going to sell it."

She looked around at the garbage and piled lumber. "Well, don't look at *me!*"

Saunders cleaned up the dishes. By the time he was finished it was ten-fifteen, and too late for anything but an hour of office work. He paid some bills, did some accounting, and was stretching his arms, pushing his chair back wearily to go to bed, when the FAX machine suddenly hummed and a tongue of paper crept out.

He adjusted the desk lamp and read the message.

HACIENDA DEL MAR, PLAYA COCOA, JAL, MEX.
POSICION: RESEARCH DIRECTOR
PARA: MICHAEL SAUNDERS   NEW AGE ASSOCIATES
LUGAR: STONEHOUSE INN, MINAKI, ONT. FAX 807-224-1181
DE: S.L. CARTER   POSICION: PRES, NEW AGE
ASUNTO: RE. NUPTIAL RITES
MENSAJE

Mikey:

Caught a sailfish this morning. Still beautiful weather. Palm trees and crashing surf have taken over my life. Leaving tomorrow, however, for reality-land, so let's get together and plan our 2nd quarter. Giselle and I have opted for a June wedding.The family wants a big blow-out wedding in Montreal but me and Giselle think we should have it someplace small and intimate, maybe at the Stonehouse Inn. Could inject some serious cash flow into your operation there, buddy. What do you say. Can you have it finished by then?

Skip

22

In spring, tiny mint-green leaves on the aspens tremble in the southerly breeze. According to Eddy Grogan, "You quit work and go trout fishing the day the poplar leaves are the size of your baby fingernail."

Not according to Saunders, you don't. This job, supposed to take five weeks, has taken all winter. And now he has a deadline. Skip's wedding will be the Grand Opening of the new Stonehouse Inn. The wedding will discharge his moral duty to Uncle Vince, showcase the hotel, bring in some revenue, and serve as his own final item from the Job Jar. But first he has to finish.

So he's fallen into a wild-haired state—renovation dementia. At five forty-five in the morning, when it's still cold enough that urine steams, he zips up his fly and pads down the stairs, pulling on his battered leather gloves. The old curling club sweater hangs down to his knees and his bootlaces dangle. He's too busy to stop for coffee or toast. The woods are gloomy. He can hear the gulls out on the river, that awful daybreak clamour that reminds him of hangovers and unhappy love affairs. His hair is snarled with wood chips and his hands are swollen from hammer blows and saw cuts. But he feels clear in his mind. He picks his way through the stacked lumber, his breath throwing steam. He uncoils the orange one-hundred-foot extension cord and hooks up the Skilsaw, unclips the steel tape from his belt and makes a careful measurement. He touches the trigger and the saw screams.

The wedding is coming. Bankruptcy is coming. But the team is on the payroll now, and it's starting to function like a smooth machine. Maggie will arrive at seven. She's taken over management of the dining room, which is now open for business, and the smell of bacon and eggs will drift across the lot. She and Saunders are both a little obsessive this time of day, and they have an informal agreement not to talk to each other until mid-morning. There are new guests at the hotel—a pair of carpet-layers, a couple of fishermen, a school consultant—and as soon as a room comes ready, Saunders stuffs someone in it. McNabb likes this new look to the inn. It means he can sell it as a functioning business.

So the job begins for another day. The sun climbs onto the turrets on the roof. Eddy and the Cruisers rumble up in Eddy's pick-up truck. They dismount, don work gloves, spit in the road. Eddy rolls a cigarette. Jim Highway studies the job list. Beaver walks around coughing into his fist, trembles and glances towards the woods, identifying potential vomiting sites. Beaver can't work until he's smoked three or four Rothman's and dry-heaved in the woods. Dwayne McCafferty straps on his gunfighter belt of tools, eyes the half-finished roof, scratches his balls.

Soon they're all at work, or maybe they're goofing off and dreaming of shallow water lake trout; it doesn't matter to Saunders. He's lost inside himself, inside nothing else but his job; he's measuring, sawing, banging nails, carrying sheets of plywood from the truck to the hotel, climbing the ladder without holding on, up, up, up to the high roof where he throws the plywood down with a BANG! If this day were a bone, he'd be growling.

For weeks, the time blurs. All day long it's screaming saws, spewing wood chips, the contrapuntal banging of hammers. Break for lunch. Break for supper. Eddy and the Cruisers go home. Saunders, the boss who doesn't get paid, goes back to work. Dirty, sore, the synapses in his muscles misfiring, he works until darkness. Then he goes inside and helps Maggie clean the kitchen. They sit down, at last, and have some dinner together. Every night, when it's time to go home, they stand looking at each other by the back door.

"Bye," he says.

"Bye," she says.

But for the briefest moment they pause. They smile. Maggie twiddles her fingers. "Good night."

And so to sleep. Sometimes in the night he dreams of Maggie. She's decided to stay one night. She kisses his wounded hands and massages his head. He always wakes up before they go further. Another night he dreams about the wedding. Skip has failed to appear. Chaos everywhere. Maggie, looking angelic in a white dress, takes him into a bedroom and holds his hand, tells him tearfully that she and her secret lover, Ben McNabb, have decided to elope. Down in the lounge, all is noise and confusion. Neil Olson, who has been charged with providing music by reviving his old band, Neil and the Nomads, is attempting to quell the riot by telling a series of filthy jokes about Italian girls. Vinnie Martens, spotting Saunders trying to sneak out the back stairway, screams a battle cry and comes cantering after him waving a portable drill.

One morning, after a night of such dreams, Saunders rolls out of bed and gimps out into the morning air. Like a watery-eyed old hound he twists his head, scowling at the yard. Something is different this morning. He's not sure what it is.

He spends the first hour building a righteous fire in the driveway, gathering up one-by-twos, stud ends and scraps of plywood, and feeding them to the hungry orange blaze. Poisonous chemical smoke rolls upward past waving spruces to the troubled overcast. A grey day, scudding clouds, more like autumn than late spring.

At seven-thirty Mrs. Froelich comes out of Cabin 3 with her easel and her folding chair. She's still here, his permanent tenant. Saunders waves to her. "Good morning, Mrs. Froelich."

"Good morning," she replies. "When is your first bingo night?"

"Friday, ma'am."

"Don't forget to remind me."

"Yes, ma'am."

At eight Eddy and the boys arrive. They all stand around the job list, a thatch of photocopied foolscap on a clipboard. Red lines are drawn through the finished jobs. Saunders scratches his head, going through the soiled pages. He has a perplexed look in his eye. What the . . . ?

Eddy and the Cruisers police up the grounds. Shingles, furls of tarpaper, scraps of pink insulation flutter into the fire. Saunders remembers a hot-water line they haven't connected. "It's done," Eddy replies, taking out his makings, rolling a cigarette.

"What about the flashing and cedar shakes on that back dormer?"

Eddy licks the cigarette and inserts it in his permanent frown. "Done."

"What about the tile on that third-floor bathroom?"

"Done."

Saunders nods. He takes his clipboard and walks across the lawn. Out behind the hotel is the nagging rise and fall of a chain-saw. Jim Highway is cutting birch firewood for the wedding. Are we really at the point we can start worrying about aromatic firewood? He can hardly believe it.

Saunders gazes at the building, then turns away and walks down the walkway toward the water. Let the boys have a smoke break for a few minutes. On the dock he sits on one heel and makes a few notations on the third page of the work list. He pops the button on the ballpoint and looks up at the fresh new roof on the inn, the rolling lawn, the neatly painted white wrought-iron benches.

He didn't think this moment would ever come. Now that it has, he's unprepared for it. He doesn't know how to stop working. He glances at his watch, feeling the urge to surrender, shake, cry.

Ten o'clock in the morning. The hotel is finished.

23

SAUNDERS SENT EDDY AND THE BOYS HOME, THEN MADE
himself an espresso in the kitchen. Skip's wedding
arrangements needed attention. McNabb wanted him
to help write an ad for the *Real Estate Gazette*. The guest
quarters needed cleaning, and he could save a few hours'
wages by doing it himself. The hammer truss in the ceiling
wasn't varnished. And then there was always landscaping, clean-up. He set the coffee cup down and stretched
his arms, having decided what to do.

Absolutely nothing.

The Jacuzzi faucets thundered as he filled the tub to
the brim. Suds, boiling water, bubble bath. Peter
Gzowski on the radio. The old portable phone, aerial
extended, perched on the shelf beside last month's *New
Yorker*. Ah yes, he thought, lowering himself into the
scalding water. Heal my wounds. He lay chin-deep in
the foam and stared at the ceiling. The place looks good,

he thought with pride. He washed his hair and was rinsing it with the hand-held shower when he heard somebody downstairs. "Hello!" he called.

A pair of light feet came running up the stairs. Maggie tapped on the door.

"Come in."

She poked her head in the door, arching her eyebrows lasciviously. "Ooh la la."

"I'm being a lazy bum."

"Do you need anything in Winnipeg?"

"Why? Are you going in?"

"I'm driving Raymond to the airport. He has a job interview in Alberta."

"So you're moving to Alberta now."

"Well . . . who knows? It's a GP job in Canmore. Mountains and all that. It's the second interview he's had so I guess they like him."

"You don't seem overly thrilled."

She shrugged. "I'm waiting to see what happens. What's the point of getting all wound up?"

"So you're going shopping in the city?"

"I need a dress for the wedding."

Saunders thoughtfully dabbed a beard of white foam onto his chin. "I need to go to the city too. I've got a meeting with Skip and Giselle the day after tomorrow."

WITH RAYMOND AT THE WHEEL, they drove to Winnipeg in Maggie's truck. They had lunch and dropped Raymond at the airport, then Maggie and Saunders went shopping. He felt as if they were a couple of kids playing hookey. It was a rainy day in the city. Saunders stopped by a clothing store to be measured for a tuxedo, and then they went shopping for a dress Maggie could wear to the wedding. For the next few hours, they just walked. At one of those horrible kiosks in the basement of Eaton's where the red-hot wieners turn on aluminum rollers, they stopped to rest on the high stools and Saunders bought Maggie a malted and a hot dog. A river of old ladies flowed by. Maggie's knee rested against his. She concentrated on her jumbo malted, sucking at the heavy straw with indented cheeks. Eventually her eyes lifted to his and she stared at him for a long minute. Finally her eyes narrowed with amused curiosity and she asked, "What?"

"What's the big hurry getting back to Minaki? Why don't you stay a few days?"

"Where would I stay?"

"Skip's apartment."

"I don't know if Raymond would appreciate that. Given our past history."

Saunders sniffed in amusement. "We don't have a past history."

"Yes we do," she said. "Now come on. Let's go spend some money."

After more shopping, they had dinner at a Chinese place on William Avenue where Saunders knew the owner and could show off to Maggie by saying hello and goodbye in Chinese. It was pouring rain when they left, almost ten o'clock at night, and Saunders could tell that Maggie wasn't looking forward to the long trip back.

They drove the truck through heavy traffic, past a tie-up with fire trucks and an ambulance. Red lights throbbed through the smeared rain of the windshield and the downpour drummed on the truck's metal roof. "Just come to Skip's for an herbal tea," he said. "Then you can hit the road."

In the parking lot Saunders hefted his bag on his shoulder and they rode the elevator up to Skip's penthouse. It was dark inside. Silent. Things never changed, here. Saunders felt his way through the familiar living room and threw his bag down on the limestone pad by the hearth. Through the big floor-to-ceiling windows the city glittered. He turned on the lights. Maggie stood with her arms folded. She looked cold and her face was solemn. "I don't want to go back," she said.

"Well, don't. Get up early. It's light at five in the morning, these days. You'll arrive at breakfast." She nodded. "And there's two bedrooms. You can try Skip's giant waterbed."

"I can't sleep on a waterbed."

"Then take the guest room and I'll use Skip's."

"I'm kind of chilled. Is there a brandy or something?"

Saunders puttered in the kitchen, brewing two big mugs of brandy-laced coffee while Maggie went through Skip's closet, trying to find a sweater that didn't reek of Giorgio cologne. She came out in an ankle-length blue terrycloth robe with a rabbit's head symbol on the chest. Saunders cackled.

"Shut up."

They sat in the conversation pit, watching the news on Skip's immense Sony. Maggie had the TV control in her hand. She kept flipping through the channels, ending up with Peter Mansbridge's deadpan delivery of the national news. Postal strikes looming. Trouble in Lebanon. The IRA shoots an off-duty soldier in front of his children. It was the same news as the last time he watched it, five months ago.

"So McNabb tells me that he's showing the hotel tomorrow," Saunders said.

"Really?"

"A couple of schoolteachers, semi-retired."

"He doesn't want you to be there?"

Saunders drank his coffee. "No. He's afraid that when they sit down to fill out the cheque, I'll start frothing at the mouth."

Maggie smiled.

Saunders took the remote control off her lap and scanned the channels. News and sports. News and sports. He laid the remote control on the floor and stared at the cold fireplace. He'd light a presto-log but Skip was evidently fresh out. There was a slight awkwardness here. All along, he'd assumed that talking to Maggie would be easier once they decided to forgo the complications of romance. But now that their time together was almost through, there wasn't really much to say. He had no interest in chatting about her future life with Raymond. What colour they'd paint their bedroom and so on. He thought Raymond was the wrong partner for her, plain and simple, and if he worked in a computer store she probably wouldn't have given him a glance. Maggie, of all people, wanted to be a doctor's wife. What a conversation-stopper. And what else did they have to talk about? The consulting business? The stock market? The simple fact was, their friendship so far was based on a shared interest in the restoration of an old stone and log building. The job was finished. The inn would soon be sold. And soon they'd be going their separate ways.

Saunders eventually got up and trucked the saucers and cups into the kitchen. Maggie followed to help him clean up. She wiped the counter and put the milk away, still quiet.

"I'm going to have a shower," he said.

He went into Skip's jungle-motif bathroom and stood under the spray for ten minutes before he towelled off and brushed his teeth. When he came out the living room was dark. I guess she's gone to bed, he thought. At least she could have said goodnight. He went into Skip's room and crawled under the quilts on the waterbed, then turned off the lights and lay motionless, listening to the distant whisper of traffic on the streets.

A faint cough came from Maggie's room. She was

still awake. There was a palpable silence in the apartment. Dark, sad as the ebbing of a huge sea. He scanned the ceiling for a long time, wishing he felt sleepy. Finally, he flicked on the light.

Maggie's voice was quiet in the other room. "Are you awake?"

Saunders paused, unsure if he'd heard her speak. "Michael."

"Yeah."

"You're not tired?"

"I guess not."

After a while he stood up. He was wearing only a tattered set of jockey shorts but at this point, he no longer cared. He padded across the broadloom in the hall and peered in the half-opened door of the guest room, which consisted of a large bare floor, a mountain of Skip's cardboard file boxes piled in one corner, and a single wooden crate beside the bed. On the crate were a clock radio and a stubby red candle. Maggie sat up in bed, scratched a match and lit the candle. She was wearing a black T-shirt with halter strings. Saunders regarded her quietly for a moment. The only reason I have the guts to do this, he thought, is because in a little while I'll never see her again. "Do you want some company?"

She nodded.

He walked to the edge of the bed and knelt on the floor. He extended his hand and she took it. They looked at each other in the candlelight.

Maggie wore a regretful smile. "I thought you'd never ask."

24

SAUNDERS WOKE EARLY IN THE MORNING TO GREY LIGHT
through the gauze curtains. Rain. The sizzle of car tires
on the street. Maggie lay against him, breathing quietly
against his neck as she slept.

The dream had come again. The dream about
showing people through the building, showing them
the interlaced cluster of logs in the upper ceiling. I
have to remember to varnish that last section, he
thought. He remembered Maggie telling him once that
the Muslims believe you should never completely
finish a building, in case you give Allah the impression
you're trying to be perfect.

He stroked Maggie's naked back, ran his fingers
down the muscular indentation of her lumbar curve
and settled his hand against her soft bum. She stirred
and cuddled beside him, her pubic bone pressed
against his thigh, but she slept on. When he woke again

it was much later and the sun was shining in the window. He crawled carefully out of bed and went into the kitchen to make coffee. Time for a swim, he decided. He changed into a pair of Skip's shorts, wrote Maggie a note and went up on the roof. It was a bright morning. He dragged an aluminum chair to a shady spot next to the pool. The asphalt was hot under his bare feet. He jumped into the pool and stroked a few lengths. The water was too warm. He'd gotten spoiled, swimming in those clear Ontario lakes.

He climbed out and towelled off his shoulders, then reclined in the yellow plastic harness of the chair. On the far side of Roslyn Road they were still building the high-rise. The spindly crane on the roof raised and lowered dangerous pallets of goods, supervised by a tiny foreman. Much gesturing and waving of arms. The high-rise was quite a distance but Saunders could hear men's voices, the whine of their saws, the knock of hammers. He was a construction man himself now, and he knew what the poor bastards were going through.

For the next few days, he'd be picking his way through a minefield: Skip's wedding, the sale of the inn, the huge debt to Uncle Vince. And now, to make the whole bloody maze even more dangerous, he'd persuaded Maggie to sleep with him. In the consulting business you learned one thing: complex problems are usually a lot simpler than they seem. If you ask someone what his balance sheet looks like, and he starts giving you a long drawn-out story, it usually means he's broke. Plain and simple. He was probably waltzing down the same path. But he didn't have a consultant to point out the obvious.

Maggie came out on the roof.

Saunders shaded his eyes with his hand. "Hi." She came up and kissed him on the forehead. "Did you find the coffee?" he asked.

"No."

"I made a pot, on the stove."

"I thought I'd come up and check on you."

"Well, I just had a swim. There's a bathing suit of Giselle's down in the apartment, if you like."

"All right."

He took her hand. "Did you have a nice sleep?"

"Yes."

Maggie went downstairs and came back wearing a yellow maillot swim-suit. She had a green towel on her shoulder and two cups of coffee on a tray. She draped the towel on the arm of the chair and knifed into the transparent water. A natural athlete, hardly a ripple. Surfacing half-way across the pool, she swam back and forth, smooth as an otter.

She rose from the pool and dried her legs, then wrapped the towel around her head and rubbed vigorously. Inside the bathing suit her breasts wobbled. She was one of those women who downplayed her figure in men's shirts and baggy tweed pants. In a bathing suit there was no hiding the V-shaped chest and long, strong legs. She pulled up a lounge chair and reclined next to Saunders. "Well, we've really done it this time."

He nodded. "I think so."

She stirred cream into her coffee and took a long sip. "So is Deborah coming to the wedding?"

"Yep. I don't think she'd want to miss it."

"And how is Skip bearing up?"

"Frankly, I don't know."

"Will he go through with it?"

"That's the first thing everyone asks me, once they hear he's getting married." He shook his head. "After all the work we've done, he'd better go through with it."

"When is he coming?"

"Tomorrow morning. We've got his stag party tomorrow night."

She smiled. "Are men still allowed stag parties?"

"You're darn tootin'."

"Well . . . I probably have to go back today."

"If that couple comes by with McNabb, can you help show them around?"

"Sure," she said. "I'll show them all the bad stuff. Maybe I can scare them off."

"Ben would really be pleased. I've stiffed him for the commission about four times now."

Maggie laughed out loud.

They were silent for a few minutes. "So after I sell the inn," he said, "what would you like to do about us?"

"Us?"

"Yeah."

"I don't know. It's only recently I've begun to realize that there is an 'us.' I used to have these little talks with myself. 'Okay Maggie, God gave you a brain. Use it. What's the smart thing to do here?' But I realize, now, that maybe that's not the best way to decide things. Do you use your brain? Or your heart? Or your conscience? Or your desire?"

He drank his coffee, listening.

"I know I told Raymond that I wouldn't sleep with you. So what do I tell him now? That I just stayed overnight in Winnipeg so that I could buy a dress? I mean, I sort of encouraged this event to happen. That makes me a liar, I guess."

"No."

"Yes," she said, with an edge in her voice. "I don't need a pat on the back, Michael. Raymond is in Alberta right now looking for a job and shopping for a house, mainly for my benefit. I *can't* tell him that I've slept with you, when he gets back."

Saunders thought for a while. "Maybe it's better not to tell him."

"And live with the deceit?"

He shrugged. "I don't know, Maggie. Whatever you decide."

She rested her hand on his shoulder.

"All the times we've talked," Saunders said, "you've never mentioned any dissatisfaction with Raymond. Are you happy with him?"

"I'm tired of living alone," she said. "I'm thirty-two years old. I'd like to have some children. Even one, before I'm too old."

"I don't blame you."

"It gets lonely," she said, "in a small town. Big cities are even worse."

"I'd be your boyfriend. In two seconds."

"Well, that's very nice, but in another week or so you'll be running back to Toronto, back to your one-hundred-pound perfect girlfriend."

"Maybe."

"So what options do we have?"

Saunders' eyes met Maggie's. "One option is, I think we should have the guts to be honest with each other. If you're truly intending to move out west with Raymond, and not answer my letters, and not phone, and not see me when I'm passing through your town, then tell me right now. Because I don't want to see you on the street six years from now, and not even be interested in saying hello."

"I can't decide 'right now,' " she said, withdrawing her hand from his shoulder. "I haven't got a bloody clue what to do about this."

There were several long minutes of silence. Then her chair creaked and she stood up.

"Where are you going?" Saunders asked.

"Inside."

"Are you angry?"

"No," she said, reaching for her coffee. The tray tipped over and the cup smashed on the pavement. She skipped out of the way. "Ouch!" she said, her voice furious.

"Did you cut yourself?" Saunders got out of his lounge chair and tiptoed on the hot pavement. Across the canyon a jackhammer chattered. He put a hand under her elbow. "Let's have a look."

She lifted her foot. He squatted on his heels, examining the cut, and dabbed at her heel with his thumb. She leaned on the top of his head for balance. A little sliver of glass was lodged in the ball of her heel. He removed the glass shard and a bright drop of blood trickled out. She was facing slightly away, her fanny in his face. Lines from the lounge chair marked the fat of her bum. The smell of wet skin. "Do you want to sit down?"

She pulled slightly away. "No."

Down in Skip's apartment she walked several steps ahead of him, leaving red spots on the beige carpet. "I'll clean it up," Saunders said. "Go ahead."

He wiped up the blood spots with cold water. Skip would have a coronary. He went into the bedroom. Maggie was sitting on the edge of the bed with her foot swathed in Kleenex. She looked sad.

Saunders sat down cross-legged on the bed, facing her. He took the wounded foot and wiped it with a wet cloth. Still bleeding. He bent over and sucked at the cut. "Might still be some broken glass in there."

She reclined on her elbows. The waterbed rolled lazily beneath. One leg was straight, the other drawn up at the knee. An errant tuft of hair escaped from the yellow bathing suit's crotch.

Saunders had a good flow going. Her blood tasted warm and salty in his mouth. "Is this kinky?" he said. "I can't remember."

"I don't know."

She stared at the ceiling. Finally she looked at him. Her eyes were green and soft. "Michael, let's save the discussion for tomorrow."

25

~~~

ON SKIP'S BALCONY THE NEXT DAY SAUNDERS LEANED back in the deck chair and rested the clipboard on his knee.

"Flowers," Giselle said.

He made a mark on his list. "Done."

"Fountain pen with blue ink."

"Check."

"Grass trimmed and raked."

"Check."

"Gravel for parking lot."

"Check."

Giselle adjusted her sun-glasses, running her eyes down the alphabetical job list. They were the sort of dark glasses that Jackie Kennedy wore after Dallas. "Oh yes. Flight connections for lobsters. You were saying there's a problem?"

"I called the supplier in Nova Scotia. As it turns out,

221

we can make that connecting flight through Toronto, so Neil will pick them up on his way to the inn."

"Will Neil be able to handle all that?"

"What do you think, Skip?"

Skip was puttering with the barbecue. "Eh?"

"Do you think Neil can pick up the lobsters?"

"What lobsters?"

"Skip," Giselle scolded, "would you please try to pay attention?"

"Neil is reliable," Saunders said. "Give him jobs enough for two people and he wouldn't notice."

"And did you see Deborah's present?"

Saunders shook his head. "No." Deborah had sent her regrets, claiming she'd hurt herself playing racquetball.

"Show Mike the beautiful plant," Giselle said.

Skip ignored her. He was tinkering with the propane fitting.

"Show us the hibiscus," Giselle said.

Saunders waited. "Earth to Skip."

"Propane tank is empty," Skip said. "The caretaker has a spare one."

Giselle looked at Saunders, shaking her head.

"What?" Skip said. "You want to eat, don't you?"

Giselle said, "Yes, but can't you pay attention?"

"I'm listening to every word!" Skip exclaimed. "This'll only take a minute."

He hefted the propane tank and went into the apartment. Saunders asked, "Should we wait until he gets back?"

"Let's go over the refreshments again," Giselle said, leaning forward to shuffle through a pile of papers. "You mentioned there's one really good recipe for punch?"

"Maggie is going to FAX it," Saunders said.

"Okay."

"Yeah, just deal with Maggie on the food and

beverages from here on. She's really in charge of that."

"All right."

"Man, I'm getting hungry," Saunders said. He stood up and sorted through the platter of fruits, fish and meat Giselle had bought for their lunch. "Would you like a shrimp?"

She nodded. "I'm supposed to be the good little girl and stick to my diet for the wedding." She smiled, her eyes enigmatic behind the dark glasses. "But who wants to be a good little girl?"

Saunders made a sandwich of jumbo prawns and raw onion. He leaned against the railing and ate quietly. Giselle picked through the carrots and slices of green pepper. From the trees below the balcony came the chirp-chirrup of nesting robins. He studied Giselle. She seemed more relaxed, confident, away from her family. "May I say something?" he asked.

"Yes."

"You look great."

She smiled. "Is that your way of saying I don't look all that horrible without make-up?"

"No. I didn't notice the make-up. Or the lack of it. I was referring to your general demeanour. You're really on top of all this."

"I'm like my mother. She was the organized type. She ran her own business for many years. And that was pretty unusual in that neighbourhood."

"And Uncle Vince is her brother?"

She frowned slightly. "No, Vince is on my father's side. My mother didn't like Vince very much. My father died when I was only three, so Vince paid the bills."

"And how does Vince feel about you marrying Skip?"

She studied Saunders for a moment. "He hates it," she said evenly. "I really think he'd have Skip quietly bribed to break up with me, or worse, if he thought it would work."

Saunders nodded. "Well, I like Skip. I don't care what anyone says."

"He can be a bit of a jerk," she said, still in the same even tone, "but he's my jerk. He talks constantly about money, but all he really cares about is having fun. Don't you think? I mean, everything makes him so excited. He's like a little boy. I find that very endearing. Especially growing up in the . . . the wax museum of Vince's family."

"You'll have to tell me about Vince's family sometime."

Her eyes were two ovoids of impenetrable glass. "I doubt very much that you'd enjoy that."

AT THE CORNER OF KING and McDermot streets at one-thirty in the morning, Saunders was walking along the sidewalk with a young woman who wasn't a hooker. "My landlord keeps saying I'm a hooker," she said, shivering like a child. She had a cold and her voice was hoarse. "Just because I dance for a living."

"Everybody's a critic," Saunders said. He paused to look up and down the street for Skip's Buick. It had been a relatively quiet stag. Fourteen guys. Skip didn't exactly have an army of friends. Saunders spotted the Buick and headed towards it.

"Well, that's what he says. He says I'm a hooker." She wore a belted raincoat and her heels clicked unevenly on the street.

Saunders took a deep breath through whisky-sharpened nostrils. He could smell the faint punky odour of distant forest fires. There were a lot of fires this time of the year, and when the wind drifted down into the city you could smell them. He looked at her. "Well, we won't worry what he says, all right?"

Saunders opened the door of Skip's Buick and wondered if they should all crowd into the two front bucket seats. "You can either sit on the console or I'll get in the back seat," he said.

She hesitated. She was tall, blonde, with smudged make-up. Kind of thin and classy-looking. She looked as much as it is possible to look like Princess Diana and still be a drug addict. "You know . . . he's always bugging me about it."

"Who?"

"My landlord."

"Oh, him."

"You know what I tell him? I just tell him hey, maybe I am and maybe not, what's it to you?"

Saunders nodded. "Tracy, I don't care what you do for a living, really. I enjoyed your dancing. You've got amazing flexibility."

"Exactly. It's none of his goddamn business."

The stag party had taken place in a meeting room at a restaurant owned by one of Skip's squash partners. Tim Talmey and the Brain had arranged to have the stripper. She had performed a twenty-minute interpretation of "Bolero," and, surprisingly, it was quite good. Particularly if you considered that she had probably never taken a dance class in her life and lived on a diet of taco chips and menthol cigarettes. Skip was still inside the restaurant, having tearful last words with Olson, Redsky, Talmey, the Brain and all his other cigar-smoking buddies. Tracy was Skip's door prize.

"Are you sure this is your car?" she said.

"It's my friend's."

"That's what they all say." She hesitated. "What's your trip anyway?"

"No trip."

"Are you on something?" He shook his head. "Then stop calling me Tracy," she said. "That's only my stage name."

"What do I call you?"

"Patricia."

"Mike," he said, offering his hand.

She got into the car and Saunders climbed in beside her and slammed the door. He rubbed the mist off the window to see if Skip was coming. He and Tracy were jammed together in the bucket seat and her upraised knee showed a foot of upper thigh, sheathed in gleaming metallic hose. He unrolled the window and they got a pair of smokes going.

"So what do you do, Mister Mike?"

"Guess."

She pondered, smoking the cigarette. "Lawyer?"

Saunders chuckled. He opened the glove box—Skip usually kept a flask there. "Why, do I look like a lawyer?"

She exhaled a cloud of perfumed smoke. "I don't know. I don't care, either. As long as you're not a vice cop."

He screwed the cap off the flask. "If you really want to know, I'm a consultant."

"What's that?"

"Basically," he said, "it's somebody who borrows your watch to tell you what time it is."

She looked away, annoyed. "I don't believe in that sort of thing."

"But I've been neglecting my work, this last while. I've been trying to fix up an old hotel."

She tapped her cigarette on the edge of the window. "So, do you want to party?"

"Well, that's why I slipped you out here before Skip comes. I wanted to talk to you about the...arrangement."

"It's ninety for a screw and ninety for a blow," she recited. "Hundred and fifty for a half-and-half. No seconds. No rough stuff. And I don't take Visa."

Saunders absorbed this. He took a sip of whisky from the flask. "Do you want some?"

She shook her head. "You shouldn't drink that stuff."

"See, the thing is, Skip is getting married in a few weeks. And I don't think this is such a great idea."

"Half the guys driving around here are married," she replied. "We give them what they can't get at home."

Right, Saunders thought. Gonorrhoea, or worse. Uncle Vince would be real pleased. They'd have to fuse Skip's knees with metal rods.

"Who paid you?"

She lifted her cigarette elegantly. "The guy with the Scotch tape on his glasses."

"How much?"

"One fifty. And that's just for your friend. No seconds."

Saunders pulled out his wallet. He leafed through it and extracted six twenties. "That's all I have. You know what I'd like you to do?"

She looked at him suspiciously. "Now what?"

"Just take a walk. That's all. You don't have to work tonight."

She shrugged, took the money and stuffed it into her blouse. "Suit yourself."

"And you better hurry, because here he comes."

Skip swaggered out the front door of the restaurant, buttoning his coat and waving a foot-long cigar. There were four rough-looking bikers straddling Harley-Davidsons just past the doorway. They looked like a knot of weedy attack dogs. Skip cupped a hand over his mouth and shouted at them. "Big Improvement!" he yelled, giving them a spirited wave. "One Hundred Percent!"

The bikers showed no expression.

Skip wagged his finger at them. "Now Run With The Ball! Go Ahead! Run With It!" He looked up and down the street and spotted the Buick, then fumbled in his pocket. His keys fell out onto the street. I should be driving, Saunders thought with misgiving.

Skip walked around the front of the car and opened the driver's door just as the stripper was getting out. "Hey, where ya going?"

She brushed past him. "Never mind."

"Hey, ya little whore. Where are you going? We hired you." He grabbed at her arm.

"Screw you," the woman replied, giving him a shove. "Don't you dare touch me."

Saunders leaned over and looked at Skip through the open door. "Skip . . . get in the goddamned car."

"C'mon, ya little tramp," Skip said, hooking his thumb like an empire. "You're in the front seat here, right between me and Mikey."

"Skip . . ."

"Get lost," she said, trying to squeeze past him. "I don't need this aggro." Skip was still holding her sleeve. "LET ME GO!" she shrieked. She reached into her blouse and threw a flurry of paper money into the front seat of the car. "NOW LEAVE ME ALONE!"

"So go!" Skip yelled. "Who needs ya?" He got in the car, jabbed the key into the ignition and cranked it. The car lit up into a high chattering roar. He leaned his head out the window and shouted at her as she walked away from the car. "Gimme gimme never gets, honey."

She looked over her shoulder and threw him the finger.

He banged the car into drive and chased her for thirty feet along the curb, then swerved out into traffic and almost broadsided a cab. He shook a fist at the taxi. "Bloody cab drivers," he muttered. "Can't they watch where I'm going?"

Saunders was silent, hunched over, looking sidelong out his window. Skip sang along with the radio, snapping his fingers. " 'Why do you build me up, but-tercup, baby, just to let me d—' "

Saunders snapped the radio off.

"Hey . . ."

Saunders stuck a finger in Skip's face. "You piss me off." Skip ignored him and hummed the song. "I know it's your party," Saunders said. "That's fine. Have a good time. But why do you have to ruin it? Why do you have to act like an asshole? You know what I feel like? I feel like, Skip . . . SKIP!"

"What?"

"Do you realize you just drove through a red light, asshole?" Skip peered in his rear view. "Pull over, I'm walking home."

"Eh?"

"You heard me. Stop the car. I'm walking home."

"But you're staying at my place."

"Then I'm walking back to your place."

"Oh come on," Skip mumbled. He slowed down.

"I don't know what's wrong with you," Saunders said. "I drive all the way in from Minaki to meet with you and discuss your wedding. . . ." Saunders lit up a cigarette and threw the match with exaggerated vehemence out the window. "I thought you wanted to plan your wedding. I drive all this way, and you won't even . . . ." He stopped talking and shook his head.

"All right," Skip said. He slowed right down to about fifteen miles an hour. "I'm sorry, all right? I didn't realize it was so important."

"Are you kidding? It's your *wedding*! What's more important than your own wedding?"

Skip didn't answer.

"What's going on?" Saunders demanded.

"I've been under stress."

"What kind of stress?"

Skip pulled into the parking garage and didn't answer.

He said nothing in the elevator. In the apartment, he made two drinks. Saunders sat in the velvet sectional and watched Skip take the portable stereo and a handful of cassettes, and go outside. Saunders stood up and followed him. Their lunch dishes were still spread out on the TV tables. Leonard Cohen mumbled nasally on the stereo. Saunders leaned against the rail and looked down at the parked cars and deserted street.

"If you're doing what I think you're doing," Saunders said judiciously, "I think you should burn in everlasting hell."

Skip looked at him, mouth slightly open. "Eh?"

"Don't say 'eh.' You know what I'm talking about."

Skip sipped minutely at his drink. He stared at the railing.

"You're backing out of the wedding. Am I right?" No answer. "You know what bothers me the most?" Saunders asked. "Not the fact that I've gotten to know Giselle, gotten to like her, and I don't want to see her get her heart broken. It's not the fact that I was counting on the wedding, and that I've been working very hard to prepare for it. And that I owe Uncle Vince forty thousand dollars. All that is secondary. You know what really bugs me?"

Skip had his feet up and was leaning back, his hands folded in his lap. He looked as if he were sleeping.

"Do you know what really bugs me?" Skip still didn't answer. Saunders leaned against the rail. He took a deliberate drink of Scotch. His face was numb. He was trying to remember what really bugged him.

Skip shifted around in the chaise lounge. "I'm not backing out of the wedding."

"Right," Saunders said. "Now deny it for a while."

"I'm not."

"Don't lie."

"I'm just trying to get used to the idea."

Saunders was quiet.

Skip had been drinking hard all night and was slurring his words. "Mike . . . I'm determined that this wedding is . . . going to be, uh . . . ," he paused, searching for the right phrase, "it's going to . . . be all right."

Saunders looked at him. "Then why are you acting like an insane person?"

Skip took a long swallow of his drink and stared through the bars of the rail. "I finally slept with Giselle."

"So?"

"You know, we're getting married and stuff. So you know—we did it."

Saunders looked at him. "So what?"

"Well . . . you know how I always told you that she's perfect?"

"Yes."

Skip made a little sniffing noise. "Well . . . she isn't."

Saunders, leaning against the rail, cast a long-suffering look out on the city. "Go on."

"She's a great gal. And I really, truly love her. And I want her for my wife. It's just that . . ." Skip took another long swallow of his drink. He looked as if he were trying to decide whether to cry. "I don't know . . . ," he said. "It's just, it's just that there's . . . someone else."

Saunders absorbed this. "What, you've got another girlfriend?"

"No, it's Giselle."

"What are you talking about?"

He shook his head. "There's not a . . . well, what I mean is . . ."

"What?"

Skip put his face in his hands. "I can't . . . talk about it."

"Oh brother. I can't believe this."

"But I'm determined to go ahead with the wedding."

Saunders stared at him. "Are you lying to me?"

Skip's eyes were downcast. He shook his head slightly.

"Let me tell you something," Saunders finally said. "You better not be pulling your usual bullshit."

"I'm not."

"This is the real thing. This is *marriage*. This is Giselle's *life* you're monkeying around with."

"I know. I know," Skip said. "And I'm determined to go into this with my eyes open. Like—I'm ready for this, Mike, I'm—"

Saunders interrupted him. "Do you have to go to the bathroom?"

Skip was pulling at his crotch. "Yeah." He stood up and drained his glass. "I'm ready for this marriage, Mike. But it's *hard*."

"Yeah yeah. It's a good thing you're so perfect, or it might be hard on Giselle too."

Skip got up and stumbled into the apartment. Saunders leaned on the rail, listening to the Leonard Cohen tape replay itself. The faint scent of smoke was in the air. Five minutes later Skip hadn't returned. Lennie Cohen mumbled something about singing another song, boys. This one was old and bitter.

Saunders went into the apartment. Skip lay sprawled like a dead man in the conversation pit. Saunders pulled off Skip's pale blue loafers and discarded them in the corner. He got a mohair blanket and spread it over the carcass. In the kitchen, he tidied up and shut off the lights.

On the way to the bedroom, he stopped to examine the blossoming hibiscus plant. The scent of the huge pink flowers reminded him of Mexico. The card was from Deborah. He read the message and was about to replace the card in its envelope when he noticed another unopened envelope inside. This one bore a single word: *Michael*.

He opened the sealed envelope and read the small, neatly lettered note within.

Michael:

I've told Giselle and Skip that I'm on bed rest after hurting my ankle. I'd appreciate it if you would let them go on believing that. The truth is, I don't have the stamina to continue with this. There's no one else. I just want to live my own life for a while. Michael, you're a decent person, but you're also very immature. I won't go into all our problems, but I think that at least half of the responsibility is yours. I suppose you wanted me to be more of a woman. But I wanted you to be more of a man.

Good luck with the wedding and the disposition of the hotel. I hope it will be an education for you.

Deborah

26

ANOTHER HOT, DRY DAY IN NORTHWESTERN ONTARIO.
Saunders sped along the Trans-Canada highway in the topless Buick with his sleeves rolled up and his hair riffling in the wind. Beside him, Skip Carter sat with his hands folded in his lap. Skip was ignoring the song on the radio, ignoring the six-pack of Coors on the console beside him. He looked like a man who was about to be executed.

At the Minaki junction Saunders swung off the highway and headed north. Another twenty miles and they'd be at the Stonehouse Inn. Tonight was the rehearsal party, tomorrow the wedding. Right after the wedding Skip and Giselle were leaving for their honeymoon. Saunders had spent the last two weeks praying he hadn't overlooked some minor little detail.

At the hill near Catastrophe Lake the little detail appeared. Saunders topped the rise and involuntarily took his foot off the gas. About fifteen miles to the northwest, looking like a great flat-topped mushroom cloud, was the towering plume of a forest fire. "What the hell is that?" Saunders said.

Skip touched his sun-glasses. "What?"

"Look at that."

"It's just a thundercloud," Skip said.

Saunders kept his eye on the smoke plume as they approached Minaki. It was growing larger with each passing minute. Just before the Stonehouse Inn road he turned off, and continued driving north. He said to Skip, "I have to get a look at it."

Each hill they topped brought the fire closer. At its base the cloud began to move and roll, blackened by the burning oils of green foliage. Saunders slowed the car and turned into a logging road, heading straight for the base of the cloud.

"Now what?" Skip asked.

"I have to see where it's going."

Saunders inched the car carefully down the rough, overgrown road. Smoke, black as tarpaper, billowed from the forest ahead. He stopped the car. A Cessna droned overhead, curving lazily through the smoke. Saunders popped the car into reverse and backed into a clearing, ready to take a quick exit if necessary. Two hundred yards down the road a clump of spruce trees exploded into flame. A great oily tongue of fire looped across the road, then another. The fire was moving southwest, towards Minaki.

WHEN SAUNDERS AND SKIP arrived at the inn, Maggie and Eddy Grogan were in the yard. "Did you see the fire?" Maggie asked.

"We just went up and had a look at it," Saunders said.

Skip gestured with his thumb. "Guy's nuts."

"Looks like a beauty," Eddy said.

Saunders nodded grimly. "It is . . . and I don't have fire insurance."

"We've done everything we can do," Maggie said. "It's in God's hands now."

Eddy Grogan looked at Skip. "So, are you ready to get married, Skipper? If we don't get burned out?"

Skip thought for a moment. "Well . . ."

Saunders glanced curiously at Skip. "He claims he's ready."

"We've almost got everything prepared," Maggie said. "Do you want to inspect?"

Maggie led them into the hotel. Saunders barely recognized the kitchen, all decked out with new utensils and neatly folded table-cloths. He'd given her a blank cheque—no point in interfering. The delicious smell of roast beef wafted through the room. Ten blueberry pies cooled on the table. Maggie's part-time helpers were busily washing dishes. On a metal tray next to the stove dozens of little sausages were wrapped in bacon, skewered with toothpicks. Saunders stealthily lifted one.

Maggie slapped at his wrist. "I've been up since *five* in the morning."

"You're doing a great job," he said. "Any problems?"

"Hundreds."

"Sorry I asked."

"Ontario Hydro phoned two hours ago and said they want that cheque you promised them."

"Did you tell them I mailed it?"

"No. I'm not going to lie. They said you have to drop it at their office by five o'clock this afternoon or they're cutting the power off."

"Oh brother."

"And while you're there can you pick up another U-Drive van?"

"What? Where's the fifteen-passenger Econoline?"

"Beaver crashed it into a tree at seven-thirty this morning."

"He fell asleep," Eddy explained. "He was up all night fixing a busted pipe on the second floor."

"Is he hurt?"

"Chipped a tooth," Maggie said. "I told him to take a couple of days off."

"Is that all?"

"No. Ben is in the lounge, waiting for you."

"Ben who?"

"Ben McNabb. And when you're through getting Skip settled, will you come straight down here? I have some fun little jobs for you."

Saunders whacked Skip on the shoulder. "Okay Skipper. Let's get you registered."

Maggie had fixed up the Lakeview Suite for Skip and Giselle's wedding night. Tonight, the DeFrancos would occupy the entire second floor and Skip would bunk in with Saunders down in the boathouse, where Saunders could keep an eye on him. Saunders hauled Skip's bags down to the boathouse. It wasn't winterized, but in the summer it was almost the nicest lodging on the property. Eight bedrooms with wicker furniture, old throw rugs and big creaky beds overlooked the water. Skip climbed onto a bed, lay flat on his back with his shoes on, and stared at the ceiling while Saunders cleaned up the room and propped the window open. "Are you going to stay here or help me with my chores?" Saunders said.

Skip nodded.

"Do you want something to read?" No answer, but Saunders gave him a *National Geographic* anyway. "And just let me know if you need anything. But try to get some rest, all right?"

Skip had a glazed look.

"But just stay here," Saunders repeated. He raised

his voice slightly, as if talking to a child. "Just *Stay Here. All Right?*"

McNabb intercepted Saunders as he hurried up the lawn to the kitchen. "Mike!" McNabb shouted. "Mike! You finally got here!" McNabb was puffing, hauling a huge briefcase. "What happened?"

Saunders kept moving. "What do you mean?"

"Well, you were going to *call* me!"

"Oh yeah."

"The Fergusons have drawn up an Offer to Purchase." McNabb waved some documents.

"How much?"

"One eighty-five. Don't you want to read it?"

"I'm too busy."

McNabb stopped. "Well . . . they want an answer. What are you intending to do?"

"You can make them a counter-offer," Saunders replied. He jogged up the stairs. McNabb stumbled behind him. "Tell them the price is one ninety-five."

"But that's your asking price!"

"I know," Saunders said. He paused. He looked out at the rolling lawn, where the McNabb Realty For Sale sign wagged lazily in the breeze. "That's my counter-offer. And would you please take down that sign? Until after the wedding?"

He went inside. Maggie was standing in the hall, talking on the telephone. Eddy leaned against the doorway, his arms folded. Maggie hung up the phone. "Well, that's just great."

"What's up?" Saunders asked.

"The fire just crossed the road."

"Which road?"

"The west highway."

"That puts it about four miles away," Saunders said. "Let's not panic just yet."

"When should we panic?" Maggie said.

A low-flying airplane zoomed over the roof of the hotel. Saunders stepped over to the window. The airplane banked over the lake and turned, approaching for another pass. It was a blue and white executive commuter, with twin engines and tucked-in gear.

"That'll be the DeFrancos," Maggie said. "They radioed in when you were in the boathouse. They need to be picked up at the airstrip."

"But how am I supposed to pick them up? The van is out of commission."

"Precisely."

"Okay, now we can panic."

AT MIDNIGHT, with the bloody moon hanging above the smoke-shrouded lake, Saunders finally lowered his weary bones onto a rattan rocking chair on the verandah and propped his feet, with a muted groan, on one of his mother's willow-twig ottomans. Maggie had hit the wall over an hour ago and had gone home to get some sleep. All the staff were exhausted. Saunders had run a dozen or so more cycles through the dishwasher and then called it a night. He poured a Scotch, unplugged the phone, and went out to join Skip, Uncle Vince and the DeFranco men on the verandah.

The verandah was dark, illuminated only by the reddish glow of the moon, and nobody paid much attention to Saunders as he settled into his chair in the corner. "There's no better fighting fish in the whole world," Uncle Vince lectured, his voice slightly above a whisper, "than the smallmouth bass. Isn't that right, Mr. Martens?"

"Yep," Vinnie Martens chortled. "You betcha."

"On a pound for pound basis," Uncle Vince added. His voice was a reverential murmur, and his finger was raised for emphasis. The men were circled around him, their heads as dark as stumps in a forest. Uncle Vince paused for a moment, flipped the cap off his Zippo and applied a blue tongue of flame to the end of his cigar. He sucked philosophically, then unleashed an enormous cloud of smoke. "Now Skipper," he went on, "some people will be so crude as to pursue the trophy smallmouth with baitcasting pole and can of worms. But let me advise you of a little fact. And please don't take this the wrong way. But since it's the eve of your wedding to my beautiful niece I feel it's best we be candid. No matter what anyone says, no member of the DeFranco clan has ever used live bait." He paused. "And I don't care what the S.Q. say."

There was a chuckle from the group.

Uncle Vince laid a broad hand on Skip's shoulder. Skip looked shrunken. "So many things to remember," Uncle Vince muttered. "I know it's not easy. Do you need another cigar?"

Saunders sipped at his drink and thought about Maggie. He had wanted her to sleep here. The air was thick with woodsmoke, but forest fires didn't move as much at night and he wasn't concerned that the conflagration would creep up on them under cover of darkness. The minister had assured him that God seldom interrupted religious ceremonies with divine action, but Saunders wasn't convinced. The minister, in any case, wasn't a very convincing individual—a bearded, plush-bottomed man in a tweed jacket and Roman collar. Saunders had tried to conceal his dislike of religious professionals when he arrived.

"God bless your fine work with this property over the years, Michael," the minister intoned.

"Thank you," Saunders replied.

"God is very pleased, I can assure you."

"Great. Would you like to see the facility?"

Saunders showed him the roped-off area on the lawn, with the carpeted wooden riser that would serve as an altar. The minister clutched his Bible, and wagged his fingers at the steel chairs and microphone.

They also toured the kitchen and office, where they'd go after the ceremony to sign the marriage licence. Eddy Grogan was up on the ladder, trying to hang some party lights along the eavestrough. The minister stuck his hands on his hips, watching Eddy. "How very, very, very special," he remarked. He made a little sign of the cross and blessed the ladder.

Shortly afterwards, the bus from Winnipeg arrived. Saunders had hired it so there'd be no intoxicated wedding guests trying to drive home after the party. The big yellow bus backed across Saunders' new petunias and wheezed to a stop, hogging half the parking lot.

The wedding rehearsal that evening had consisted of a drill of the proceedings, followed by drinks and hors-d'oeuvres on the terrace. Thick smoke obscured the lake. Saunders was worried about the fire, worried about the guests being even more worried than he was. But the water bombers were at work. And everybody seemed to think it was kind of exciting. At the rehearsal party Maggie's special quiche and blueberry pie were a big hit. Then it was back to work. Now here he was, exhausted. After Uncle Vince concluded his lecture on smallmouth bass the DeFranco retinue arose and escorted Skip down to the boathouse, no doubt to keep an eye on him until the wedding. Finally, Uncle Vince and Saunders were the only ones left on the verandah.

"You've done a good job," Uncle Vince remarked.

"Thank you," Saunders replied. He wasn't sure if the old man was talking about Skip or the hotel. "I'll be able to settle my account soon, and I really appreciate your help."

"What account?"

"The forty thousand, sir."

"Oh that," Uncle Vince said, puffing thoughtfully on his cigar. "I've been meaning to talk to you about that."

Saunders waited.

"I was very unhappy, at first, with the concept of my Giselle marrying Sidney. I didn't believe that he was stable and cooperative. But I must say, I've been changing my mind these last few weeks. He's very agreeable, not at all the flippant little fellow I took him to be. I'm making an effort to create a place for him inside our organization, and since you're his partner, I think it would be logical to extend the offer to both of you."

Saunders was silent for a moment. "Well, thank you."

Uncle Vince shrugged. "It's not my generosity at work here. The strength of our business has always been teamwork. We like to include rather than exclude. I'd feel better about Skipper's long-term stability if you were somehow brought into the company."

"Can I be frank?" Saunders asked.

Uncle Vince tapped his cigar. "It's late. There's no one here but us."

"I feel really tired right now. I don't know if I can conduct a serious business conversation. But I'd certainly love to discuss this with you, maybe tomorrow."

"The only reason I bring it up," Uncle Vince said, "Giselle mentioned to me that you're still having some cash flow problems."

"Yes sir," Saunders agreed.

"And if you're selling the place, you don't want to bargain from a position of weakness."

"That's true," Saunders replied. "But I don't have much choice."

"You've had offers?"

Saunders nodded. "I counter-offered someone today. I'm hoping to get one ninety-five."

Uncle Vince took a long slow pull on his cigar, then lowered it and exhaled a thoughtful spew of smoke. He looked at Saunders. Finally he said, "I'll submit an offer of two hundred."

"I had no idea you were interested."

Uncle Vince shrugged. "I'm interested in bringing you and Skip into the company. If purchasing the Stonehouse Inn will ease problems for both of you, then I want to look at that as an option."

Saunders hesitated, off balance. He had been fairly confident of finding a buyer for the inn, but he hadn't expected a bidding war.

"I should be honest," Uncle Vince said. "I wouldn't run it as a hotel. I'd keep it as my own personal vacation property. I'd find someone like that fellow Grogan to do caretaker duty. Would he be open for something like that?"

"Maybe," Saunders said. "You could ask him."

"What about the cook?"

"Maggie? She's moving away."

"I'd like to use this as a hideaway. Someplace to entertain clients, get in a few days of fishing."

Saunders nodded.

"And don't worry about the forty thousand," Uncle Vince said. "We can waive that." He shifted his huge bulk out of the chair. "Think about it," he said. "I'm going to get some rest. Big day tomorrow."

"Good night, sir."

Saunders sat alone in the verandah, wondering what the hell he should do now. It was very quiet. Just him, and a loon somewhere out in the dark, sending its long lonely cry across the lake.

27

THE NEXT MORNING, SAUNDERS AWOKE TO A RAPID knocking at his bedroom door. Eddy Grogan's voice. "You wanna get up, Mike?"

"What time is it?"

The sun was bright in the window. "Almost ten," Eddy replied. "There's some guys here with a truck."

"Who is it?"

"I don't know. They got a U-Haul and a bunch of equipment."

Saunders sprang out of bed. Neil and the Nomads. He dressed hurriedly and went outside. He felt bad about sleeping in. But things seemed quiet enough. The grass was spiky under his bare feet, and the tables and chairs on the lawn were empty. A water bomber droned lazily overhead. Smoke hung over the lake. It was near the solstice and through the smoke haze the sun was hot on his bare arms. He found Neil and Iris and a couple of the musicians in the parking lot. Neil and Tim Talmey were manhandling a big amplifier out of the trailer. Saunders walked up behind Iris and touched her shoulder. "Hello you guys."

Iris peered at him from under a broad-brimmed straw hat, and extended a white glove. "Hello Michael."

"You look good," he said as he shook her hand.

"Hi Mike," Tim Talmey said. "So . . . Hangin' Day."

"Yes it is. Did you get in all right?"

"We almost didn't," Iris replied. "The police have the road blocked because of the fire."

"We begged and pleaded," Tim Talmey added.

Neil lowered his end of the amplifier and brushed the dust off his clothes. With a tidy and characteristic seriousness he adjusted the tight cuffs of his double-knit slacks over a vicious-looking pair of bullhide Tony Lamas. "Hope we didn't disturb your beauty sleep, Mike," Neil said. "Are you sure we got the date right? I was under the impression there was a wedding here today."

"I was up all night," Saunders said. "Getting things ready. Did you bring the lobsters?"

Neil nodded. "Sure did. Where's Skipper?"

"Probably asleep."

"Still?" Neil looked at his watch.

"Big day," Saunders replied. "And they're leaving for their honeymoon right after the wedding."

Neil raised an eyebrow. "Where are they going?"

"Apparently it's a secret. Some tropical hideaway."

Iris said, "How romantic."

Neil looked around. "Anyway, the Stonehouse is looking good."

Saunders grinned at Iris. "Neil's changed his tune. Last year he wanted me to tear it down."

"Hey," Neil said, "I didn't know you could handle something like this."

"Is it really for sale?" Tim Talmey asked, unwrapping his microphone cord. "How much do you want for it? I could use a joint like this."

"I think it's a shame to sell it," Iris murmured.

Saunders thought of the red flowers in the garden, the freshly painted windows, the new cedar shakes on the roof. "Well, I don't have much choice. Unless you know someone who'll give me a thirty-year mortgage with nothing down."

"Yeah," Neil said. "The Bank of Never-Never Land."

"We've been missing you around the office," Iris said. "I guess you'll be back soon."

Saunders nodded. "If I don't get back there soon, Neil and the boys will invoke the shotgun clause and buy me out."

Neil agreed. "You got that right."

"So it's a done deal," Saunders concluded.

"You got some work for us?" Neil asked.

The consultants set up the bandstand, and then organized the dining area—twelve folding wooden tables they'd commandeered from the community hall, covered with crisp white table-cloths and bouquets of wild flowers gathered by Giselle and Maggie. Around lunch Skip made a frail and shaky appearance, and managed to spill coffee on one of the table-cloths. Maggie catered lunch for everyone on the lawn, and shortly after Chief Leo and the Brain rolled into the yard in Chief Leo's brand new midnight blue Nissan Pathfinder. Factory air, compact disc, telephone, the works. Saunders leaned against the window and congratulated Chief Leo, who in recent weeks had decided that New Age Associates was a dying swan and had decamped for Ottawa, where he now held a nicely upholstered government job with DIAND.

"Try this one for size," Chief Leo said. He cranked up John Conlee until the hillbilly voice bounced off the trees.

"I like it," Saunders said curtly, meaning, Turn it down.

Chief Leo turned it a bit louder and stared at Saunders with an obstinate smile. After a moment or two he chuckled and turned it off. He got out and gave Saunders a cigarette, the all-purpose Indian peace offering, then popped the tailgate and handed the Brain his luggage. Chief Leo and the Brain were second-class citizens so they had to stay in the boathouse.

The Brain pulled Saunders aside. "Hey listen, is Neil jumping on Iris?" he asked.

"I have no idea," Saunders replied.

"It's not very professional," the Brain said.

"Listen to him," Chief Leo said. "Never had a girlfriend in his life."

"No, it's just I don't want to lose the world's best secretary."

The boys hauled their suitcases down to the boathouse, then pitched in with the work. Inside the hotel Maggie and Iris finished their food preparations in the kitchen, Brenda Star vacuumed in the halls and the two local girls Maggie had hired set the tables in the dining room. Saunders and his fellow consultants hauled beer, set up the bar, and climbed high shaky ladders to hang the last party lights. The minister came out and blessed their ladders.

Chief Leo helped Saunders hold the ladder for Eddy. It was getting windy, a strong wind that rattled the party lights against the eavestroughs and carried the pungent stink of firesmoke. Eddy kept yelling at them to hold the ladder steady.

"So where's that girlfriend of yours?" Chief Leo said. "That Deborah?"

"She's boycotting the wedding," Saunders replied. "She's mad at me."

"What's the latest on the property sale?"

"I've got two offers," Saunders said. "I haven't really decided yet."

"Maybe I should check around. This place would make a nice half-way house."

Saunders smiled. "Forget it, Leo. You had your chance."

Early in the afternoon Saunders laid out his tux and shaved. The water pressure died, of course, just as he was patting a nice thick layer of Foamy on his face. In his gotch, looking like a bare-legged Santa, he cantered down to the boathouse and put on the snorkel and face mask. He dove down into the freezing water, struggled with the intake, surfaced periodically to demand tools from Neil and Chief Leo, and finally got the clogged unidentifiable substance out of the waterline. He was frantically getting dried off and dressed when Eddy rapped on his bedroom door. "Yes?"

"Al Bonner is here," he said.

"Who's Al Bonner?"

"The sergeant," he said. Eddy knew everybody and assumed that Saunders did too. "The police sergeant."

Saunders rushed downstairs. The police? What the hell did the police want? A big round-shouldered man in a blue uniform stood in the kitchen. Saunders recognized him. "Hello Sergeant," he said.

Sergeant Bonner gave Saunders a big grin. "Hi Mike. Guess what? We may have to evacuate the town."

"Are you kidding?"

"The ministry says they can't hold the fire in this wind. If it crosses the road by the junction, we're going to have to evacuate."

"How far is it from town?"

"Five clicks, maybe."

"Oh no."

"Oh yes," said the policeman happily. "We've lost half a dozen cottages already."

"I just finished rebuilding this place."

The cop lifted his shoulders slightly, as if to say, There's not much you can do.

"And I've got a wedding going on."

The policeman looked at his watch. "What time is the ceremony?"

"Right now."

"Well, go ahead then. I'll keep you posted." He wagged his finger in Saunders' face. "But you be ready to clear out on short notice, you hear?"

THE SHOW MUST GO ON. The congregation gathered in the yard. Saunders hurried around making sure everyone had a seat. At precisely three twenty-five in the afternoon, running almost half an hour late, he went around the back of the hotel and up into the kitchen, which was crowded. At the head of the crowd the minister was whispering and shaking his Bible.

"They can't hold the fire," Saunders said. "The police are talking about evacuating the town."

The minister turned to Saunders and enclosed his hand in a clammy handshake. "God preserve us from this wrathful force of nature, Michael."

Giselle clutched Skip's sleeve as if to prevent him from escaping. "Have we got time to get married?"

Saunders said, "Yes, as long as we get on with the show."

The minister hurriedly gave them the drill. "Through this doorway, we'll all move at a slow-w-w-w, but not too slow, walk and you, Michael, will hold the ring and stand beside Skip while Giselle mo-o-ves gradually this way with Mr. DeFranco to the altar, with Giselle on my right, your left, Skip on my left, your right, is that clear?"

Saunders nodded. He unbuttoned his jacket to release the heat trapped inside the heavy fabric. He looked at Giselle. "Are you ready, Giselle?"

She nodded bravely. "I'm ready."

"Are you ready, Skip?"

Skip didn't speak. His eyes were blurry, unfocussed. He looked as if he were in a trance. The sharp stink of woodsmoke came in through the screens.

"Are you ready, Skip?" Saunders said.

Everybody turned en masse and stared at Skip. Saunders nudged him. "Skipper . . . are you ready?"

Skip was motionless.

Oh my god, Saunders thought. He's going to balk.

Skip's hand moved up towards his boutonnière. He adjusted it. He stared at Giselle. "Okay baby . . . let's do it."

28

At FOUR-THIRTY IN THE AFTERNOON, WITH A DRY, HOT westerly wind pushing it through the bush, the forest fire known as Kenora 31 staged a frontal assault against Ontario Ministry of Natural Resources fire squads deployed in a north-south line along Highway 596. Eighty men in the government's standard blaze-orange FIRE SUPPRESSION coveralls fought the fire with shovels, water pumps and several miles of hose. Overhead, large yellow water bombers roared, dipping low to spew fusillades of lake water on the leading edge of the fire.

In some places there was no fire visible at all, but several feet underground, scrawny white pine roots snaked like nerve ganglia through the humus, each root a fuse. Way out on the edges, far from the hubbub of men and machines, long-dead rotted cedar trees smouldered secretly under the lichen, loosing only an occasional wisp of blue smoke to reveal what was underfoot. Elsewhere, purplish gases tongued out of birch thickets and threw tiny fragments of burning spittle upwards. Caught by the wind, the embers drifted across the road, over the heads of the labouring men, under the winds of the roaring airplanes, and settled delicately in the fresh dry forest on the other side of the highway. By five o'clock in the afternoon, the Fire Boss suspended four hundred feet above the blaze in a tiny Hughes 500 helicopter picked up his radio transmitter and keyed the handset.

Kenora 31 had officially jumped their lines and crossed the road. Ahead of the fire now was nothing but two miles of virgin timber. And then the Stonehouse Inn.

Saunders was in the hotel dining room, witnessing the signing of the wedding licence, when a black and white OPP cruiser went by the window, roof lights flipping as it drove around the front of the hotel. Eddy Grogan came hurrying in the door a moment later. "Mike, the cops are here."

Saunders went outside and talked to the police, then went into the hotel and discussed the situation with Skip, Giselle, Maggie and the staff. He went to the microphone, which was set up for his best man speech and Uncle Vince's toast to the bride, and tapped the mike for everyone's attention. "Excuse me, ladies and gentlemen. Excuse? Could I have your attention for a moment? I've just been talking to the OPP and it seems that they're having some problems controlling this fire. They're recommending that we evacuate the hotel. In fact, they're evacuating the town and all the cottage areas to the east of us. There's no cause for alarm. We've got lots of vehicles, a bus, and the VIA train, apparently, has been commandeered on behalf of the community and is waiting at the station for those who don't have cars."

Saunders cupped his hand over the mike. Skip had walked up and was whispering to him. Saunders nodded. "Okay folks, Skip has offered his apartment for a place to have our reception. I know it's a long drive. But it looks like we have to go anyway, so . . ."

Skip took the mike. "Come on you guys, there's lots of food. Wine. Champagne. What do you say?"

The crowd answered with a round of applause.

Saunders stepped down from the microphone and went into the main lounge, where he stood for a moment, trying to decide what he needed to do. He stared up at the ceiling, at the apex of complicated logs. He'd never had a chance to finish that last section, way up there among the timbers, where the light through the stained-glass windows was turning bloody in the late afternoon. The new drywall, the new plumbing that you couldn't see, the octagonal carpet in front of the massive stone fireplace . . . it was all going to be lost after all.

He went into his bedroom and threw a few things into his overnight bag. Miles away, he could hear the train moaning, not the usual honk-honk, but one long moan that didn't waver. He looked around the room. What should he take?

What about the old photograph on the wall, the family portrait, taken many years ago on the front lawn on the occasion of his parents' twenty-fifth anniversary? And the wooden book shelf in the corner, the one he made in grade eight shops class? Could he fit it in the back of the truck with all the food? He looked at the clutch of round stones on the window ledge, his collection of stones from the oceans of the world. Throw them in his kit bag?

The enormity of this was too much. He couldn't believe he had to make these last-minute choices. What should go? What should stay?

The right thing was to simply walk away, hope that it all survived. Because all this stuff was of equal importance. And it was all irreplaceable.

He went downstairs, wiping the wetness out of his eyes. Maggie and the girls were cleaning out the kitchen. Out in the back yard Eddy Grogan, in his ill-fitting K-Mart wedding suit, dragged a big gasoline-powered water pump out of the machine shed. Saunders said, "Eddy, what are you doing?"

"I'm going to get this pump goin', start soaking down the woods."

Saunders nodded. Well, he thought, I have to decide. Eddy and I can stay here and fight the fire, which is what I feel like doing. We could fight it to a standstill. And if we can't stop it we can at least be here. Be here to see it. Take seats up on that third-floor balcony, pour ourselves a couple of drinks, pull up a couple of chairs, and watch the fire come down the hill. Watch that big two-thousand-gallon fuel oil tank by the motor lodge explode.

He said, "I don't think the police will let you stay."

"They can't stop me."

"I think we better head into the city, though, and do the job we were hired to do."

Eddy studiously removed a blackened, soddened cigarette from the corner of his mouth. "I'd rather stay here."

Saunders looked at him. "I need you in the city. To help out."

"I'd be more use here."

"But I'm paying the bills, right?"

"Then I quit," Eddy said. "Now gimme a hand with this pump."

Saunders and Eddy hauled the pump down to the lake. A haze of firesmoke drifted above the flat water. Little pepper-sized flakes of ash sifted down. They laid the hose out and Eddy started the pump. The hose swelled. Water coughed out the up-hill end. Eddy took off his suit jacket and rolled a cigarette. He looked at Saunders with a lopsided smile. "Now, bring on your inferno."

Up the hill the bus had backed around in the parking lot. Everyone was queuing up to climb aboard. The wedding guests seemed to regard this as more entertainment. Saunders located Maggie. "What are you going to do?"

"Well, I'm coming with you, of course."

"Good."

She brushed a strand of hair from her eyes. She had that messy-haired, exhausted look that chefs always have.

"Are you all right?"

"Never mind me," she said. "How are you?"

"Ask me tomorrow."

They brought Maggie's big four-by-four truck around, loaded it and headed up a wagon train of vehicles. He refused to take one last look at the inn. They drove slowly down the road and through the town. It was like a scene from a war movie. Crowds of evacuees lined the road, walking to the railway station, carrying loads of clothing, babies, books, boxes and suitcases. Through thick smoke the sunset burned. At the train station the VIA train idled, with its locomotive loosing that great unwavering prehistoric moan.

Saunders and Maggie continued out of town. Just beyond the town limit a pair of OPP cruisers blocked the road. Past the police cars, Saunders could see where the fire had crossed the road. Thick clouds of white smoke drifted through black skeletal trees. Two cops stood by the police cars. One was drinking coffee from a Styrofoam cup. The other, Sergeant Bonner, was talking into a portable radio. Saunders rolled down his window.

Sergeant Bonner walked up. "Hi Mike. Did you get everyone cleared out over there?"

"Everyone but Eddy."

The big policeman nodded. "Just give us a minute and we'll escort you through."

They waited. Sergeant Bonner got in his car and they followed its flipping red light through the white smoke. Eventually they emerged into clear air. The police car pulled onto the shoulder and waved them past. Saunders slowly accelerated, watching the procession follow in his rear-view mirror. The forest on either side of the road was lush and green. The sky was clean and blue. The fate of the Stonehouse Inn was out of his hands now.

Several hours later they arrived in Winnipeg, unloaded the liquor and food, and herded ninety wedding guests into Skip's apartment. Saunders ran up and down from the apartment to the parking lot, unloading supplies. Maggie reheated all the food. Instead of a sit-down dinner, they arranged a smorgasbord. Maggie showered and put on a dress. Skip and Giselle and the DeFranco family formed a gabby mob in the conversation pit, with Uncle Vince presiding over all, smoking a big cigar and looking pleased with himself. The Minaki evacuation was a top story on the CBC news. Saunders kept ducking into the kitchen, listening to the radio for updates. Nothing definite.

At eight-thirty, the band plugged in its instruments. Tall Timmy Talmey hit a rim shot on the drums and started a funky African beat. Chief Leo thumped on the bass. And then the Brain fell in with the electric organ. Neil's brothers built the melody with the lead guitar and saxophone. It was the introduction for Paul Butterfield's "Born in Chicago." Out on the balcony Saunders could see Neil lurking in the shadows. Everybody was clapping. The band played the introduction for a full minute. Suddenly Neil leaped up in front of the microphone. He wore wrap-around sun-glasses and a gold metallic jacket. "Thank you ladies and gentlemen, I'm sorry for the delay. I was outside," he said, "talking to Elvis."

Everybody laughed and cheered.

Neil shot a finger at the crowd. "And do you know what Elvis told me?"

Tall Timmy rapped the snare drum. The Brain wailed on the organ.

Neil was moving to the music. "Elvis told me, he said, It's a hot night tonight, there's fire abroad in the land. I want you to play HOT, son. I don't want you to play no Bobby Vin-tonn . . . I don't want you to play no Bobby Vee-ee-ee."

Everybody cheered again.

Neil shook his head. "No . . . I want you to play that straight, natchural rock and roll-ll . . . HOT ROCK AND ROLL!" he said, shaking his fist. "HOTTER THAN A FOREST FIRE!"

The crowd roared.

Neil broke into the song. Born in Chicago. Nineteen and forty-one. His daddy told him, son you'd better get a gun. At the end of the song the band went straight into "Black Is Black" without a break, then "Down the Road a Piece." The living room became a dance floor. Saunders went around and emptied ashtrays.

A little before midnight Skip and Giselle got up, arm in arm, and gave a toast to everybody, thanks for the wonderful party. Skip hugged Giselle and lifted a hand in farewell. "But we've gotta go, folks. We've got a plane to catch."

Saunders went downstairs and got the Buick from the parking garage. Somebody had booby-trapped the car, hung a gang of tin cans from the rear bumper, put the licence plate upside down and scrawled *Just Married* with a bar of soap on the rear window. Probably Chief Leo or the Brain, the company's comedians. Saunders drove the car through the parking garage with the cans ringing on the pavement, up the ramp and outside, around to the front entrance. A small crowd of wedding guests waited with Skip and Giselle. Saunders got out and presented the keys to Skip.

Skip squeezed his arm. "Thanks for everything."

Saunders smiled. "My pleasure, Skip."

"Have you heard anything about the hotel?"

"Nope."

Skip embraced Saunders. "Come here," Skip said, dragging Saunders to the rear of the car. Skip had the heavy smell of liquor on his breath.

"What's going on?" Saunders said, cautious.

"I just want to thank you for everything."

Saunders glanced around. Uncle Vince was watching them. Saunders looked at Skip. "What's the problem?"

Skip shook his head. At a loss for words. "Oh man."

"Listen," Saunders whispered. "You and I talked about this. Are you all right?"

"I love Giselle," Skip muttered. "I know that."

"Then what's the problem?"

Skip grimaced, squeezing Saunders' arm. "Oh man . . ."

"What?"

"Sidney! Let's get the show on the road!" Uncle Vince laughed, gesturing with his stogey. "You're keeping your bride waiting!"

"Don't let me near that old—" Skip said.

"Who?"

"Vince," Skip said.

"What are you talking about?"

Skip's breath was like a wine barrel. "I'll kill 'm. After what he did to Giselle."

Saunders paused, incredulous. "Who . . . are you crazy?"

Skip gave Saunders a frown of almost comic seriousness before the DeFranco brothers ushered him into the waiting automobile.

Saunders paused for a moment, watching, then shook his head. What was that all about?

In a procession they followed the big wedding car out to the airport. Saunders and Maggie rode with Neil and Iris, all four of them wedged into the front seat of Maggie's pick-up. On the open-air observation deck at the airport, they stood out in the midnight dark, in the cool wind, watching the tiny running lights of the DeFranco commuter crawl down the runway. Far away in the west, lightning flickered in the clouds. Probably more fires in the offing. Still no rain. At the end of the runway the little airplane turned and paused, then began its take-off roll. Saunders put his arm around Maggie. They all lifted their hands and waved. Good luck, lovers, Saunders said silently. Wherever it is you're going.

They went to a motor hotel near the airport, where Chief Leo and a few of the out-of-town wedding guests were staying. They raided the bar fridge in Chief Leo's room, then everybody went down to the bar, which had an old twin-engine plane impaled in the wall, as if some pilot had crashed into the building. There were pictures of old World War II bomber crews on the wall and the music was all circa 1940s, Glenn Miller, the Dorsey band. Saunders called Skip's apartment to see if any guests were left but Tim Talmey said he was just packing up the equipment. Everyone had gone, the party was over.

Saunders joined Neil and Iris at the bar. Maggie wasn't around. Neil and Iris were too busy staring into each other's eyes to talk to him. He ordered a Scotch and watched the people dance.

Maggie sidled up and sat beside him. "Hello."

He sipped at his Scotch and gave her a neutral look. "I thought you'd left."

"I was talking to Raymond."

"That's nice."

259

"Don't be snide."

"So what's up with Raymond?"

"He's in Canmore, still. He's looking at houses."

"Find anything?"

"Yes. He wants me to fly out there next week."

Saunders nodded. "Is that why you phoned him?"

"I wanted to tell him how the wedding went. The fire and everything. He's been hearing the news on the radio. He's quite concerned."

"I'm sure," Saunders remarked. "Did you think about what we discussed the other day?"

She lifted her glass of wine thoughtfully. "Yes."

"And?"

Maggie give him a cool look. "What is your problem, anyway?"

He shrugged. "Sorry, it's just that my hotel is on fire. I guess I'm being self-centred."

"Oh, I see," she nodded. "You're worried. But no one else is, right?"

He drank his Scotch, silent.

She finished her wine. "Well, I'm going to go."

He stood up. "Don't."

"Why?"

"Because we haven't danced yet."

"Are you going to be rude?"

"No."

They went out onto the dance floor. She folded easily into his arms. They waltzed, close together, past all the other couples bopping to the music. "I appreciate all your help," he said.

"Do you?"

"Of course I do. And I've been meaning to thank you, all night."

"Is that why you're being so rude?"

"No," he said mildly. "That's the Scotch."

"Well, shape up."

He nodded. The other dancers began to jitterbug to a feverish version of "In the Mood." Saunders continued waltzing with Maggie. He could feel the slight pressure of her body against his. The flex of her waist, the smell of her hair. "I really want to thank you for all those days and nights you helped."

Her hand moved slightly on his neck.

"It was fun," he said. "I like spending the winter with you."

She nodded. "Me too."

"And whatever happens, we can be proud of one thing."

"What's that?"

"We can say we finished that inn."

"No . . . you can say it."

"I couldn't have done any of it without you. Remember that time I got the BMW stuck in the snow? I was ready to quit. And the time you got us our first booking? From Mrs. Froelich? And all the work you did for this wedding? You should probably get more credit than anyone."

She smiled.

"But mostly you were a friend when I needed one. So I just want to say thanks."

"Well . . . you're welcome."

The other dancers jostled against them. "And whatever happens, let's not forget, we did a good job."

"You talk as if something terrible and final is going to happen." Maggie pulled back to look at his face.

"I hope not."

"Are you worried about the inn?"

"Of course."

"Do you want to drive back there?"

He shook his head. "We don't have much time left. Let's just be together."

"Can I ask you something?"

He nodded.

"If I tell Raymond that I still want to maintain my relationship with you, do you think we can stand to see each other, once in a while, and not sleep together?"

He shrugged. "I don't know. When would we ever see each other?"

"You travel so much."

"Not in western Canada. You'd better tell Raymond to get a job in Thunder Bay."

She cocked her head thoughtfully. "What if I told Raymond that I wanted to retain the freedom to have a part-time relationship with you?"

"Sleeping with both of us?"

"Well, not in the same room, preferably."

He smiled. "It wouldn't work. I want you all to myself."

"I sort of feel the same way."

This might have been an indirect reference to Deborah. He didn't tell her that Deborah had taken her exit. He didn't want Maggie's pity. Poor Mike. Lost his family place in that forest fire. No insurance. Property is worth practically zip with all those blackened trees on it. And what with the loan shark thing, and Deborah taking a walk, it's no wonder everyone whispers when he walks through the room.

"We can make all kinds of noble promises to each other," Saunders said. "But let's just try to be honest. I like you. We had a good partnership, rebuilding that old hotel, and I thank you for it. What else is there to say?'

"I think you've summed it up."

The music stopped. They separated and walked back towards the bar. "I don't turn into a pumpkin until three-thirty tomorrow afternoon," she said. "Do you want to skip off somewhere?"

"Yes."

"I'll be back in a few minutes."

Saunders polished off his drink and paid the bartender. He looked around for Neil and Iris. Maybe it was late, but he didn't feel tired. He wanted the night to go on forever.

Maggie suddenly appeared, smiling. "Come with me," she said, extending a hand.

"What?"

"I want to show you something."

She took Saunders' hand and led him across the dance floor. She went out past the coat check, down the long hall, pulling him by the hand. The bellhop smiled and nodded as Maggie manoeuvred past. The smell hit Saunders in the face the moment they stepped out the front door. The air was thick. It rustled. The sky boomed and rolled. The parking lot swam with mirrored light, shiny as oil.

Rain.

29

THEY WERE ALL GONE. SKIP AND GISELLE, ON THEIR honeymoon. Maggie, off to Alberta to meet Raymond and scout for a new home. The DeFrancos, back to Montreal.

Saunders drove east on the Trans-Canada highway. It was a beautiful summer morning, the sun warm, the fields as green as spinach. Maggie's absence nagged at him like a sore rib. It would take time to get over this one. He had decided to quit smoking, and so far so good, but every time he thought about Maggie, he wanted to smoke in misery.

When he got to the Stonehouse Inn, Eddy Grogan showed him the boundaries of the forest fire. Apparently, after the wedding the fire was more or less curled up for a few hours, spending the night along the edge of the valley where Saunders had lost his hub-cap, when the rains arrived. Come daybreak, the fire smouldered under dripping foliage. And around noon, four school buses loaded with fire-fighters arrived after having driven non-stop from Kirkland Lake. From Eddy's truck, Saunders and Eddy watched them at work, digging with spades, hefting axes, tearing moss and vegetation off the ground as if stripping a fallen enemy. They were soot-smeared and tired-looking men, but the fire was out.

Saunders erected a scaffold in the main lounge and climbed up into the apex of the ceiling to sand and varnish the last section of roof timbers. If he was going to walk around saying he totally renovated his family's old hotel, he wanted it to be true. Lying on his back, face-to-face with the massive A-shaped hammer truss of Eastern white pine, he ran his fingers along its centrepost and limbs, marvelling that this one simple, uncompromising trinity of peeled tree trunks had kept the inn perfectly square for all these years.

When he was in college he studied these things in his History of Architecture class. He remembered being surprised that the distinctive delta-joint of logs up in the ceiling of the Stonehouse Inn was the same truss that you could see up in the apex of Europe's largest cathedrals. He learned that the hammer truss was an ingenious device for strengthening large buildings without the use of vertical posts and supports, and was regarded by architects as a piece of folk craft gradually transformed into art of the highest form. He remembered his father telling him about the one in Westminster Hall, sixty-five feet wide, and how "nobody to this day understands how the hell it holds the building together."

Being a typical young college student, he was surprised that his father actually knew anything about the material in his textbooks. And even though he was secretly intrigued that the Stonehouse Inn was architecturally interesting, he had never gotten around to climbing up and looking at the beams, face-to-face, until now.

So he worked, and sanded it down, and applied four coats of finish until the big logs gleamed.

McNabb had re-erected the For Sale sign in the front yard and seemed to drop by on an hourly basis. Of course, Vince DeFranco was in the front running for the purchase of the inn, especially since New Age Associates was probably going to be working for him regularly, but as soon as the two schoolteachers found out they had a competitor, they upped their offer to two hundred and five thousand, and Saunders wasn't sure what to do. Overnight, McNabb had become a champion of "precious heritage buildings" and he carried on as if Saunders had under-valued the inn from the very start.

"You handle it," Saunders told him. "Tell Vince there's a better offer."

When Saunders pulled out of the Stonehouse Inn driveway, towing the U-Haul trailer loaded with bureau drawers and quilts and books and photographs, McNabb was jogging alongside, frantically requesting instructions.

In Winnipeg Saunders rented a locker at a Safestore compound and packed away his family possessions. He'd volunteered to run the New Age office in Winnipeg while Skip was on his honeymoon, and then he planned to ship everything back to Toronto. In the meantime, he tried to get his mind off Maggie and the sale of the inn by throwing himself back into the consulting business. He set up a card table on Skip's balcony and sketched site plans, septic fields and motel units. He sketched the interior of dining rooms, using the always popular Knights of the Round Table motif. He threw himself into his work but the best he could manage was about three minutes of sketching for every three minutes of staring at the green foliage of the city.

A hundred feet below him was an old neighbourhood with big trees and shabby roof tops and telephone wire.

Somebody had spray-painted a message on a garage door: DEATH IN THE SUBURBS. He felt like a solitary tourist. This city wasn't his home.

A WEEK LATER Skip and Giselle came back from their honeymoon. They'd gone to Las Vegas, which Saunders considered to be about as attractive for vacation purposes as one of Chief Leo's bingo halls. But Giselle and Skip said they had had a "fabulous" time. Skip lost two thousand dollars on the crap tables, was personally introduced to Wayne Newton, and did an amateur night stand-up at the Comedy Store. Saunders asked Giselle how funny Skip had been and she said, "It was pretty scary. I was the only one who clapped."

Saunders wanted to update Skip on office activities so they sat up late that night and killed a few beers on the balcony. "I've got a decision to make," Saunders said. "Uncle Vince has made a pretty good offer on the inn, and I feel obliged to accept it, given that we're going to be working with him."

Skip's face was solemn. "Yeah, we've gotta straighten this out."

Saunders raised a hand. "Okay, let me finish. I've had a hell of a winter, fixing that place, and I don't want to give it away to just anybody. That building might have seemed run-down last year, but structurally it was perfect. I measured it. It's less than one centimetre out of square, after fifty years."

"That's pretty good."

"And that's because it's got this one great big truss in the ceiling, holds the building together. I sometimes think that's what is lacking in my approach—one strong principle. Like, I'm always convincing myself that things are complicated. Maybe it's simple."

"I don't follow you."

"Well . . . I have to decide whether to sell it to Uncle Vince or not. What if I just follow my conscience, and do the right thing?"

"What are you talking about?"

Saunders poured the remaining contents of his beer bottle into the glass. He hesitated. Skip wasn't going to like this. But he had decided that he wasn't going back to the old way of doing things. "I'm not selling it to Uncle Vince, Skip. He's not the person I want owning the Stonehouse Inn."

"Good," Skip said, lifting his glass.

Saunders paused. "I beg your pardon?"

"I don't want to have anything at all to do with the old bastard."

"Why?"

"He's a pervert. He used to go into Giselle's bedroom when she was a little girl."

As soon as Skip said it, Saunders knew it was true. "Why didn't you tell me?"

"Giselle didn't want me to."

"Why? It's nothing to be ashamed of. She should report him to the police."

Skip nodded. "It was a long time ago. She almost told you a couple of times, but she didn't want to discourage you from getting money from him. She knows you're in a tough spot."

Saunders frowned, trying to absorb all this. "Well, that's terrible."

Skip shrugged. "It's getting better, though. We're married now, so Giselle is free of him."

"You're not going to take up Uncle Vince's offer and move down east?"

"Are you kidding?" Skip said. "Giselle would settle for a basement apartment and a job at Burger King, rather than spend another year living near that old pervert."

Saunders reached for one of Skip's cigarettes. He hadn't had a smoke for over a week. But he needed one now. "Well, that explains a few things."

"Uh huh," Skip agreed, accepting a Player's and leaning forward for the match.

"Like, why you were acting like such an asshole that night."

Skip's brow wrinkled. "Which night was that?"

SO IT WAS SETTLED. Richard and Ella Ferguson, of Sioux Lookout, Ontario, would be the new owners of the Stone-house Inn. All Saunders had to do was drive out to Kenora, meet McNabb at the lawyer's office, sign a few documents, and he'd be two hundred thousand dollars richer. Twenty-five of that would go towards miscellaneous accounts payable, forty plus interest would go to the DeFrancos, five to Skip, six to Eddy and the Cruisers, about the same to Maggie Chavez. (What did he owe her? Anything? Everything?) When all the ciphering was done, he'd still land at Pearson with a hundred grand and change in his briefcase. Not bad for a winter's work.

The night before the deal was finalized, Skip and Giselle threw a small party on Saunders' behalf. Skip invited the two flight attendants from next door, and then Chief Leo showed, hauling a case of beer. Neil and Iris appeared at the door a little later. Iris was a full-fledged partner in New Age Associates now, having bought herself a share, and Skip couldn't leave it alone.

"Hey Iris," he kept saying, "if you're going to be a partner, who's going to do all the work?"

Skip pulled Saunders aside once things were underway and admitted that some unexpected guests were coming later. Maggie and Raymond.

"What are they doing in town?"

"Some last-minute stuff, apparently. Raymond bought a house in Canmore."

"Where did you see Maggie?"

"She came to the office, looking for you."

By the time Maggie arrived, alone, Saunders had collected himself to the point where he could greet her at the door, bearing a drink and a cigarette, and act the perfect gentleman. "Maggie!" he enthused. "You made it."

She gave him a prim embrace. "Hello Michael." She took off her doeskin jacket and smiled, her hair glossy and her cheeks flushed.

God, I miss this woman, he thought. He guided her into the living room. "Where's Raymond?"

"He has a few errands. He's managed to get a flight back to Calgary tonight."

"What time is the plane?"

"Ten forty-five."

"Well, I'll drive you to the airport."

"That's not necessary."

"Don't be ridiculous," he said. "I don't mind. I'll borrow Skip's brontosaurus. Do you want a drink?"

Maggie sat down and was immediately besieged with questions from the other consultants. What's the latest news from Alberta? Where's Raymond's new job? Skip wheeled in the TV and showed a video tape of the wedding. The room was dark. Saunders watched it all up on the screen, the wedding party on the afternoon lawn, the old Stonehouse Inn, its battlements hung with crêpe paper and flowers, the speeches, the smoky fading light of the forest fire afternoon, the solemn faces of the bride and groom, the ceremonial dresses of the bridesmaids and the rest of the wedding party. Saunders watched himself standing by Maggie, both of them smiling, clapping. He could look at her face and say, yes, we were happy. I was a successful innkeeper. And for just a little while we were happy.

After the video Skip cranked up the Beatles on the

stereo. "All right," he said. "It's time to get down to some serious partying."

Skip got one of the stewardesses to dance with him, then Chief Leo showed Giselle some moves. Chief Leo danced like Elvis, barely moving his feet, making his knees shimmy wildly. No matter how obscure the song, Skip knew all the words, and proved it by singing loudly and shaking his finger in people's faces.

"Just let me know when," Saunders said, walking by Maggie.

"That's all right," she said, dancing dutifully with Neil. "I don't need a ride."

"Don't be silly," he argued. "What time's the flight?"

"Ten forty-five," she said. "I already told you."

He glanced at his watch. "You've got a little time yet. Do you need a drink?"

She turned away. "No, thank you."

Saunders went out onto the balcony to have a smoke. Kristin, one of the stewardesses, was there. He lit a cigarette and talked to her for a while. If someone put a gun to his head, he realized, he couldn't bring himself to touch this person. He had totally lost interest in women. Maybe he needed counselling. Or electro-shock therapy. Kristin went inside. He stayed on, smoking another one, shooting the butt into space. It twirled and crashed down on the side wind, bumping down through layers of air and disappearing into the night. The door opened and Maggie stepped out. "Time to go?" he asked.

"If you say so."

He looked at his watch. "Yeah . . . I'll ask Skip."

Saunders went inside and petitioned the keys. Skip warned him that the Buick had a broken muffler. "The old bitch doesn't like those speed bumps."

"Well, maybe if you hit them at thirty-five miles an hour," Saunders replied. "Where are your keys?"

Maggie thanked Skip and Giselle for the party while Saunders waited outside the door. They went out into the thick carpeting and pagan statuary of the long hall, and walked in silence to the elevator. Saunders pushed the button. "So Skip and Giselle seem happy."

She nodded. "I think so."

"They went to Las Vegas."

"I know."

"Skip lost a lot of money."

"I know. I talked to him for about an hour this afternoon at the office."

They rode the elevator down to the cavernous parking garage. Their steps echoed as they walked to Skip's Buick. "I've been thinking," Saunders said. "I don't want to go back to the old way of doing things."

"What's that mean?"

He put his hand on her shoulder. "Well, even if you're living with somebody else, I don't care. I'd still like to be friends. Stay in touch." He unlocked the car, held the door open for her. "I don't want to be a sore loser."

"That's good. But I should tell you something."

"What?"

"You finish, first."

He walked around to his own side and got in. "So if I call you, and we meet for dinner, I don't want you to think I'm going to try and talk you into staying all night." He paused to see if she had an answer. She didn't, so he started the car.

Surrounded by bare walls of echoing concrete, the Buick sounded like a fuel dragster. Saunders thundered up the ramp and out into the night. He made a left on Roslyn, drove down to the intersection and stopped at the light before he said anything else. "I'll get a traffic ticket for sure with this thing." He looked over at Maggie. "Where's Raymond?"

"Probably at the airport."

"What do you mean, 'probably'?"

"Well, I'm not sure."

"You're not sure?"

"He's mad at me," she said.

"Why?"

She was quiet for a while. "Because I'm not going to Alberta."

Saunders stared at her. He noticed the light was green and eased the car forward. "What the hell are you talking about?"

She was way over on the passenger side, her arms folded tightly across her chest. "It has nothing to do with you."

"Well, thanks."

"What I mean is, I don't love him."

"It took you a while to figure that out."

She nodded.

"So what are you going to do?"

"Go back to Minaki."

He drove north on Osborne Street, heading for the airport. He was driving slowly, his posture stiff and cautious. "I'm really confused now."

"Why?"

"This changes things."

"How? You're still selling the inn tomorrow. What's the difference?"

"I don't know." He accelerated, the car rumbling. It was raining lightly and the wipers smeared arcs of neon across the windshield. Saunders opened the ashtray and stabbed the cigarette lighter into its socket. He waited until he had lit his cigarette before he said anything else. "Based on what you've told me, I shouldn't be selling the inn to these people at all."

"Why?"

He looked at her. "I should sell it to you."

"That's not possible."

"Why? You're going to live in Minaki. You're a good chef. You're a hard worker. You love the place. So what's your problem?"

"I don't have any money."

"Do you have a dollar?"

She nodded.

"I'll sell it to you for a dollar."

"No."

"Why?"

She didn't answer.

"If you feel guilty for ripping me off, don't, because once you own that place, your life will become sheer, utter hell."

Her tone was impatient. "I know that."

"Then what?"

"What will you do? You owe everyone money. You need the revenue from the sale."

He shrugged. "Five minutes ago, I had a hundred thousand dollars in my pocket, and it made no big difference. Basically, it was a lousy feeling. Right now, I have a chance of being flat broke and seeing you own the inn, and it feels just right."

"But what about Uncle Vince?"

"He gets nothing. I've got a piece of paper says I owe him money. Fine, the first instalment's not due for another two months. I'll get the money. I'll go back to Toronto and work my butt off. There's things I can do there. I could even sell my share of New Age, if it comes to that. I've been looking for a reason to bail out of the consulting business. Maybe this is my big excuse."

Maggie was quiet.

"So what do you say?"

She finally spoke. "I'll buy fifty cents' worth."

Now Saunders said nothing.

"You need to do the right thing," she said. "So do I. The Stonehouse Inn is not my family's property. It's yours. You need someone to help you run it. So I'll do it. But I think you should retain half interest."

"Okay," he said. "Yes. Absolutely. I agree with you."

They drove in silence for several minutes. Then Saunders slowed down, confused again. "But if you're not going to live with Raymond, why am I driving you to the airport?"

"I have no idea."

He stopped in the middle of Portage Avenue.

Maggie said, "You've been insisting all night that you're going to drive me to the airport in time for Raymond's flight. I keep explaining, I don't think he wants to see us."

"Why didn't you tell me?"

"I can't get a word in edgewise."

Cars sailed by on either side and piled up in a long row behind him, horns honking. Saunders checked the rear-view mirror and pressed the accelerator. The big car swayed and detonated like a wounded dinosaur. "So where do you want to go?"

"I don't know."

"Do you want to see if Skip will lend us the car for twenty-four hours? We could drive to Minaki? And tomorrow we can settle that business with the Offer to Purchase? Cancel the deal?"

She nodded. "I think that makes sense."

He turned the wipers on full speed. It was raining hard now, the downpour drumming the fabric roof. So we'll go there right now, he thought. This is unbelievable luck. He turned the heater on and grinned at Maggie. He took the off ramp down to the bridge across the river.

"Oh no," Maggie said suddenly. She laughed softly.

"What?" he asked. "What's the matter?"

"Who's going to break the news to McNabb?"

More Recent Fiction from Turnstone Press

The Pumpkin-Eaters by Lois Braun, $12.95

Black Tulips by Bruce Eason, $11.95

Bone Bird by Darlene Barry Quaife, $12.95

Older Than Ravens by Doug Reimer, $12.95

Fox by Margaret Sweatman, $12.95

Murder in Gutenthal by Armin Wiebe, $12.95

Tell Tale Signs by Janice Williamson, $12.95